THE JOURNEY
OF THE ELDEST SON

J. G. FYSON

THE JOURNEY
OF THE ELDEST SON

Illustrated by Victor C. Ambrus

London
OXFORD UNIVERSITY PRESS
1974

Oxford University Press, Ely House, London W. 1

GLASGOW NEW YORK TORONTO MELBOURNE WELLINGTON
CAPE TOWN IBADAN NAIROBI DAR ES SALAAM LUSAKA ADDIS ABABA
DELHI BOMBAY CALCUTTA MADRAS KARACHI LAHORE DACCA
KUALA LUMPUR SINGAPORE HONG KONG TOKYO

ISBN 0 19 272061 9

© *J. G. Fyson 1965*
First published 1965
First published in this edition 1974

To

MY FATHER

Printed in Holland
Zuid-Nederlandsche Drukkerij N.V.
's-Hertogenbosch

CONTENTS

1   THE FATEFUL CHOICE   1

2   THE WOLF'S TOOTH   14

3   IN A TWILIGHT WORLD   23

4   ENOCH SON OF ENOCH   32

5   THE ISHAKKI OF KENAN   51

6   THE NOISES OF THE NIGHT   59

7   ZEPHO AND HIS FATHER   69

8   THE BEACON   85

9   THE STAR OF SHAMASHAZIR   102

10   THE PURSUIT   113

11   IN THE FOREST   132

12   WILD MEN OF THE MOUNTAINS   150

13   ENOCH HAS A DREAM   165

14   BACK TO UR   173

AUTHOR'S NOTE

The people of Ur believed that the sun, the moon, the mountains, the rivers, the rain, tools, scribes, insects, accounts, and almost anything you can think of that existed in those days, had its own god or spirit to look after it. They were called *dingirs* (the Sumerian word for gods) and the people of Ur worshipped them and fed them with sacrifices. Each Sumerian city had its own special dingir to look after it—the City of Ur was taken care of by Nannar the Moon Dingir. But because these mighty creatures were so busy with great affairs that they had no time for every one of the thousands of inhabitants of Ur, each family had its own guardian spirit, which I have called a teraphim, which it fed with its own food (mostly porridge, fish, and beer).

The people of Ur believed that the earth was flat, and that underneath it lay the Land of the Dead, or Underworld. There were two judges in the Land of the Dead—one of them Nannar the Moon Dingir. And there were two dingirs in charge, one of them called Nergal. But many other dingirs visited the Land of the Dead, or found themselves living there from time to time.

Shamashazir's family and their ages at the beginning of his journey.

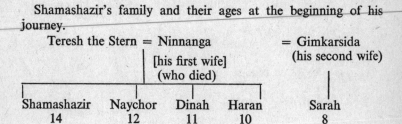

Teresh the Stern = Ninnanga [his first wife] (who died)   = Gimkarsida (his second wife)

Shamashazir	Naychor	Dinah	Haran	Sarah
14	12	11	10	8

1 THE FATEFUL CHOICE

Shamashazir (pronounced Shamas-hazir) had walked from the great and ancient City of Ur to the foot of the White Mountains; and his muscles were as hard as his cousin Serag's. Shamashazir was fourteen; and this was his first journey with one of his father's caravans.

Through the hot plains they had travelled in the cool of the morning and by moonlight, past shadowy date gardens and apple orchards, past canals where frogs croaked. But at first the mystery and excitement of moonlight and dawn had been lost on Shamashazir. He had walked with his head bent down, watching his steps in the dust of the beaten earth, avoiding droppings of dung, and

1

seeing only the rhythmic movement of camels' legs and the sway of men's skirts. For every bone in his body had ached, his legs had moved stiffly; his skin had been sore with sweat and dust; and the straps of his sandals had chafed his feet till they bled. During the long, hot hours of rest, he had lain aching and exhausted, and tortured by flies, while the men parched corn and told stories to pass away the time.

But gradually his feet began to harden, and his muscles to strengthen. He took notice of the country they were going through: how the Great River had dwindled in size, and how the sun shone through the leaves of the date-palms, catching the sparkling bright wings of insects in the deep shade; and how the people they met talked with strange dialects. And he began to think of his father, back in Ur, and to wonder if he had discovered the broken Image of the sacred Teraphim in the vault under the Chapel; and if his younger brother Haran had confessed. And then a momentary shudder of apprehension would cloud his enjoyment; for his longed-for journey had started under ill omens.

But the City of Ur was very far away. Swinging into his stride on those long, dusty tracks, listening to the chanting voices of the camel men, what happened at home was soon forgotten. What mattered now was to prove his courage and endurance, and to earn the respect of his companions. He was the eldest son of Teresh the Stern, whose caravans of camels, laden with merchandise, travelled on all the trade routes from the City of Ur to the land of Egypt and the foot of the White Mountains. One day he, Shamashazir, would own these camels, and be the master of these men. As he trudged along beside his cousin Serag, he knew they watched him critically, judging his worth, and discussing him among themselves. He had heard them, had smiled to himself, and gone doggedly on.

When the track began to rise too steeply, they left the camel men with their camels at the Village of Changing Beasts, and loaded the packs of merchandise that they were bringing from Ur on to donkeys, in charge of wild-looking tribesmen of the hills. Now they slept by night and walked by day. But Shamashazir had a new and yet harder standard to live up to. These men were used to fighting lions and wolves, and being ambushed on their journeys through the mountains. They were expert at using their slings and spears. And their tales round the camp fires were of violence and of death. Shamashazir listened; and wondered how *he* would behave, if night suddenly descended on them from the sky in broad daylight with a darkness that hid the flames of the fire.

Back in Ur, listening to his cousin, Serag the Lucky, talking of his adventures, Shamashazir had longed to go with him. But now he began to have doubts of his courage—and of his wisdom. The broken Image and all it might forbode, was more and more often in his mind. And now that his bed was the warm, bare rock, and the roof overhead a vast dome of stars almost curving in below him, he began to lie awake, thinking of all that had happened during his last week at home, weighing every significant incident, wondering what the meaning might be.

It had begun on the day that his father and Serag were called away, and he was left as head of the household. He had been suprised and proud of his sudden responsibility. But from the start everything had gone wrong—seriously wrong. Illness had struck down the two youngest children; and evil spirits had taken possession of all their tongues, so that they had quarrelled—the kind of things that happen to a family when the Teraphim (the guardian angel) flies up to heaven and deserts it. Then something far worse had happened. For no sooner had his brother Haran been healed of his sickness, than he had gone into the family Chapel and not only touched the sacred Image of the Teraphim, but smothered it with porridge and honey; and then broken it! There had been a great evil in the house.

Sitting on a bollard down by the quay, Shamashazir had felt the dark shadow draw near; and he had got up to go home. But he had been made to wonder; for evil had not led to evil. And he had thought he felt the presence of an unseen friend beside him, helping him. He had thought he felt—but he did not know. For evil spirits can be like wolves in sheep's clothing, coming with smooth words and open hands to get their revenge. But why, when the Teraphim was broken, had the current of misfortune changed and everything begun to go well? Sarah, his youngest sister, had also been healed. Haran's friend Uz had made them a new Image—so exactly like the old that not even Shamashazir could see the difference. And when his father came home again, the Image was standing on the altar.

Shamashazir had tried to tell his father about the broken Image; but something stronger than himself seemed to prevent him. And then his father had said he could come on this longed-for journey;

for the Teraphim had spoken. Out on the hills at sunset the Teraphim had spoken to him: 'Let Shamashazir, your son, go with the caravan.' No one in Ur would dream of setting out for the White Mountains, or the Sea at the End of the World, without the goodwill or advice of their family guardian; for if they did so they would certainly meet with disaster. His father brought wonderful news for Shamashazir. Or it would have been, but for the knowledge that at that very hour of sunset, at the very time the Teraphim had spoken, the Image in the family Chapel had stood on the altar helpless and insulted, with a crack clean through its middle! And also that, at the same time, he had seen the gold-and-silver shrine of Nannar, the Great Dingir of Ur, the guardian of the whole city, turn from silver to blood-red, against the sky. And he had come away without saying a word of this to his father.

When the air was cool, and the morning dew was on the grass, Shamashazir was tempted to believe it was a friendly spirit, who meant him good, who had decreed he should come on his journey. But when he was tired, or dark clouds piled up ahead, he was sure it was evil. And the guilt in his mind painted the clouds even darker; and he heard the cry of angry spirits in the moaning of the wind.

Day by day growing in size, the white-topped mountains rose ahead in foreboding grandure. The travellers were approaching the home of ancient dingirs,* avenging and cruel, whose sudden bursts of anger would come sweeping down from the cold, white peaks, destroying men who dared to come into their realms with guilt in their souls or lies on their lips. Shamashazir looked up at these once longed-for peaks, then shivered slightly as he walked, in spite of the sunlight, and turned his mind to the country round him, trying to forget his qualms. For it was in the mountains, he felt, that he would face his trial.

Not much could grow in these high places. But here and there, in the valleys, a tribe had built itself a village of rough stone huts; and sown a few oats or barley in small patches of soil composed of the droppings of donkeys, and dust brought down by the streams. When they saw the caravan coming in sight, the tribesmen would climb the rocks on each side of the path and wait for it to pass, twirling their spears in the air and shouting. His cousin Serag

* See author's note.

greeted these wild men as old friends, with a courteous welcome; and he always stopped to trade with them. Shamashazir, standing behind, watched his clean-cut solemn face, as he bargained for lumps of green copper ore in exchange for dates and corn and sometimes a knife for the chief.

Less fierce, and more hospitable, were the great tribes of wandering shepherds, from whom Serag bought fleeces of wool in exchange for gold rings or lengths of cloth. They would order a sheep to be killed; and the whole caravan feasted. The women would dance and sing, and the men tell stories. Shamashazir was interested in these shepherds—thinking that his grandfather, as a boy, had lived as they did; and that if his grandfather had not decided to marry a Sumerian woman and settle in the City of Ur, he himself might have been living the same kind of life with his sheep on the bare hills.

As the ground grew rougher and steeper, the tribes became fewer and smaller. On the fifth day, at noon, they came in sight of about forty people—men, women, and children, going westwards towards the mountains, with a few sheep. The men had crooks, and the women and children carried baskets and bundles and water-pots on their heads.

'The tribe of Enoch!' said Serag, sounding pleased.

Shamashazir had heard the name of Enoch in his grandfather's stories of the time before the Flood. He began to scan the vast empty horizon, looking for the clouds of dust raised by another great people.

Serag laughed. 'That is the whole tribe.'

'Those?' said Shamashazir, astonished. 'They are nothing but a handful, with hardly enough sheep to keep them.'

'So are the mighty fallen,' said Serag.

The Ishak, their chief, called a halt when he saw that Serag was with the caravan that was overtaking them. The women put down the burdens that they were carrying and began to search for dung to make a fire. Like a dark statue in the glaring light, the Ishak waited to greet the traders. He wanted corn for his people—only a little corn—in return for a few fleeces; but he welcomed Serag with the dignity of a king, and invited him to be his guest.

Shamashazir, as usual, stood a little behind his cousin, as a servant would stand; for among the wild tribes Serag kept secret Shamashazir's identity. 'If it gets known that you are the son of Teresh the Stern,' he explained, 'they will surely lay an ambush to capture you and hold you to ransom.' But now Serag called him to come forward, and introduced him by name to the Ishak Enoch. Shamashazir bowed low.

Behind the Ishak, he noticed a boy of about his own age, standing erect and proud, looking at him. His dark eyes were fierce and challenging. No flicker of a smile disturbed the hauteur of his countenance. The Ishak turned to him and introduced him to Shamashazir as his son, also called Enoch. Shamashazir bowed again—not so low as he had done to the Ishak; but the boy Enoch only inclined his head slightly. 'As if he owned the whole world,' Shamashazir thought.

When Shamashazir and his cousin had washed in a stream, they joined the tribe of Enoch, seated round their fire, where a sheep was being lightly scorched to give it a flavour. The Ishak sat on a throne made of coarse linen stuffed with sheep's wool, to raise him above the rest. He had put on a white linen cloak. And under it, a chain of finely wrought gold lay on his bare chest. 'Beautiful enough to have been made in Ur,' Shamashazir thought.

Beside him on the ground, cross-legged and silent, sat his son. Occasionally, from under his lashes, he darted a swift look at Serag; but Shamashazir, sitting next to him, he ignored.

'He can see that I am city-bred,' thought Shamashazir. 'I am not worthy of his attention.' And he smiled to himself, tickled at the thought that he, the eldest son of the great and wealthy Teresh the Stern, who was treated with respect by the governor of Ur, should be considered of so little consequence. Nevertheless, he liked this boy. He was fascinated by the watchfulness of his eyes, which took in all that passed without seeming to notice. He tried to start a conversation. 'My grandfather was born a shepherd,' he said.

Enoch slowly turned his head and looked over his shoulder at the heathen merchant's son beside him. 'Of what tribe?' he asked.

'An Ishak of the Hiberu,' Shamashazir answered with casual pride.

An Ishak of the Hiberu, it seemed, was something more honourable to be than a merchant in Ur, because Enoch remained a moment looking at him, weighing him up as though he were on a more equal footing. But he said nothing. Men who live among the hills are not used to speaking when there is nothing to say.

Shamashazir tried again, more boldly: 'I would like to know more of your people and your customs.'

Enoch's eyes narrowed into a look of suspicion. The customs of his people were sacred. He did not wish to discuss them with strangers.

But his look only excited Shamashazir's curiosity the more. What did these people know about the ancient gods, the dingirs of the mountains? he wondered. 'Are you going to the mountains?' he asked; and watched Enoch's face to see if this also was a forbidden subject. But Enoch turned his head away.

'We go,' he answered. There was a new note in his voice which Shamashazir had not heard before, almost a note of shame. Then suddenly Enoch said, 'In the days of my grandfather, the tribe was a mighty one.'

'Oh,' said Shamashazir eagerly. 'Do you remember it?' He was hoping that Enoch would go on talking.

But he only said, 'I was too little. There was much shouting and singing,' and lapsed into silence again.

'I remember my grandfather,' said Shamashazir, trying to draw him out. 'He had a long white beard and told stories of battles. And he had arrows made with bronze!'

'My grandfather had a sword with a hilt of gold!'

'A sword! It must have been made in Ur. All the finest swords are.'

'If that is so,' said Enoch with dignity, 'it must have been; for there is no sword to match it in the whole world.'

And so for some time the two boys talked happily of swords, about which Shamashazir knew much, and battles, of which he had learnt only in history lessons. But Enoch had experienced the terrible slaughter of his tribe. Then the talk drifted to hunting; and then to fishing—as it was done by spearing in the mountain rivers, and as it was done by boat on the Great River at Ur, with nets and hooks and bait. This was fascinating to Enoch; and he so completely lost his former aloofness that Shamashazir dared to ask him the question often asked of strangers in Ur: 'What dingir does the tribe of Enoch serve?'

Enoch suddenly stiffened and drew himself up proudly. 'The tribe of Enoch serves no man.'

'I forgot,' said Shamashazir. ' "Dingir" is the Sumerian name for the "Great Ones" who govern the heavens and the earth.'

'There are no "Great Ones" in this country. *They* live on the fertile lands to the east and the west.'

'Are there no dingirs in the mountains,' asked Shamashazir in an awed whisper, 'who roll stones down on to men, and carry them away to the Land of the Underworld, so that their bodies are never seen again and no burial rites can be said over them?'

'Evil spirits!' said Enoch with withering scorn. 'The tribe of Enoch pays tribute to no evil spirits.'

The conversation seemed suddenly to have taken a perilous turn. Shamashazir could not think how to bring it back to a safer footing. He floundered about, saying: 'I'm sorry. I did not know. In Ur, the dingirs are never evil. They are good to their friends and bad to their enemies. In Ur, the mountain dingirs are said to be just, but without mercy to wrongdoers . . .' But Enoch's face was darkening with suspicion. Shamashazir stumbled on: 'In Ur, we serve Nannar the Dingir of the Moon. He is no evil spirit, but guards the City of Ur from all enemies, and sees to it that the other dingirs do their work.'

'Other dingirs,' questioned Enoch. 'Are you speaking of the idols of the heathen?'

Shamashazir did not like being called a 'heathen'. 'No,' he said angrily. 'I'm talking of the dingirs of Ur: Enki the Dingir of Wisdom, Enbilulu the Dingir of the Great River, the dingirs of cattle and corn.'

'The Corn Dingir!' Enoch's dark skin paled and his eyes blazed. 'We serve the Great Spirit,' he cried, suddenly leaping to his feet and seizing the hilt of his knife.

'Ah,' said Shamashazir, at least pleased that he had surprised Enoch's secret. 'The Great Spirit? Who is he?'

'Let his name not be sullied by your lips, you unclean sacrificer of bodies,' Enoch shouted, and would have fallen on Shamashazir where he sat, if Serag had not been too quick for him.

For a moment it seemed as if the whole tribe were going to take up the quarrel. But the Ishak sat calm and unmoved on his throne of wool until the hubbub had quietened down. 'It is not the will of the Great Spirit,' he said, 'that guests should be killed at the feast.'

An immediate hush fell on the angry men, and they went back to their places shamefaced. But the effect of the Ishak's words on Shamashazir was to leave him even more curious about this unknown Great Spirit who despised all the dingirs in the world, and yet was so chivalrous to his guests.

During the disturbance Enoch had vanished. He did not appear again that night. Nor could Shamashazir see him the next morning. And although he thought he saw a lad of about Enoch's height, sitting afar off on a rock, beside a flock of grazing sheep, there was no means of satisfying his growing curiosity.

The caravan left early, and with a clip-clopping of donkey hooves, followed the ever-steepening road through a forest of cedar-trees. Tall and dark they grew on the lower slopes; but as the track climbed higher, the flat-roofed cedars gradually gave place to pines, which became shorter and fewer; until the forest suddenly came to an end at a wall of rock, rising sheer above their heads. Serag ordered a halt.

'Do we camp here?' asked Shamashazir. 'It is early.'

'We camp up there,' said Serag. 'But we must stop to pick up wood.'

Shamashazir stood craning his neck back, trying to see how they could climb so sheer a cliff with packs and donkeys—and now Serag was talking about carrying wood! Were they to carry wood up that height?

The foreman of the donkey men came and asked if they should collect enough for one night, or two. For a moment Serag stood irresolute. Then he said, 'It is not yet decided which way we go. Tell the men to carry sufficient for two nights.'

'Have we come to the place where the way divides?' Shamashazir asked. Serag had talked of this place in Ur. There was a high way over the mountains; and there was a low way through the valleys. It was the custom for the leader of the caravan, when he came to this place, to consult the Teraphim and take his advice as to which path they should take, for both were dangerous. The mountain way went through the haunts of the dingirs, where black darkness fell by day; the other way through a valley of wild tribes who frequently ambushed the caravans. On the last journey that Serag had made he had taken the wrong path. The brown eyes of a maiden who lived in the valley had lured him, so that he could not hear the advice of the Teraphim. For the voice of the Teraphim is small. It speaks in the silence; and only he who has a heart free of fear, and free of desire can hear it. So Serag had taken the valley way. And the caravan had been attacked, goods lost, and three men killed. Now that he had Shamashazir, the eldest son of Teresh the Stern, with him, Serag felt the responsibility heavy on his shoulders. He sighed with the weight of his thoughts.

'How can I decide the way we should go?' he murmured. 'The nearer I get to the valley where the daughter of the coppersmith lives, the more clearly I see her dark eyes, and hear her soft voice calling me.' He pulled his knife out of its leather sheath and viciously sliced a flake off the bole of a tree while he spoke. 'If I were alone I should go to the maiden by way of the valley. What is the loss of the lives of a few donkey men—or of my own life, for that matter? But if *you* should be killed in a scuffle, I should for ever live under your father's curse.' Then, jabbing the knife violently into the scar that he had made on the tree, he said, 'It is better we go the mountain way; and, if I have chosen the wrong path, hope that your father accepts the sacrifice of my desires.' He gave a deep, shuddering sigh at the thought of the maiden he would not see, and thrusting the knife back into its sheath, turned, leaving Shamashazir thoughtfully staring at the wound in the tree.

Two men carrying wood passed him by. He heard them discussing his cousin Serag: 'Serag the Lucky has become Serag the Proud. He has made a quarrel with the Dingir of the Trees. Evil will surely come to him.'

Shamashazir did not like these words. He had always admired and trusted his cousin Serag. Serag the Lucky he was called, because, until his last journey, he had never lost a man or a donkey in all his travels. He had imagined that Serag's luck might be strong enough to protect him from the anger of the mountain dingirs. But Serag had made his decision without consulting the Teraphim. Thoughtfully Shamashazir selected a small cedar branch, and joined the file of men who had begun to climb by a tiny zigzagging path up the face of the steep wall of rock. His mind was on Ur again, thinking of the broken Image. He began to realize that, having obeyed his impulse and deceived his father, no one could save him from the consequences. And if anything happened to him he must not let his cousin suffer for his own guilt. 'For if the mountain dingirs take their revenge on me, and Serag goes back to my father with the news, my father will surely kill him, in his anger, or make him a slave for the rest of his life.'

Trailing his branch up the steep rock-face, farther and farther behind the rest of the caravan, alone and afraid, Shamashazir suddenly felt the presence of spirits again—the happy presence that he had felt in Ur at the making of the new Image. Doubt left him, his courage rose, and he suddenly made up his mind. '*I* will consult the Teraphim,' he said to himself. 'And I will let it be known by all the men that *I* am deciding the way.' Now that he had made this decision strength came into his legs; and he threw all his attention to struggling up the path with his heavy load and trying to catch up with the caravan. But the donkeys moved surefootedly ahead; and the men climbed that dizzy height with easy confidence. No amount of effort by Shamashazir could lessen the distance between them and himself. In spite of his new-found strength, he gained no ground, battling with the awkward branch and the slippery rocks.

When he at last reached the top, it was with an almost trembling voice that he announced his decision to Serag, doubting if his cousin would agree to it. But to his astonishment, Serag left the skinning of a goat killed for supper, which he had been watching, and said, 'I also have been thinking that *that* would be the wisest course. You have neither knowledge nor desire, to mislead you in your choice. *You* will hear the voice of the Teraphim clearly and lead us to the path of safety.'

Shamashazir did not contradict him. And Serag continued: 'Let us go to the place of decision before it gets dark.' Then beckoning Shamashazir to follow him, he led the way across the camping-site and along a hardly perceptible path, towards another great wall of rock, which rose into the final summit of the ridge. Just as Shamashazir was wondering if they would have to climb over it, a huge black shadow down its centre opened up into a deep gash cut through the cliff as though by a stroke of lightning. Serag led the way into it. It was cool and dark and their footsteps echoed eerily in the hollow stillness. 'It is called the Passage of Troubled Voices,' he whispered to Shamashazir; and his words were taken up and bandied, hissing, about the high rocks that nearly met overhead, long after he had finished speaking. Shamashazir drew closer to his cousin (as near as the uncertain ground allowed) and walked behind him, almost touching his feet, until the sides of the gorge began to slope away, there was more light, and the sight of the setting sun sinking behind a rugged line of dark peaks.

They walked between jagged boulders for the distance of an arrow's flight, and then Serag stopped. 'It is here,' he said.

Shamashazir looked at the rocks ahead, to the right, and to the left. He could see no signs of any path over them. They stretched hummocking away to the edge of a ridge—a desolate waste that gave him the feeling that he was no longer on the earth he had known from boyhood.

Serag pointed to the ground at his feet. Here and there the sharp edges had been worn away; and in a crack to the left were a few dried fibres, from the droppings of a donkey that he said must have passed by a moon ago. 'The other path goes straight ahead towards that great boulder over there,' he added; and pointed out the direction it took when it dropped over the ridge in front of them. 'The sun will be nearly set when you come back. I will fetch a torch from one of the fires to light you through the Passage of Troubled Voices; for it will be dark in there.' He turned to go. And Shamas-hazir was alone on the top of that strange mountain, that seemed to him to be no place on earth, waiting for the advice of the Teraphim to come to him.

He sat down, shut his eyes, and crossed his hands over his chest in the Sumerian attitude of prayer, listening to the soft rustle of Serag's footsteps on the hard rock, dying away behind him. When silence had settled again, and he knew his cousin must be in the Passage of Troubled Voices, he began the prayer for guidance that his father prayed in the family Chapel in Ur:

'O Teraphim, guardian of the house of Teresh, make known your will to me, concerning the path that I am to take in this strange and terrible country.' Then he thought for a little and altered his words: 'Not that I am to take, but the path that my father's caravan is to take. For I have deceived my father and am not worthy of the guidance of the heavenly rulers. But my cousin Serag has done no wrong. Do not lift your hand against him because of my fault.'

When he had said these words, he opened his eyes to look again at the two paths. Bare boulders stretched to the sky in wild solitude. The Passage of Troubled Voices stood between him and the comfort of any human being. He was alone with the terrible dingirs of the mountains. He found himself trembling all over. How could *he* know which path the caravan was to take?

Slowly the sun sank towards the rugged horizon. The clouds reddened and the pale moon appeared high in the sky. He had never before looked into such a wide-stretching globe of fiery gold. 'Surely no evil thing could live in the presence of such majestic beauty,' he thought. His shaking limbs steadied. He remembered another, but smaller, sunset back in Ur, and the unknown presence who had seemed to help him. He shut his eyes again and crossed his hands. 'O Unknown Dingir, if you are my friend, guide me through these mountains,' he prayed. Then he sat looking for a long time into the distance, where the two paths must go. The path to the left was really the one that went through the valley, where the wild tribesmen and the beautiful maiden lived. Yet Shamashazir could not imagine anyone living along that path. It seemed to lead to a blank emptiness. It was along the path straight ahead that he felt people must live—people living and a great glory, and danger— terrible danger. But now that he felt the mysterious presence again, the danger seemed to draw him towards it like a temptation—for of course the caravan must go the safer way.

He got up to go back to the camp, picking his way between rocks and boulders in the fading light, until he saw Serag's flaming torch in the Passage of Troubled Voices. But as he went, he felt a great bitterness of disappointment that he would never meet the people who lived along the dangerous path, nor see the great glory.

Serag asked him eagerly: 'Which is the way?'

And he heard himself answering: 'The path straight ahead.'

'The right-hand path?' said Serag, his voice almost fading away with a lover's regrets.

'Yes.'

'It is the mountain way.'

Shamashazir knew that he had made a mistake; but he could not alter his words: for Serag believed him to be giving the advice of the Teraphim.

2 THE WOLF'S TOOTH

In the morning, when Serag told the men which way had been decided on, they were far from pleased. They said the wind was in the wrong direction, and that there might be a darkness of mist.

'There is no wind,' said Serag. 'Not enough to blow out a lamp.'

But the men pointed to the clouds and said that they were coming from the south-east.

'The wind will change,' said Serag. 'For the dingirs have told the son of Teresh to go the mountain way; and the son of Teresh knows.'

The donkey men looked at Shamashazir suspiciously. In the hill tribes the son of a chieftain was not considered a man until he had proved himself in battle, which Shamashazir had not yet done. They went with discontented looks, grumbling to one another. But they had not gone far before they met a party of shepherds bringing their sheep across the mountains. The shepherds said that they had come from the valley—where the Ishak of one of the mountain tribes had just died. 'His son is only a boy; and all his brothers fight to be Ishak. It is no safe place to keep sheep in that valley.'

The grumbling stopped. The donkey men looked at Shamashazir with approval. 'It is better to fall into the hands of the Dingir of Darkness,' the foreman said, 'than into the hands of a tribe without an Ishak. For without an Ishak there is no law; and each brother will plunder the caravan for goods to bribe his followers.'

After the first drop over the summit, their path went steadily upwards. It was very steep, and for most of the way ran along the side of a towering cliff, overhanging a precipice. It was a ledge about as wide as the height of a man, and sloped sideways away from the cliff. It gave Shamashazir a constant feeling that either he or the donkeys would slip over the edge. But the donkeys went along happily enough—almost as if they were walking up the narrow streets of Ur. The younger men amused themselves by throwing stones into the precipice, and waiting to hear them fall on the rocks below. Several of them stood on the brink and looked over. They dared Shamashazir to do the same. But Serag forbade him. 'These men have been born in the mountains,' he said. 'They have played among the rocks ever since they could walk. They are used to great heights, but you have stood on nothing higher than the parapet of your father's house. And the mountain dingirs **do not** care for strangers to peer into their secrets.'

'That is true,' said one of the older men. And he began to tell the story of a young merchant from Nippur who had boasted that he could stand on the edge and look down into the precipice like the mountain-born guides. And how the Dingir of the Rocks had come up behind him and pushed him into the abyss. 'I saw him myself,' he assured them, the pupils of his eyes dilated with horror at that distant memory. 'He was grey, the colour of the clouds, with a face like a wolf. And his clothes were made of rock. One moment he was there; and the next moment the mountains and valleys gave forth fearful cries and screams; and he was not.'

After that, the young men stopped throwing stones over the edge; and a kind of hush fell on all of them. Shamashazir and Serag were in front, with two or three of the camel men, who were carrying spears and slings, in case they met a mountain bear. But they saw nothing but wild goats leaping over the rocks with their kids.

In the middle of the day they came to a wider strip of ledge; and Serag consulted the head guide about whether they should stop and eat. But the head guide said the wind was rising, and coming from the wrong direction; and he thought they had better press on. So Serag ordered them to eat as they walked, and to give the donkeys handfuls of the grass which they had brought with them in sacks.

Shamashazir was surprised that the men did not start grumbling again at having no time to sit down. But they seemed pleased. The sooner they got safely to their camping-ground the happier they would be.

During the latter half of the day, the donkey men all began to shout in a curious singing call, that went from low to high and down again, and echoed round the mountains from peak to peak.

Serag explained to Shamashazir that they were warning any caravan coming the other way to hold back. 'The path goes out of sight round the rocks ahead, and there is no room to pass.'

'By Nannar! there isn't,' said Shamashazir. But he liked the shouting and singing. It was difficult to believe that so clear and sweet a noise could be made by the throats of men.

When at last the sun began to get lower, the path eased up and began to slope downwards, gently at first—and then almost as steeply as it had come up. Shamashazir's knees, unaccustomed to going down, began to ache, and his legs to tremble. But the men behind were talking eagerly, knowing that their journey was nearing its end. The path took a sharp turn; and they came to a broad rocky shelf, overhanging a gently sloping valley surrounded by towering peaks. On the shelf were the charred marks left by centuries of wood fires. Shamashazir did not need telling that this was their camping-place. He heaved a sigh of relief; for he felt as if his trembling legs would hardly carry him another step. Only his pride stopped him from sinking to the ground.

The men lit a fire with the wood they had brought with them, and cooked a goat which one of them had killed. And then they settled down to tell stories, while Shamashazir lay flat on his back on the sun-warmed rock.

But Serag did not seem in the mood for story-telling. When he had finished his food, he wandered off by himself, until he found a comfortable ledge where he could sit apart from the others, and gaze at the distant mountains and the valley below. He was thinking of the maiden who lived in the valley.

Shamashazir watched him go off, then lay back, listening to the story-tellers. But the drone of their voices became blurred and more difficult to hear—and he fell asleep—worn out with the hard climb in the thin, mountain air.

The sun moved downwards towards the west, hiding behind the higher peaks, which cast a deep shadow over the camp, filling all the valleys with a twilight gloom. But looking up, the very topmost peaks were still bathed in a golden light, that made them stand out like fiery spear-points and rosy islands of rock, floating on a sea of shadow.

Shamashazir was woken up by Serag's prodding him gently with the butt-end of a spear, and rubbing his eyes, gazed around at this faery world in astonishment.

Serag had a linen bag in his hand, into which he was putting corn and dates and cheese. 'The time has come to sacrifice,' he said. 'The dingirs of the mountains prefer the fruits and grasses of the plains to the flesh of goats.'

Shamashazir got to his feet and stretched himself. His knees were a little stiff; otherwise he had quite recovered.

Serag led the way towards a little peak that stood by itself, rising out of the valley below like the tooth of some great beast. 'It is called the Wolf's Tooth,' he said. 'And the camping-site is called the Wolf's Tongue.'

A steep and slippery path wound round the peak in a spiral, sometimes taking a short cut and going upwards in a flight of steps roughly hewn out of the rock.

'It is quite safe,' said Serag, seeing Shamashazir's look of apprehension at the sheer height. 'Keep your eyes on the rocks above you. Never look down and you won't feel dizzy.'

Shamashazir did as he was told. The path was safe. But as they neared the summit, the rocks sloped away so steeply that he could not help glancing down. There were birds flying below them; and a dark ravine with a glint of water at the bottom. 'Oh, Sumugan!' he muttered under his breath; and Serag turned round quickly to see if he was all right.

'It is better here,' he said. 'The ground slopes away more gently.'

Shamashazir looked up at him and regained his confidence.

The top of the peak had been flattened out like a huge platform, and an altar of stones had been built in the middle. They reached it at last; and the view burst upon them in over-awing magnificence. They spoke only in whispers; for this was a solemn and holy place. All around them, peak after peak of shining, fiery gold caught the rays of the setting sun. Far away to the west was a thin, glimmering line, which Serag said was the Sea at the End of the World. Below them hung a shadowy-blue haze that partly hid the earth; so that they seemed to be perched on one of many shining islands above a blue sea of deepening dusk. Between the mountains and the Sea at the End of the World was a glimpse of rich green vineyards and pale ripening corn; which Serag said was the Land of Milk and Honey, where there were few cities and much pasture.

Shamashazir was enraptured. This was the dream that he had dreamed about for so long and the glory he had come to find. He could have stayed up there and gazed at this promised land for hours. But Serag said they must make their offering to Sumugan.

They laid the cheese and corn and dates on the flat stone of the altar, and asked the Dingir's blessing on their journey through the mountains—both sitting on the ground with their hands over their chests in the attitude of prayer.

To Serag, the prayer was a form of words that had to be gone through if the journey was to prosper. But to Shamashazir, thinking of the possible danger ahead, it was a cry from the heart; for he knew that whatever was going to happen would happen very shortly. 'Perhaps this very night,' he thought; for the name 'Wolf's

Tooth' had a ring of doom.

Suddenly Serag jumped to his feet, saying under his breath: 'Look at that!'

Shamashazir opened his eyes, drawing himself into a crouching position in automatic response to the note of urgency in Serag's voice. His cousin was pointing to a thin wisp of cloud that was settling round one of the highest peaks. 'See that! The dingirs are about! We must go down at once.'

Silently, they began to climb down the zigzag path, going as fast as they could. Shamashazir's already tired knees were trembling again. It was as much as he could manage to keep up with his cousin. Serag stopped frequently to look round at the mountains for signs of more mist. But always he seemed satisfied, and went striding on with a bending, springy stride, amazing Shamashazir by his balance.

When they got to the bottom safely, Shamashazir stopped and looked back to the peak they had just left. A ghost-like scarf of thin mist hung round it.

'Sumugan, the Dingir of the Mountains!' whispered Serag. 'He has accepted our offering. That is good.' Then both he and Shamashazir crossed their hands on their chests and bowed low to the mountain, saying again: 'Let Sumugan, the Dingir of these mountains, be praised for his gracious hospitality to Shamashazir son of Teresh, and his cousin Serag the Lucky. And we humbly petition him to grant his protection to them through his country.'

The men seated round the fire crossed their hands and said, 'Let the dingirs be praised.' Then they made room for Shamashazir to join their circle.

Shamashazir was glad of its warmth. He had never felt so cold before in all his life. He fetched out his embroidered cloak and hung it round his shoulders, then sat down to listen, with his legs stretched out before him to ease his knees.

But the story-telling did not go on for long that night. The high, cold mountain air made them sleepy. And one by one they curled up and lay down, until only the watcher was left awake.

And Shamashazir? He lay down under the great silence of the stars, with his cloak pulled tightly round him, and dreamed—not of evil spirits and mountains and dingirs—but of the promised land, the Land of Milk and Honey, that lay between the mountains and the Sea at the End of the World.

He was the first to wake that morning, pleasantly surprised to find himself alive, and the dawn so unbelievably mysterious and beautiful. His mind was full of his happy dream. He felt as though he had missed the crisis and been pardoned.

It was half light, and very cold. Over in the east a pale moon was fading into the blue of the sky—Nannar of the Moon, the Dingir of Ur, was with them. Shamashazir's heart rose high with excitement; but his whole body was stiff and ached with the hardness and coldness of the rock. He stood up and stretched, then picked up his cloak and wrapped it tightly round his shoulders. It made little difference. 'I must move about and get warm,' he thought, stepping away from the fire.

Looking up, he could see the first rays of the rising sun lighting up the peaks. 'It must be warmer up there and wonderfully beautiful,' he thought. He could see each peak clearly, some still dark and blurred, some glowing clear-cut against the pale sky. There was no sign of cloud overhead. The dingirs of the mountains had left them.

He stepped silently away from the fire. The watcher huddled in his cloak glanced at him over his shoulder; then, with a charred stick, raked the embers of the fire together again, and fell into a doze. Shamashazir passed the donkeys, huddled together to keep warm, and set out towards the peak that he and Serag had climbed the night before.

It was very still and quiet; so quiet he was afraid to break the silence with even a footfall. He trod softly, climbing the first steep steps, and creeping round the spiralling path. Higher up, the rocks were wet and sparkling in the sun, here and there covered by a thin coating of a shining, jewel-like glaze. Shamashazir touched it with awe, and then suddenly withdrew his hand. It had burnt his fingers —and yet it was cold. For a moment he was afraid. And then he remembered how, in Ur, Serag had spoken of the whiteness of the White Mountains that sparkled and glistened—and vanished away in the heat of the day.

He went on more cautiously, helping himself with his hands because of the slipperiness. Suddenly, ahead of him, there was a cascade of falling stones. He looked down towards the camp; but he was on the wrong side of the Wolf's Tooth and cut off from its view. And then he laughed; for a small flock of five or six wild goats came in sight, leaping daintily from rock to rock.

It was owing to these goats that no one at the camp discovered Shamashazir's whereabouts until it was too late. The goats were accustomed to feeding on the food left on the altar of the mountain dingirs. They were always there in the morning when a caravan passed through. So when the watcher heard the fall of small stones and looked up and saw the goats, he did not bother to see if Shamashazir was back in his place. Why should he? And when small stones were dislodged by Shamashazir's feet later on, no one woke up. They said to themselves, 'It is the goats.'

In spite of the slipperiness, Shamashazir found the climb much easier than the night before. He was fresher after his sleep; and his knees had lost their stiffness. Down below him, the deep gorges and valleys of the mountains were all filled with a soft white mist—like the mist that used to lie over the marshes round Ur. With this soft blanket below him, he felt no dizziness from the height. He was able to walk along the treacherous rocks faster, and with more confidence. Even when the path passed the edge of the abyss he felt no fear, because of the mist, which gave him the feeling the earth could not be far below it.

As he reached the summit, the first rays of the sun fell on the altar; and he could see the thin arc of its brightly shining ball just sticking up behind a bank of blue haze to the east. All the land between him and the Sea at the End of the World was covered by the same pearly white blanket, and was still in shadow. He was a little disappointed. He would have liked to see the sun lighting the vineyards and cornfields of the Land of Milk and Honey. Nevertheless, it was marvellously beautiful up there, alone among the shining peaks, completely cut off from the earth, looking down at the whiteness that was billowing and boiling and throwing itself up into strange humps and curves below him. He stood watching for some time, fascinated, until the sun's rays struck so warmly on his shoulders that he slipped off his woollen cloak and held it over his arm. The sun was well above the horizon now; and here and there its rays were picking out fluffs of mist that had boiled up above the general level, making them shine with a pure pearly whiteness, whiter than the wings of a swan. It was unbelievably wonderful. He wanted Serag to see what he was seeing; and he looked down at the camp to find out if his cousin was awake. Several of the men were beginning to move, although it was still very dark at the camp. He picked out Serag from the rest. He was yawning and stretching and rubbing his thigh. Shamashazir laughed to himself, remembering the hardness of the rock. And then he called to his cousin, trying to imitate the way he had heard the men call the day before; and his voice echoed through the mountains.

Serag looked up, then suddenly leapt to his feet. He and all the men began shouting and waving their arms. Shamashazir could not hear what they said. But he shouted back at them: 'Come up here!'

And then, suddenly, they disappeared. A great billow of mist had risen up from the valley below and engulfed them. Shamashazir was terrified, and began to run down the dangerous and slippery path as fast as he could. They were still shouting something. But their voices were muffled; and his feet made too much noise on the hard rock, kicking loose stones that fell with a rattle into the abyss. It wasn't until there was another great upsurge of mist below him, blotting out the bottom of the peak nearly up to his feet, that Shamashazir himself began to realize the danger that he was in; and that he ought to keep still.

He was standing at that moment at the very point where, the night before, he had called upon Sumugan—the curve in the path that overhung the steepest precipice. He did not fancy stopping there. Farther along it would be safer. He went on more carefully. But the mist swirled suddenly above his head, plunging him into a dim whirling greyness, so dense that he could only just see the path at his feet. His cloak was slipping from his arm; he let it fall, to give himself more freedom and a better balance—forgetting how he would need its warmth, waiting in that icy dampness. But by now he was so frightened he felt neither heat nor cold. He dropped down on to his knees and began to crawl, using his hands to feel the uncertain way in front of him. But the path, instead of getting easier, got more difficult. And the darkening, clammy mist was making the rocks run with water. A stone gave way unexpectedly beneath his hand, upsetting his balance. He clutched at the air frantically, and fell, giving a cry as he went—head first—feet first—then head first again. And all was darkness.

The men in the camp heard the cry; and they heard the long rattle of stones falling down the mountain-side. Then silence—the close dead silence of the mountain mist.

Serag shouted and called. And they waited—all listening. But there was no answer; and no sound except the drip drip of water from the wet rocks. There was nothing more they could do except wait. They hadn't the heart to talk.

As the sun got hotter, the mist began to rise and to thin out.

Serag at once took a couple of guides and began to search the peak for Shamashazir. They did not have to go very far, for one of the guides immediately spotted his cloak lying in the stream at the bottom of the deep gully. Serag ordered them to take all the harness ropes off the donkeys and knot them together, so that he could climb down. But they shook their heads. The ropes were not strong enough; and if they were all knotted together they would not reach half-way down that steep cliff. Sumugan had taken Shamashazir, they said. It would displease him if they tried to get his body out of the gully. They looked anxiously towards the altar on the summit, which was still smothered in clouds.

Serag was more afraid of returning home without Shamashazir and meeting his uncle Teresh, than he was of either Dingir or death; but alone he could do nothing. He had to be content with reciting the prayers for the dead; and with throwing food down the precipice, for Shamashazir to eat on his ghostly journey to the Land of the Underworld. Dates and barley, bread and cheese they threw down. There was nothing left of the goat they had killed and eaten the day before. But while they were still standing peering into the gloom beneath, trying to make out where Shamashazir's body lay; and wondering if the food had fallen near enough, another puff of mist came swirling round their heads.

They looked up anxiously to the sky. 'Let us go,' they said to Serag. 'Sumugan is angry. The wind comes from the City of Darkness. Let us not stay too long or we shall all be lost. It was not right for the Ishak's son to choose the way before he had been proved in battle.' They began to move down the mountain, back to their donkeys; and Serag knew there was nothing else to do but to give the order to proceed, and to follow them.

Serag realized that not only was Shamashazir lost, but his own luck was broken. Teresh would never trust him again, and even the donkey men were looking at him suspiciously. He pulled himself upright, and his face set stern and immovable; so that the men were as afraid of him as of Teresh himself. There was no more murmuring. But there was no more singing on that journey either; and Serag kept himself a little away from the story-telling round the fires at night, grieving over the loss of his cousin.

After his fall, Shamashazir thought he was floating about in a place of wonderful colours, feeling very happy. For years and years he seemed to be floating in happiness. And then he gradually became aware of a dark shadow that seemed to be slowly rising up under him and closing in on him, becoming more and more terrible —getting nearer and nearer—until at last it caught up with him, and he knew what it was. It was pain. Pain steadily growing and spreading into every part of his body. His head throbbed as if a hammer were hitting it. His arms ached, and his back hurt. His neck was so stiff that he could not move it; and one leg felt as if a red-hot knife were being stuck into it.

It hurt so much that he cried out; and to his astonishment a voice answered him in Akkadian—a soft, woman's voice, like his mother's. But, as the voice went on, he remembered that his mother had never talked Akkadian to him, and that she was dead. He tried to remember where he was ... It couldn't be Ur—he had left that long ago. He had crossed a river. And there had been mountains. And the Land of Milk and Honey. But he hadn't got there. He had gone to look at it and there had been a mist—and he had fallen. And then he had floated through bright colours for a long time. He must have come to the Land of the Dead. Yes, the Land of the Dead. And that was his mother's voice. If his mother was in the Land of the Dead it must be a good place. He was not afraid. He opened his eyes to see what it was like in the Underworld of the Dead. It was dark and there were no stars, only a flickering red light, dancing on a rocky roof above his head.

He shut his eyes quickly again; for the pain in his leg was terrible. He screamed: 'Have mercy!' But hands came out of the darkness and held him, so that he could not move.

Then suddenly the hands and the pain began to melt away into the bright colours, and he was floating in the air again—for a long time—until he heard his name being called by a man's voice. He opened his eyes. And there was the red light again, flickering on the roof; and the pain came surging back all over his body. But the terrifying hands had gone, and so had the intense agony in his leg.

He felt himself raised up by the shoulders and a curiously rough cup of creamy liquid was put to his lips. It tasted of goat's milk.

He drank it eagerly, and felt better. The pain in his leg was a great dull ache and he could not move. He could not move at all. He lay back and listened to the voices. He seemed to have heard them before; but he could not remember where. They were not the voices of Haran or Naychor, his brothers, or his father or Serag. . . . But of course they weren't. These were all people who were living. And he was in the Land of the Dead. But he was glad that they had goat's milk to drink in the Land of the Dead. It tasted good. And the red light danced on the rocky roof when he opened his eyes. . . . And his mother was there—somewhere. He closed his eyes and fell asleep.

He woke several times. Always he saw the flickering light on the rocky roof above him. Once someone came and gave him cold water to drink, and moved him into another position. He found that he was lying on a sheepskin, spread over something hard and sharp which stuck into his back like the points of arrow-heads. He wondered why they had put the sheepskin over the arrow-heads. Perhaps his mother had done it for him to lessen his punishment. He put out his hand and felt bare, hard rock beside him; and wondered why he couldn't lie on that. But when he tried to roll off the spikes on to the smooth rock, it seemed as if they grew longer and pierced his back even harder. So he gave up trying to move and fell asleep again.

He was woken by music—beautiful singing that seemed to fill the air above him and all round him. But he could see no one singing. The warm red glow of fire had changed to a cool, pale, pearly light; and the rocky roof overhead had disappeared into shadows. He tried to listen to what they were singing. It seemed to be in Akkadian. He thought he could hear the words: 'The Lord, the Mighty One, hath spoken.' But that was all. They must be singing to the Dingir of the Underworld. Perhaps he was coming. The pearly light seemed to be getting stronger. 'He must be beautiful if he brings this light with him,' Shamashazir thought. Then the singing stopped. And he heard voices talking and footsteps coming towards him—the footsteps of the Dingir Nergal * himself.

The hammer in Shamashazir's head seemed to beat louder and harder. He discovered that his arms and legs were trembling with fear. He struggled to sit up. But he could not move. The dim form

* Nergal was the King of the Underworld.

24

of a huge man stood over him. Something that shone like gold hung round his neck.

'Forgive me, my Lord, for not rising to bow to you,' said Shamashazir in terror.

'You are courteous, O Shamashazir son of Teresh,' came the man's voice, surprisingly gentle. 'For my wife says that you are in great pain.'

'Yes,' said Shamashazir. 'I am.' For a moment the hammer in his head grew muffled and he felt himself drifting. But when his head cleared again the Dingir was still standing beside him.

'The pain,' said Shamashazir. 'The pain . . .'

The Dingir said nothing; but his head came lower and lower towards Shamashazir, so that he could see the bright gold round his neck. It was a chain, and the pattern on it he knew well. The face above it he knew. It must be Nannar. * Very gently the head was laid on Shamashazir's chest.

If Shamashazir had not been in such a queer state of mind, he would have been astonished that the Dingir of the Underworld should lay his head on his chest. But he was still so confused and muddled in his head that he thought of himself listening to his young brother Haran's chest, to hear if he was alive. And when the Dingir said to him, 'The life in you beats louder today,' he answered, 'I have broken the Image.' Then he remembered that it was Haran who had broken the Image. And he corrected himself: 'No, I did not break the Image. That was not me. I broke the laws of my father's house.'

But the Dingir did not answer; for a woman came with a cow's horn filled with goat's milk. It was the woman whom he had thought was his mother. But he could see now that this was not his mother. 'Where is my mother?' he asked. 'Won't she come again?'

'Maybe, if you go to sleep again, poor lad.' She gave Shamashazir the milk, looked at the Dingir and shook her head. Then they both went away and left him.

Shamashazir slept most of that day. And the woman fed him from time to time with more milk. He was very puzzled about her, because, although he now saw that she was not his mother, he felt sure that he had seen her before somewhere. But he was too sleepy and confused to ask any questions.

---

* Nannar, the Moon Dingir, was also one of the judges of the dead.

Gradually, as the silvery light grew brighter, and then faded and turned again to a dull red, the hammer in his head stopped beating; and he began to take more note of things about him. The red light that flickered—it was surely fire-light . . . he could smell the smoke. But he could feel no heat. In fact he was shivering with cold, in spite of the warm sheepskin that covered him. And the singing came again, echoing through the caverns. He listened to the words. He could hear them clearly, now that the hammer had stopped:

'Mine are all the fowls upon the mountains,
And the wild beasts of the field are in My hands.'

'Birds and animals,' thought Shamashazir. 'I am glad that there are birds and animals in the Underworld. But I suppose there must be; or they would not have given me goat's milk out of a cow's horn. There must be goats and cows, anyway, although I have not seen any.'

The singing went on:

'If I am hungry I will not tell thee,
For the whole world is Mine.
Thinkest thou that I will eat the ram's flesh;
And drink the blood of goats.'

'They must be singing about the Dingir Nergal. But that's a most extraordinary thing to say,' Shamashazir went on. 'Perhaps the King of the Underworld likes corn and dates and wine. And yet I can smell goat's meat cooking. Perhaps that is for the dead and not for the Dingir. I will ask the woman when she comes again. And then the song says that the whole world is his. It must mean the whole Underworld. But I suppose everything that lives comes to the Underworld in the end; so that in a sense the whole world is his.'

Shamashazir felt so much better that he was able to wriggle himself round a little, and raise his head to look round the cavern for the singers. He thought he saw them, a group of shadowy figures kneeling on their knees with their hands over their faces. He could not see the Dingir that they were speaking to. But after the singing was over, Nannar came again and asked Shamashazir if he felt any better.

'Yes, I do,' said Shamashazir. 'My head is clearer.' And then he added, 'I am sorry that I have no corn for you—nor dates—nor wine. I must humbly ask your forgiveness. It is the custom to bury people in the City of Ur with corn and dates and wine for their journey to the Underworld. But I wasn't buried.'

Nannar frowned. Then he said, 'There are dates that we bought from Serag the Lucky half a moon ago. And there is a handful of corn left. Would the son of Teresh be content to be buried with corn and dates and a dish of goat's milk for the journey?'

Shamashazir could not understand this answer. He could not understand why they mentioned Serag's name. 'Is Serag my cousin dead?' he asked. 'Where is he?'

'I have not heard that he is dead. We did not see him; nor did we see any sign of the caravan; nor did my men find his body when they brought in the cloak. I do not know if he is dead.'

The Dingir went away and Shamashazir shut his eyes. He began to think this could not be Nannar. He did not know if Serag was dead or alive. He must be some lesser dingir. Perhaps he was Neti. He fell into a doze, but was awakened again by voices near him.

The Dingir's voice said, 'He is preparing for death. He wants the burial of his people, with corn and dates and goat's milk.'

The woman's voice answered, 'Did he say the words that must be spoken?'

'No,' said the Dingir; but he spoke so softly that Shamashazir could not hear what followed. He wondered who they were talking about. A long conversation went on between them, half in whispers. And Shamashazir fell into a doze again. He was woken by a prayer being said across his head. He opened his eyes. He could just see two shadowy figures silhouetted against the dim flicker of the fire-lit walls. He listened intently.

'O Lord of all the Earth,' the Dingir's voice began. 'This son of Teresh is dying far from his people and from the gods of his father's house. Forgive the sins that this son of Teresh has committed against you, and take him into your care.'

But the Lord of all the Earth could not have been listening, for the arrow-heads stuck into Shamashazir's back as cruelly as ever. Or were they less sharp than yesterday? His head was better. Perhaps his punishment would soon be over, and the Dingir of the Underworld was relenting. The prayer went on about the greatness and the mercifulness of the Lord of all the Earth, and how He was a Shepherd of His people. Shamashazir lay listening to the droning voices, and drifted off into a long, sweet sleep.

He woke the next morning feeling much better. His headache

was bad; but the arrows were no longer sticking into the whole of his body. There seemed to be a kind of springiness to his bed, as if it were made of sticks and roots, instead of stone. He longed for parched corn.

The Dingir came again and looked down at him, holding a flaming torch from the fire. Shamashazir no longer felt afraid of him. He smiled, and the Dingir gave a sudden start as if he were surprised.

'Come,' he called into the darkness of the cave. And the woman was beside him. She knelt down and felt Shamashazir all over.

'He is warm,' she said, 'and he breathes like one who is not sick. Has the Lord of all the Earth, in His mercy, restored him to life?'

'Can a man who is dead come back from the dead?' Shamashazir wondered, listening to her words. Or perhaps he was not quite dead. He was very hungry. 'Your mercy and kindness are great,' he said aloud, and then he whispered: 'But I am hungry.'

The woman heard him, and laughed.

She brought him some milk, which he drank quickly instead of sipping a mouthful as he had done before. And she stood smiling at him, while the Dingir still held the flaming torch. She looked so pleased to see him drink that he dared to ask for parched corn.

'There is only a handful.'

'Let him have it,' said the Dingir. 'Blessed are they who show hospitality to the stranger.'

She went away to fetch it; and while she was gone, Shamashazir had a good look at the face of the Dingir, which he could see more plainly now, lit by the light of the torch. Where had he seen it before? Was it that of a statue in the Temple of Ur? Was it somewhere on his journey? Or was it on the hill above the gate of the Old City, where he had met Uz; and where all the dingirs had fought in the sky? Could this be the face of the 'Other One?' 'Who are you?' he said at last, in a quavering voice.

'Do you not know me? I am Enoch, the Ishak of the tribe of Enoch.'

Shamashazir was astonished and quite bewildered by the answer. He had seen the Ishak Enoch only for that short time when they had been his guests on the way to the mountains. What was he doing here. His mind was in a complete muddle, until he realized that if he were dead then the Ishak must be dead too. 'When did you die?' he asked.

'I am not dead,' the Ishak answered gently.

'Not dead!' Shamashazir gave up trying to understand what had happened, and just stared at the Ishak in blank confusion.

'Did you think you were dead, my son? I am not surprised. You must have been to the very gates of death. It is a thing of great marvel that a man can live after so terrible a fall.'

'If I am not dead what place is this then?'

'A cave in the mountains.'

'Oh!' said Shamashazir. 'I have heard of men who live in caves in the mountains. But the voices singing—whose are they?'

'They are my people praying to the Great Spirit, the Lord of all the Earth.'

The woman came back with the parched corn. And when Shamashazir had eaten it, he shut his eyes and tried to think what it meant to be alive again. He had thought for so long that he was dead that it took him some time to get used to the idea of living. When next he saw the Ishak he began to question him.

'How did I get here?' he said. 'And how did you get here? When we left you, you were many days' journey away.'

'At this time of the year we come up into the mountains where the air is cooler; and we make our way across to the Land of Milk and Honey to buy more corn. I sent my son ahead, to see that there were no wild beasts lodging in this cave, before we brought the sheep into the valley. And he found you lying at the foot of the peak where the people of the caravans sacrifice to their dingirs. You were lying like one who is dead. But my son, who has seen death strike both man and beast, knew there was life in your body. And he lifted you on his shoulders and brought you here. Then my wife, who is skilled in herbs, set the bone in your leg straight, as she would set the broken bone in the leg of a sheep. And she washed your wounds and tied them up with the leaves of herbs.'

Shamashazir lay and looked at him for some time, trying to take all this in. 'Then I am alive!' he said.

'Yes, my son; by the mercy of the Great Spirit you are still alive.'

'And shall I see the Land of Milk and Honey?'

'We are going that way.'

'And your son who found me—he is the Enoch who talked to me at the feast. Where is he now?'

'He is with the sheep.'

'Why doesn't he come? I should like to thank him.' But Shamashazir did not wait for an answer. 'And the woman who brings me food and prayed over me in the night, who is she?'

'She is my wife.'

'The Ishakeen . . . I think I understand,' said Shamashazir.

When the Ishakeen brought him bread soaked in milk, for his supper, he thanked her for setting the bone in his leg and binding his wounds; and then he ate the bread and milk greedily. He was certainly getting better.

In the morning they sang again. He did not see Enoch among them; but he listened intently, trying to catch every word, hoping to learn something about the Great Spirit who was Lord of all the Earth; and who, unlike the dingirs and Teraphim, did not need to be fed by men. He did not want goats' blood or the flesh of rams, but only a contrite heart. The Dingir—no, the Ishak of Enoch— he had said that Shamashazir was alive by the mercy of the Lord of all the Earth. Shamashazir marvelled that so great a dingir, whom he had never heard of before, should take so much trouble over him. No, he must not call the Lord of all the Earth a dingir. He was different. He might perhaps be the 'Other One' whose presence he had felt in Ur and who had been his guide.

Shamashazir wondered as he lay; and thought for a long time about his miraculous escape. For it seemed impossible to him that anyone could fall from such a height and not be dashed to pieces on the rocks below. 'The Lord of all the Earth must want me to do something for Him,' he thought; and began to wonder what it was, and how he could thank the Lord of all the Earth for His goodness in giving him his life.

For a quarter of a moon (which is about seven days), Shamashazir lay on his bed without being able to sit up, and thought, and listened. And every night at sunset, and every morning at sunrise, the whole tribe of forty—men, woman, and children—gathered in the centre of the cave, where the roof was highest and the sound of their singing echoed loudest; and each time they sang a different song to the Lord of all the Earth.

The one that interested Shamashazir most was the song of how, having made darkness and light, air, water, earth, grass, trees, and every kind of animal, the Lord of all the Earth last of all made man, and breathed into his nostrils a living soul so that He might talk to him on the hill-tops and in the caverns.

Talk to man! This was extraordinary and wonderful and quite different from what he had been taught in Ur about the beginning of the world.

So Shamashazir thought, as he lay helpless in the darkness, longing for the time when he could get up and join in the singing, and talk to Enoch the son of the Ishak, who had saved his life. He often saw him among the worshippers in the cave. But immediately the singing was over he would disappear.

Shamashazir asked the Ishak where he went.

'He is looking after the sheep.'

'I should like to thank him,' said Shamashazir. 'He must think I am ungrateful.'

The Ishak said nothing. But the next time that Enoch came in for his meal, he was sent first to speak to Shamashazir. He stood with his fine strongs arms folded across his chest.

'I want to thank you,' said Shamashazir. 'I owe you my life. If I ever get off this bed and can walk again, and if I ever go back to my father, I shall reward you for what you have done. My father owns silver and gold, and many cattle and sheep and camels and donkeys, and tents and carpets and many slaves. I am his eldest son and one day these things will belong to me, to do what I like with.'

'You may keep your reward,' said Enoch. 'I would have done the same for a goat.' And he turned on his heel.

A hundred needles seemed to stab Shamashazir's bones at this cruel rebuff. 'He's no bigger than I am,' he thought to himself—when he could begin to think at all. 'I must have been a great weight to carry. And yet he said he would have done it for a goat! I suppose he *would* carry a goat if it had broken its leg. They must always be carrying sheep that get hurt. But a goat!' Enoch had a very queer temper; but Shamashazir could not help liking him in spite of it. 'He behaves as if he were a king.' Then he remembered that Enoch had told him that once—before they had all been killed in battle—the tribe had been a great one. '*He* would have been their king; and I was boasting of my father's wealth!' Shamashazir gave a deep sigh of loneliness.

But the long, dark days of lying on his back came to an end at last, and the Ishakeen said he could walk with a pair of crutches, cut from two saplings by an old man of the tribe. Then one of the young men helped him to his feet; and he hobbled to the mouth of the cave and looked out over the valley.

That evening the children of the tribe collected heather and laid it in a heap up against the rocky cliff, outside the mouth of the cave, by the Ishak's throne—that same bundle of wool tied up in a linen cloth that Shamashazir had noticed when he first met the tribe of Enoch. Then one of them brought out the sheepskin from Shamashazir's bed in the cave, and laid it over the heather. 'Shamashazir is well today. He is coming to eat with us,' they shouted. And Shamashazir thought that now, at last, he would have a chance to talk to Enoch and perhaps to make friends with him.

But when the men had driven the sheep into the fold among the rocks for the night; and the tribe had gathered round the fire, Enoch took his place on the other side of his father, without a word to, or even a glance at Shamashazir, behaving as if he were not there.

The women had cooked rabbits, seasoned with herbs and wrapped in clay, and fish, which they laid on hot stones. The shepherds pulled the rabbits apart with their fingers and gnawed the flesh off the bones. But the fish fell to pieces, and had to be put on rough wooden platters. A whole family of children ate from the same platter, picking up the bits with spoons made of polished bone.

They talked of lions and their habits; and the Ishak listened, putting in a word now and again. Shamashazir tried to join in the conversation, but it was difficult as they had no lions in Ur except golden ones. But throughout the whole meal, Enoch spoke not a word.

When they had finished eating, the Ishak made a sign: and they all got up and went down to the stream to wash, so that they would be clean before singing to the Great Spirit. A girl brought Shamashazir a goatskin of water, and poured it over his hands. But when he made as if to struggle to his feet, the Ishak signed to him to keep still. 'We go to pray,' he said, as if he did not expect him to come. 'It is better for the son of Teresh to remain on his seat of heather.'

But Shamashazir refused to be an invalid any longer. He clung to a protruding rock and pulled himself upright. 'I can walk to the cave,' he said. 'Let me come with you to thank the Great Spirit who has saved my life.'

The Ishak seemed to hesitate.

Shamashazir reached for his crutches.

Then Enoch suddenly stepped forward, speaking for the first time. 'How dare he, Father!' he shouted. 'He is a heathen and a worshipper of idols and evil spirits.'

The Ishak held up his hand to silence him. 'The thanks, even of a heathen, are acceptable to the Great Spirit,' he said.

Enoch stood up very straight, clenching his fists. 'That is not the law.'

And the tribesmen echoed: 'True, O Ishak, that is not the law.' And they closed in behind Enoch, taking his side against his father.

The Ishak looked at them a moment, thoughtfully weighing the justice of their words and the power of their anger. 'It grieves me that the words of my son are true,' he said at last to Shamashazir. And he went into the cave, followed by all the men, women, and children, leaving Shamashazir standing alone among the discarded bones and debris of the meal.

He let himself gently down on to his seat of heather, and leant back against the rock, seeking comfort in its warmth. If he hadn't felt so weak and helpless, he would have been angry; but as it was it was hard to keep the tears from coming to his eyes. 'Stupid!' he said to himself. 'If so great a God as the Lord of all the Earth wants me to serve Him, what right has any man to stop me?' But as the sound of booming voices came from the cave and he listened to the familiar cadences of the sacred songs, he became calmer, considering what he should do next. The drowsy bleating of the contented sheep, folded in a near-by cave, seemed to speak patience. The swift, sure flight of one or two birds of prey, returning to their roosts for the night, attracted his attention by the delicacy of their movements, making him feel that he was clumsy and impetuous, and that these wild people must be spoken to with an art equal to that in the flight of the birds. The Ishak had at first seemed to be on his side. It was the law of the tribe that was against him. 'An Ishak cannot break the law,' he said to himself, thinking of the laws of Ur. But in Ur there were many skilled in argument who could prove that the law did not mean what it said. If the Lord of all the Earth wanted him, He would surely find some answer, even to the law. Shamashazir tried to think of the right words to explain all that he felt.

The glowing light of the setting sun turned the distant peaks to gold—and then to red. And it seemed as if the Great Spirit Himself were passing over the valley and standing beside him.

The booming of voices stopped; and the men began to come out of the cave, leaving the women and children to settle down for the night. They put more wood on the fire. And two of them took torches, and went to have a last look at the sheep in the fold.

The Ishak sat down beside Shamashazir, and began asking him questions about Ur. 'It is a very great and ancient city,' he said. 'Many kings and heroes must have lived and died there.'

'Oh yes,' said Shamashazir wonderingly. 'The archives of the Temple are full of the stories of great men. They are written on clay tablets.'

'Written?' said the Ishak. 'I have seen this writing in the City of Jericho. It is a great wonder that men can look at it and repeat the words of a man who is dead. And yet it is not the same as the telling of stories. Is there no telling of stories in Ur, from father to son, as we tell round the fire at night?'

'The old men tell stories on the roof-tops after dark; and my cousin Serag tells of his travels.'

'Ah! The old men! And what are the stories of the old men on the roof-tops, after dark?'

'Oh,' said Shamashazir, curiously watching the Ishak's face, 'they teach the children the great sagas of the people—about the Moon Dingir—and the Great Flood—and how the Ziggurat was destroyed and rebuilt—and about Cain and Abel.'

The Ishak smiled significantly, and sat silent.

Shamashazir thought that his opportunity had come. But as he was about to open his mouth to speak, he looked up, and was startled to see Enoch standing in front of them, watching him suspiciously. The words died on his lips.

The men were gathering round the fire now, some sitting, and some half lying, propped up on one elbow; talking quietly to one another about the lateness of the season; and the need to move on to the Land of Milk and Honey before all the corn was sold.

'What are the words that Shamashazir of Ur was about to utter to my father?' Enoch demanded quietly.

The Ishak looked up, and turned towards Shamashazir inquiringly. Shamashazir would have preferred to speak to the Ishak alone without Enoch's interference; but he felt he had to speak, now. 'Is it *never* permitted,' he began slowly, his voice slightly trembling, 'for a stranger to kneel beside the tribe of Enoch, when they pray, and to give thanks to the Lord of all the Earth?'

Enoch took a step forward. 'It is *never* permitted for a worshipper of unclean gods to approach the Great Spirit. Never!' He
glared at Shamashazir defiantly, his head well back and his chest
thrust out, as if he were ready to fight him. The men round the
fire stopped talking; and those who were lying down sat up and
listened.

Propped up as he was against the wall, Shamashazir could not
see the Ishak's face; only the clear-cut line of his cheek, and the
taut muscles of his powerful neck, silhouetted against the fire-light
in front of him, as he slowly turned his head towards his son, and
fixed him with a hawklike gaze of ferocity. But Enoch held his
ground, shifting his body slightly sideways, with his right shoulder
towards his father, as a man does in battle, and looked him steadily
in the eye.

What daring! And what outrageous boldness. Shamashazir would
never have had the courage to defy his own father in such a
manner. More than ever he wanted Enoch as a friend. But the
Ishak was speaking. 'It is not for you, my son, to declare the law
of the tribe,' he said.

Enoch's dark skin darkened angrily.

'He has already lain on the floor of the cave and heard the
secrets that no man should hear, and seen the rites that no man
should see,' he said.

The seated men began to murmur: 'The lad is right. The worshipper of unclean gods has heard too much. It is the law that he
should be killed.' They spoke without anger or malice; and none
of them moved to lay a hand on Shamashazir.

Enoch took a step backwards away from his father. 'That is the
law,' he said. 'He should be killed!' But he hesitated slightly and
seemed less certain.

The men backed him up again. 'The law must be performed,'
they said. 'Let the unclean stranger die.' They began to rock their
bodies to and fro, with their eyes half shut, chanting. They could
not kill a man in cold blood. They had first to work up their
passions.

But the Ishak remained still as a statue. And Enoch took another
step backwards, so that he stood in the gathering gloom of the
falling darkness. Shamashazir could see nothing but the fire-lit faces
of chanting men, and the dark line of the Ishak's cheek-bones. Still

and quiet, he stood as if he were trying to hold the tribe by his quietness. Gradually the shouting died away; and the Ishak spoke. 'Let the law be kept,' he said, raising his hand. And there was a deadly silence, broken only by the screeching of a distant owl, and the hissing of the flames. Shamashazir swallowed. His throat felt very dry.

Then the Ishak spoke again: 'In the days of my father, this was a great and powerful tribe with a long history of heroic deeds, and many laws which the elders of the tribe knew. And every day my father kept a court, and gave judgements between men and their neighbours. For when a multitude of people live together, there are disputes.'

'True, O Ishak!' said the voice of the old man from out of the gloom. But the younger men said nothing.

The Ishak went on: 'Since the battle of Jericho, when only a few lads and women escaped death, we have lived together as a family. No man has tried to take the life of his brother, nor stolen his wife, nor come to me for judgement. The laws of the tribe have been put away and forgotten. Now hear the law of the tribe of Enoch.' He raised his voice to a chant: 'No man shall lift his hand against a stranger who has eaten food by his fire.'

A sigh of relief went up from the tribesmen. And Enoch, who had been standing, sat down cross-legged, with his hands, palms upwards, in his lap—but still outside the circle.

The Ishak held up his hand again. He hadn't finished yet. 'And there is another law, that no kinsman of the tribe of Enoch shall be barred from worshipping the Lord of all the Earth.'

'Shamashazir of Ur is no kinsman,' said Enoch.

'Ah!'

'How could he be? Look at his face and his dark brown skin. It is the face and skin of a strange people.'

'It may be so. It may be not,' said the Ishak.

The shepherds mumbled something. They couldn't believe that Shamashazir was any sort of a kinsman; but they respected their Ishak. Their mumbling died away.

'I will tell you a story,' the Ishak went on. 'And Shamashazir will prove to you whether he is our kinsman or not. And you shall judge for yourselves.'

'That is fair and just,' said the men.

'And what do you say, my son?'

'It is impossible!'

'It is how it may be,' said the Ishak. 'But I have seen the hand of the Lord of all the Earth in this.' And he settled himself down and began:

'And the Great Spirit said unto Noah, "The end of all flesh is come before men, for the earth is filled with violence through them. And, behold, I will destroy them with the earth. Make thee an ark of gopher wood . . ."'

It was the story of Noah and the ark. It was the Akkadian version; word for word, the story that Shamashazir had learned from his grandfather. The only difference was that instead of the Dingir Enlil warning Noah of the Flood, it was the Great Spirit.

Shamashazir listened, astonished, leaning forward eagerly on his comfortable seat of heather and taking in every cadence of the Ishak's voice. Now and again the Ishak glanced down at him and then smiled, as if he were pleased at his rapt attention. He went on describing the animals going in two by two, and the fury of the storm.

When he got to the part where Noah lets out the raven, to see if there is any land showing above the water, he stopped and turned towards Shamashazir. 'O Shamashazir, son of the black-haired women of Ur and the shepherds of the hills, let my people hear the rest of this story from your lips—as it was told you in your father's house.'

Shamashazir gasped, shut his eyes, and began very nervously.

He was not a skilled story-teller like the camel men; and there were several versions of the Flood. He must not get them mixed up; and he must not on any account mention the name of the Dingir Enlil. So he shut his eyes and imagined himself sitting again on the clay bench at school, chanting the Akkadian version against that of the Sumerian boys. He seemed to hear the voice of Naychor ringing in his head, beside him. But he spoke the words slowly, giving a pause now and again to hold his listeners in suspense. Twice he caught himself saying 'En-' but he changed it to 'En— and . . . the Great Spirit', as if he had a stammer before mentioning the Divine Name. He was thankful when he had got safely to the end; and dared to open his eyes again.

Enoch's face was hidden in the darkness beyond the fire. But the Ishak was smiling; and all the shepherds gazed at him open-mouthed.

'That is good,' the Ishak said, raising his hand. And the shepherds murmured their approval.

Enoch suddenly jumped to his feet. 'It is a lie,' he said. 'In Ur they do not speak of the Great Spirit, but of Enlil. And I heard the lips of Shamashazir make the name of Enlil before he said the Great Spirit. The Great Spirit is not known in Ur.'

'My son,' said the Ishak, 'the Great Spirit is not known by *name* in Ur. But no living thing can breathe without his consent; and wherever men speak to one another, there the Great Spirit moves. He walked with Enoch our father upon the hills; and we are His chosen people. Every man on earth dances to the music of the Great Spirit. And the sons of Enoch were not all keepers of sheep. Listen now, while I question Shamashazir, and you yourselves shall be his judges.'

'That is fair, O Ishak of thy people,' the tribesmen answered; and Enoch squatted down on his haunches among the boys to watch and listen.

The Ishak swung round sideways, facing Shamashazir, and asked him if he knew the name of Noah's father.

'Lamech,' he answered at once.

'That is good, O Ishak!' said the tribesmen. 'We judge well. But that is not enough.'

'And who was the father of Lamech?' went on the Ishak.

'Methuselah.'

'And the father of Methuselah?'

There was a sudden tense silence among the listening men. Nothing could be heard but the gentle flicker of the flames over the wood.

'Enoch,' said Shamashazir very quietly.

There was a deep sigh as he spoke, as though all the watchers had been holding their breath.

'He knows,' said a tall shepherd called Eb—wonderment in his voice.

'He learnt it listening in the cave,' said another.

'We've said no word of it,' put in a good-natured man who went by the name of Sam. ''Tis no man that knows the secrets of our tribe but an angel of the Great Spirit.'

'I'm not an angel, nor a dingir, nor a teraphim. I'm a man, Shamashazir of Ur, and my father's name is Teresh. I had this knowledge from my grandfather, Nahor son of Serug.'

'And what was his father's name? And the father of your father?'

Shamashazir began to repeat his own ancestry backwards. A long string of names, over two thousand years, back to Noah. They went in a sing-song rhythm—Nahor, Serug, Reu, Peleg, Eber, Salah; but when he had got half-way through, the men of the tribe joined in. They had the same ancestors. Shamashazir was kin of their kin. And by the time they had reached Shem and Noah, they had pulled Shamashazir to his feet, and were kissing him on both cheeks, and welcoming him to the tribe like a brother.

All except Enoch. He stood alone and quiet among the boys, until the excitement had died down. Then the Ishak turned to him and said, 'Why does my son stand apart, and hold back from welcoming his kinsman?' And all the men looked at Enoch—mostly with sympathy; for they knew he was a proud lad, and they loved him.

With head erect he came towards Shamashazir, and with great dignity bowed to him, and said, 'Welcome, O Shamashazir of Ur, to the tribe of thy people.'

Shamashazir held out both hands to him; he hated apologizing himself. But Enoch having made his bow, turned again on his heel, and withdrew into the shadows.

'I give my thanks to the tribe of Enoch for the honour that they have done me; and especially to Enoch son of Enoch, who carried me from the rocks of death,' Shamashazir said. And then he felt so tired that he asked the Ishak if he might go to bed.

The shepherd called Sam took a burning torch out of the fire, and lighted the way into the cave where the children were sleeping; and where some of the women were talking together in low voices, waiting for their husbands.

In the morning Shamashazir had his breakfast with the tribe, outside, round the fire. And afterwards he exercised his leg, by walking two or three steps up and down in front of the cave with his crutches. He was very weak and every movement was an effort. The crutches were difficult to hold in place and kept slipping. Very soon he felt utterly exhausted and lay down to rest. After the long, dark days in the cave, it was wonderful to be in the sunshine again. The grass in the valley was so green and the sky so blue; every stone on the dusty earth seemed to have its own delicate colours, which he had never noticed before. And the sounds of birds and insects, and the half-muffled voices of men talking in the open air, were a new experience. And then, while he was resting, the Ishakeen brought a basket that she was making, and came to sit beside him, singing softly to herself a song that began:

> 'O come let us kneel before the Lord our maker,
> For we are the sheep of His pasture.'

And Shamashazir lay with his eyes shut, listening to her. He thought that she had a most beautiful voice; he had never heard her sing alone before. But even more beautiful, he thought, were the words. The Lord of all the Earth was looking after His people; as these rough shepherds gently cared for their sheep, carrying the lambs on their shoulders and leading the sheep to green pastures. But most of all, the words that pleased him were:

> 'In His hands are all the corners of the Earth,
> And the strength of the hills is His also.'

They reminded him of the mountain peaks from the top of the Wolf's Tooth. He sat up and began to tell the Ishakeen what he was thinking, his eyes glowing and his weakness forgotten.

'O Shamashazir, son of Noah,' the Ishakeen said gently, 'the Ishak has sent me to teach you the songs of the tribe of Enoch. The tribe of Enoch is your tribe; and its songs are your songs.'

The Ishakeen had taught all the children of the tribe; but she had never had a pupil so eager to learn as Shamashazir. He lapped up her words as a thirsty lion laps the cool waters of a mountain stream, until the Ishakeen said, 'You have learnt much in this day. Tell me again about your father and your brothers and sisters in Ur, and the death of your mother.'

So Shamashazir began to talk about himself and his family. And she listened with such sympathy that at last he confessed to her how he had deceived his father. 'But if I not done so,' he ended, 'I would never have come on this journey; and I would never have found the Lord of all the Earth.'

The Ishakeen was silent for a few moments, twisting the willows of her basket. 'There comes a time to every boy as he grows into a man,' she said, 'when he must obey the Lord of all the Earth before his father.'

'I wish I had known,' said Shamashazir.

'No *young* man can know. Many evil voices speak to the soul. Only by experience and a humble heart can wisdom come. But you, O Shamashazir son of Teresh, have a humble heart. You have heard the voice of the Lord while you are still a young lad. You will be the father of a great people.' She spoke slowly, looking straight before her like one who sees a vision. And Shamashazir felt that her words were the words of the Great Spirit Himself.

That evening he was allowed to go with the tribe into the cave to join in the singing. He sang with eyes shut, remembering the words without mistake, standing, balanced by his two crutches, a little behind the kneeling tribesmen. As the singing came to an end, and the last echo still rang in the hollows of the cave, he became aware of Enoch gazing at him. He looked up, smiling. The torch-bearer was coming towards them, illuminating both their faces; but Enoch quickly turned away his head. He had not spoken to Shamashazir all that day. Nor did he the next.

But at sunset, Shamashazir saw him coming with the sheep, and hobbled out to meet him, proud that he was learning so quickly to use his crutches. Because the uneven rocky ground was so slippery and difficult to walk on, he had to walk with bent head, watching every step; and progress was slow. He had only gone the distance of twenty-strides-of-a-man when he heard the sound of the approaching sheep, and looked up to greet Enoch.

But it was not Enoch who faced him with the sheep. The shepherd Sam stood where Enoch had been, and was leading them in. Enoch had vanished.

That night the men complained that the sheep had eaten all the best pasture, and that they had to go farther and farther up the valley every day to find food for them. But the Ishak let another quarter of a moon go by, before he gave the order to pack up, and get ready to move on the following day. The children gave a whoop of joy, and rushed into the back of the cave to bring out pack-baskets, to be slung on to the donkeys; and more baskets that the women would carry on their heads.

Shamashazir asked, a little uncertainly, where they were going.

'To the Land of Milk and Honey,' answered the Ishak.

'That is towards the west?' There was alarm and dismay in Shamashazir's voice. 'But my Father! My cousin Serag will return to Ur without me. If I could go back to the Village of the Changing Beasts, I could meet my cousin Serag. And when I got home my father would give you as much corn as you wanted, and a thousand sheep besides.'

'A thousand sheep! A *thousand*!' the youngest of the shepherds cried excitedly. 'We should be a rich and powerful tribe again with a thousand sheep!'

He was quickly silenced by the shepherd Eb. 'A thousand sheep —and ten men to look after them!'

'Your offer is gracious,' said the Ishak politely, 'but what my men say is true. We are too small a tribe to look after a thousand sheep in these hills; and too small a tribe to fight for the rich pastures of the plains. We are nothing but a handful of men, until our sons have grown. But nevertheless, you shall see your cousin Serag again, and you shall return with him to your father's house. But first we must buy corn from the Village of Kenan. Then we will turn northwards up the trade route to the White Mountains of the Bull; and there we shall meet your cousin on his way down.'

Shamashazir gratefully bowed his thanks to the Ishak. He would see the Land of Milk and Honey, and then go home to his father. And perhaps he would see the peaks of the White Mountains in the distance.

All that day the women spent in preparing for the journey. Flint knives, axe-heads, scrapers, bone picks and bone tools for digging, tents and sheepskins, bone combs, reed-pipes, skin water-bottles, cheeses, and the Ishak's throne of wool, were all packed into baskets, with as careful regard to balancing the loads as was taken by the packers in the warehouse of Teresh the Stern.

The old man who had made Shamashazir's crutches, and taught him how to get his strength back by resting, then bathing in the stream and walking, then resting again and bathing, watched him to see he did not overtire himself before the journey. For he was venturing farther and farther along the banks of the stream every day, exploring. There were fish in the water—different from the fish in the canals at Ur. They were spotted and barred to look like stones. And they moved across the bed of the stream as smoothly as a ripple made by the wind.

This day, going farther than ever, he went slowly upwards until he came to a great cliff—dark and mossy, and dripping with water from a stream which plunged into a narrow gorge, too rocky for him to follow. But high above his head, and growing from the top of the high wall of rock, was the familiar shape of the Wolf's Tooth.

It was the place from which he had fallen.

For a long time he stood staring at it, propped on his crutches, his neck bent back, marvelling at his own miraculous escape. Then gradually his thoughts were broken into, and he became aware of the bleating of sheep not very far away. He must have found the flock. Full of curiosity, he swung his crutches round and limped down again, round the base of the Wolf's Tooth. Long ago there had been a fall of rock. The land sloped in an ever steepening sweep almost sheer to the summit. The lower and more gradual slope was covered in grass—and the sheep were peacefully grazing. Two men with crooks were seated on a ledge high up the slope watching them. They had slings and piles of stones by their sides. Three other men were lying on the ground lower down, talking to one another. But between Shamashazir and the flock sat Enoch, alone, with his back to him, mending a reed-pipe and completely absorbed in his work.

One of the resting shepherds hailed Shamashazir and called a greeting to him, and then went on with the tale he was telling. But Enoch neither looked round nor altered the pace of his movements. 'What an opportunity to speak to him,' thought Shamashazir. He began to climb the hill, struggling with his crutches till he was out of breath.

But Enoch took no notice. Only, when Shamashazir was just five paces behind, he slipped down from his perch; and began leisurely to climb farther up the steep, rocky hill.

Shamashazir knew he could not follow. 'Enoch son of Enoch,' he called. 'It is I, Shamashazir, come to look for you.'

But Enoch never turned his head. He went on climbing, as if Shamashazir were nothing more than a mountain raven calling to its mate.

Disappointed, Shamashazir turned round and made his way back to the cave: where the old man scolded him for being away so long and going too far. 'I was coming to look for you,' he said, 'when I saw you down by the stream again.'

That night the inside of the cave seemed full of baskets. Some large and some small, and some lined with clay for carrying water. The children danced round them excitedly, explaining to Shamashazir which of the women was to carry each load, and which were going on the donkeys. He was surprised that the women, not the men, had to do the carrying. But the Ishakeen explained that the men had to be free to use their spears and sling-stones quickly.

The tribe set out along a narrow goat-track, in carefully arranged order: the Ishak and his son in front, with two men carrying spears and slings, and another loaded with a basket containing stones—to be hurled at any wild beast, or enemy, that they might meet. Behind them came the women, carrying baskets and babies, followed by the children and the old man leading the donkeys. Then came the sheep, jumping over the rocks and stopping at every possible opportunity to snatch mouthfuls of grass by the way. And last of all came five more men with crooks, among them Shamashazir, helped along by the shepherd Sam. Sam was good-natured, gentle, and talkative, and a marvel with the sheep. He told Shamashazir that he understood their language, and that they were better company than men. And as for the donkeys! It was wonderful what sense they had—cunning and obstinate they were. 'It is as if you had found a plover's nest, when a donkey makes a friend of you.'

Shamashazir liked Sam. He reminded him of the Sumerian people in Ur. He laughed at his stories about donkeys and ill-natured rams. Sam was considered a poor story-teller by the rest of the tribe, who admired tales of daring and adventure. He was pleased at Shamashazir's appreciation. And that night, round the fire, he invited Shamashazir to sit between him and his friend Eb. Eb was the opposite of Sam—a spear-man and the tallest and strongest in the tribe. He seldom laughed, and talked little; but when he did, according to Sam, he was the best story-teller of them all. 'After the Ishak,' he added. 'And when he was a lad, he was chosen to be the Ishak's armour-bearer.'

Shamashazir looked surprised.

'The old Ishak,' Eb explained, 'in the time when the tribe was nine hundred strong. I had to keep my basket filled with stones and hold the Ishak's spear when he used his sling.'

'Did the *Ishak* fight with stones?'

'When his arrows were spent. But he was a strong man and better with a sling than an arrow. He had another lad to carry his bow; but he was killed in the great battle of Jericho.'

'Tell me about it,' said Shamashazir.

But Eb shook his head. 'It is not a story that the Ishak likes to hear round the camp fire. I'll tell you tomorrow while the sheep are grazing.'

The next day they went only a little way, wandering slowly along a green valley, to give the sheep a chance to eat their fill before making a long, high climb over bare rocks where there was no pasture. Shamashazir was able to stop and bathe in the cool water again; and to talk to Eb, while he was resting from his turn at minding the sheep. He remembered his promise about the battle of Jericho, found a quiet place in the shade a little away from the others, and began:

'The tribe was a great tribe in those days—nine hundred strong. And when we were hungry, we raided the barns for corn and burnt the villages. It was cheaper and quicker than trading our wool. But we grew too bold. The villages that lay around the walls of the City of Jericho grew the richest crops. It is always so round a great city.'

'I know,' said Shamashazir. 'But in Ur we do not leave our corn out in barns. We bring it straight into the Temple granaries.'

'So did the people of Jericho. But we fell upon them in a great force, as they were taking the corn along the road to the city. Once we did it. Twice we did it. But the third time a great army was lying in wait for us.' Eb paused. 'I was a lad of your age. It was the first real fighting that I had seen. The old Ishak went down with a bronze spear between his ribs. And I turned and ran, and ran, and ran. I ran till I had no breath left in my body. Then I crept under some bushes, and was sick with the sight of what I had seen. I heard the horsemen and chariots of Jericho thundering past me, and the screams and cries of the wounded. They surrounded our sheep and drove them down to the city; and they carried off our women and children. I lay and watched from under the bushes. And afterwards, when all was quiet and darkness had fallen over the groaning and bloody plain, I made my way back to the hills, to a cave in the rocks where we had sometimes folded our flocks. I wondered how I should live. And I looked out for any sign of sheep which had broken away.' He stopped again, thinking of the desolate hillside, and how he had come to the cave and heard voices that he knew. Then he told how he had found the Ishak's son with his wife and their child Enoch (little more than a baby), with a handful of lads who had been left to guard the flock during the battle, and who had escaped the charge of the men of Jericho; and how together they had searched the mountains for stray sheep; and how they had found one of the shepherds who had run away from the battle, and had collected a small flock. 'There he is,' said Eb, pointing to the old man who had made Shamashazir's crutches. He flicked a green and yellow beetle off his knee and got up to take his turn with the sheep. Shamashazir watched him go down the hill and greet Enoch, who was now free to rest.

Sam, and the other shepherd who had been watching the flock, came over to Shamashazir and asked him how he had enjoyed Eb's story; but Enoch sauntered over to the opposite side of the valley. Shamashazir watched him stretch himself out in the long grass; then, measuring the distance with his eyes, took up his crutches. He decided to go over and try to speak to him again. But Sam called out to him to rest his leg, for they had a hard day ahead of them.

Obediently, Shamashazir sat down and lay back. The long grass stood up like a miniature forest all around him. He could see nothing but the sky above him—neither Sam nor Enoch. 'If I can't see them, then they can't see me,' he thought; and leaving his crutches behind, he began to wriggle and crawl on his belly through the grass, towards the opposite side of the valley, where he had last seen Enoch. The earth was warm and dry. Grasshoppers jumped into his face; and the long grass tickled his nose. Now and again he raised his head and looked around. As he got nearer, he could see the hump of Enoch's brown shoulder turned towards him. Nearer and nearer he crawled. Then suddenly Enoch stood up. He stretched and yawned and, without glance at Shamashazir, began to walk leisurely over to the other side of the flock. Shamashazir lay still in the grass; and presently crawled back to his crutches and to Sam.

The next day they followed the stream, going upwards towards its source. As they got higher, the view through the mountains widened. Shamashazir thought he could recognize some of the summits, that he must have seen from the Wolf's Tooth before his fall.

The grass on these upper slopes was thin, and the ground became steep and rocky. They went on—higher and higher—until they were faced with a cliff of sheer rock that towered over them, and completely barred their path upward. Then they turned off sideways, along a goat-track that skirted the bottom of the sheer rock and took them right round the mountain, to the head of another stream going downwards. They followed it into a deep valley, where the sun never shone, but the grass grew lush. And there they put up their tents and stayed for two nights.

The valley was narrow. The cover was good; and the sheep were never far away from the camp. Shamashazir determined to hunt Enoch down in good earnest, as Sam hunted the rabbits. 'I'll make friends with him if I have to fight him first,' he said rather boastfully to himself—considering Enoch's natural strength and quickness. So all that day he crawled through the grass, trying to get near enough to Enoch to speak to him. But Enoch had ears as sensitive as a deer's and eyes as keen as a hawk's. A leaf could not fall on the ground without his noticing it; for his very life depended on the acuteness of his senses. What chance had the clumsy Shamashazir to track him down?

When they met together round the fire to eat their parched corn and goats' cheese, he saw Enoch's face, lit by the flames, turn towards him for a moment. And he thought there was a slight twinkle in his eye.

The talk that night was of stalking rabbits. 'It's queer,' said his friend Eb, 'the way a fox knows to keep down-wind of his prey.'

'Nothing queer,' said Sam. 'He learns it from his mother.'

'Your fox, that you took as a cub, had no mother to teach him.'

'He learnt it from me,' said Sam. 'I took him hunting with me. That fox understood every thought that entered my head. . . . until the night he heard a vixen cry. Then he went like an arrow from a bow.'

'Down-wind,' thought Shamashazir. 'I must try that.'

So the next day, he noticed carefully from which direction the wind was blowing, before he set out to hunt Enoch. But it was useless. Enoch's face unmistakably bore a smile of amusement, when they met across the fire again; and all the shepherds seemed inclined to tease him. Sam asked if he would like to come rabbiting with him the next day, or if he had caught anything on his own.

Shamashazir felt he was making himself ridiculous. But he was not going to be stopped by that. 'I am not hunting for rabbits,' he said. 'My quarry is a greater quarry than any beast of the field, or of any hunter with a spear. For my quarry is the quarry of friendship.'

There was silence after Shamashazir had spoken. Then the Ishak began to tell a story about the loyalty of two friends whose tribes were enemies. All the while he spoke, Enoch sat with bent head, gazing into the palms of his hands, which lay limp in his lap.

When the story came to an end, with one friend dying to save the other's life, he gave a quick glance towards Shamashazir, caught his eye, and lowered his head again.

Then the Ishak pronounced a blessing; which meant that it was time to lie down and go to sleep. But Enoch remained seated; for it was his turn to share the first watch that night.

In the morning, Shamashazir's leg was so much stronger that he was able to throw away his crutches, and walk with a couple of sticks that Eb cut for him. They followed the sheep again. Enoch in front with the spear-men, and Shamashazir walking with Sam. He was very puzzled as to the direction in which they were going. Sometimes it seemed towards the north and sometimes south or west; and once or twice east—directly back towards the way they had come. He even thought he saw the Wolf's Tooth again. They seemed to have gone round in a circle. Sam explained that they had to do this to avoid taking the sheep over the high mountains, where there was no food. There were one or two of these twisting low routes through the mountains. But not many tribes knew of them. 'The big tribes keep to their own grazing grounds, which they have fought for. But we have to find food where we can.'

At midday they stopped on a sunny slope.

It was hot. The cicadas shrilled. Enoch was sitting on a rock with the sheep. Shamashazir lay lazily dozing, half listening to the talk of the men around him. Suddenly he felt a shiver of cold. Although the sun was high, the shadow of the mountain was creeping over the valley. He sat up.

'Not hunting today?' asked Sam, who was kneeling down sharpening a fishing-spear in the newly-lit fire.

'The grass is short; and my leg aches,' said Shamashazir.

'Hunting on your belly would give it a rest,' Sam answered.

But Shamashazir did not move.

'The ways of men are even stranger than those of beasts,' said Sam thoughtfully. 'They will face arrows and swords and knives and the teeth of a lion. But laughter and a few words will turn their courage to water, and make them as fearful as naked birds in the nest.'

Shamashazir looked at his kindly face and smiled. Then he stood up and stretched. 'If only I could learn some of your hunter's cunning,' he said.

'No cunning of mine would catch Enoch son of Enoch. Only patience will catch a fish such as he.'

Shamashazir began to limp down the valley, making no attempt to hide himself. But he had left his sandals behind and was walking barefoot through the dusty, dried-up grass, stepping as softly as he could. Enoch, who had been carving a pattern on a goatskin pouch, put his work down, thrust his knife into its sheath and picked up his reed-pipe. Then, without altering his position or turning his head, he began to play two or three soft notes over and over again.

Shamashazir advanced step by step, moving in time with the tune, hoping the music would drown the soft rustle of his footsteps. Nearer and nearer he came; and Enoch did not move. But his body was tense like a listening deer's. Then, still without turning his head, he withdrew the pipe from his lips and said, 'Why is it, O Shamashazir son of Teresh, that you follow me about like a ram follows a ewe?'

Shamashazir was taken aback. 'I want to be your friend,' he said at last.

'How can the son of Teresh, who owns five hundred camels and ten thousand sheep; and who can read and write magic words, be the friend of Enoch the shepherd?'

'Friendship is greater than sheep or camels. Besides, there are not five hundred camels nor *ten* thousand sheep.'

'A great Ishak will make a friend of the meanest of his servants if it pleases him. And yet when the time comes, he will order his friend to be killed, and take his wife to live with him.'

'If my father did such a thing in Ur, he would be punished by the law.'

Enoch turned round and stared at him. 'Punished!' he said, astonished. 'Can a man like your father, whose caravans are known from Egypt to the White Mountains of the Bull, be punished by the law?'

'Of course,' said Shamashazir. 'The law is more severe on rich men with important positions. They have more knowledge, and less temptation to break the law than the poor, the ignorant, and the hungry.'

'Oh,' said Enoch thoughtfully. 'Ur is a strange city where the great are punished.'

'The possession of camels and sheep is not considered of any great account in Ur. Magistrates who serve the law, and priests who serve the Dingir, and clerks who keep the accounts and archives of history, are of higher rank than merchants. In the time of the

Sumerian kings there were no merchants, for all sheep and camels and donkeys belonged to the Temple.'

But Enoch was not listening. He was working something out in his mind. 'The tribe of Enoch serves the Great Spirit and I am the Ishakki of Enoch; so my rank is higher than the high priests and magistrates of Ur.'

Shamashazir wanted to laugh at Enoch's audacity; but he wanted his friendship even more. 'To Shamashazir son of Teresh you are of more account than priests and magistrates,' he answered.

Enoch darted a piercing glance at him, suspecting he was being mocked. But Shamashazir met his inquisitorial stare with eyes of unwavering candour.

Like two rams taking one another's measure, the two boys faced each other, Enoch questioning, Shamashazir letting the flame of his spirit shine in his eyes. Then Enoch smiled, nodded his head slightly, and moved a little sideways on the rock to make room. Shamashazir climbed over and sat down beside him.

'My father made me foolish before you,' Enoch said in a friendly voice.

'My father also forgets that I am a man. But all the boys in my school make the same complaint of their fathers. We say it is the way of fathers in Ur.'

'Explain this school,' said Enoch.

Shamashazir explained. It took a long time; because Enoch did not know what brick was, nor a bench, nor had he ever seen a clay tablet or a stylus. Shamashazir had to describe rooms and houses and crowded streets.

That night, Enoch came back to his seat by his father at the camp fire; and Shamashazir sat beside him. And the next day, Shamashazir began, very tentatively, to ask questions about the Great Spirit, explaining that he wanted to give up serving the dingirs of Ur, and to serve the Great Spirit for the rest of his life.

To his surprise, Enoch looked as pleased as if he had been his brother. 'I have looked into your eyes and seen that they are good,' he said. 'And the Great Spirit likes good people better than images and temples of gold or silver. He likes better the things that He has made with His own hands. Look——' and he waved his arm, pointing to the valley where the sheep were grazing. Butterflies flew from flower to flower, and a cruising eagle swooped on its prey.

'So do I,' said Shamashazir.

5 THE ISHAKKI OF KENAN

Shamashazir's leg got rapidly better. His knee was still a bit stiff, and tired easily. But if he took his time, he could climb without help over most of the rocks that lay in their path. The two boys spent all day together, following the sheep as they slowly wandered through the valleys on their winding journey. Enoch was like a brother. He had never had the companionship of a boy of his own age; and he threw himself heart and soul into his first friendship. He began by teaching Shamashazir the laws and secrets that had been handed down from father to son for generations—to know the plants and roots and berries, which were good to eat, which were poisonous, and which were healing—and the language of birds and how to use it.

'When you see a small bird fly up suddenly from out of the bushes, you know that there is something moving about that you can't see,' Enoch explained. 'It might be a lion, or an enemy from another tribe; or it might be only a fox. And then you give a warning call, like this . . .' And he imitated the high mewing of an eagle so exactly that a bird wheeling above them answered back, and the shepherds resting in the grass leapt to their feet. But Enoch waved to them; and they sat down again.

'Phew!' said Shamashazir. 'I wish I could do that.'

Enoch tried to teach him. He tried to teach him how to make the calls of all the birds, and the foxes and wolves. Enoch could call to a fox as if he had been its mate. But Shamashazir was no mimic, and he was so little used to hearing the calls of birds and beasts that his efforts were ridiculous. Enoch found it difficult not to laugh at them. If he had been a Sumerian, he would have held his sides and shaken with merriment. But the Akkadian shepherds looked upon laughter as an insult. So Enoch politely changed the subject, and began to talk about the songs of the Great Spirit, which pleased Shamashazir much more. He had learnt them rapidly because he was so keenly interested. But Enoch said that it was not fair that he should do all the teaching and Shamashazir all the learning. He would like to hear more about the City of Ur.

But when Shamashazir began to tell him something about its complicated laws and society (always taking great care not to mention the dingirs), Enoch kept interrupting him with 'What is a magistrate?' and 'What is a baker?' or 'What is a porter?' and 'What is a boat?', until Shamashazir had to give it up. It was impossible to describe so vast a city to a boy who had lived all his life in caves and tents.

'We don't seem to be able to talk each other's language,' said Shamashazir, thinking of the bird-calls.

But Enoch misunderstood him. 'Language . . .' he said. 'I like the sound of the strange words: Gi-mil-Ma-ma, and hul-lu-pu, A-me-lu. Teach me the language, so that I can talk to you as your cousin Serag the Lucky does, and no one will understand what we say.'

Shamashazir jumped at the idea; for it was very difficult to talk about Ur without mentioning the dingirs. They were in everything and the cause of everything.

Enoch's mind was fresh. He was wonderfully quick at learning. Shamashazir had only to repeat a word three or four times, until Enoch had got the sound of it into his head, and he never forgot it. He was very particular to imitate Shamashazir's exact voice as well as the words. So that a conversation between them sounded as if Shamashazir were talking to himself in broken Sumerian.

And so gradually, with Enoch's teaching, and as his leg got steadily stronger, Shamashazir began to feel less awkward and clumsy among these swift and silent moving men of the wild places. He learned to spot fish as they lay in the rocky pools of the mountain streams; and after that, to spear them with a sharp stick.

At dawn and dusk they used to go out rabbiting. Shamashazir learned to lie flat over the burrows and catch the rabbits as they came out of their holes. He thought he would like to live like this for ever: sleeping under the stars at night, listening to tales round the fire, fishing and hunting, and following the sheep. He liked it even better than walking with the caravan; for they went more slowly. There was time to stop and look at the exciting things that were going on in the streams, behind the bushes, and even under the rocks in the mountains. They found a snake's nest. And inside the transparent eggs they could see the young snakes coiled round and round like tiny springs. They found a toadstool as big as a man's head, which they cooked and ate; and a young kid whose mother had been killed. They gave it to one of their goats to feed; and it followed with the flock. Hidden by bushes, they lay and watched young foxes at play together, and ate the mountain berries. They bathed in cool mountain streams, and lay on the hot rocks to dry in the sun. And Enoch taught Shamashazir how to make a fire by striking iron-stone and flint together.

But all things come to an end. And one day, after going through a long valley and a deep gorge, they came out of the mountain country—and suddenly found themselves looking down on a wide plain, with a great stretch of open sky above their heads. The plain was filled with vineyards and cornfields and olive groves; and here and there a few cattle were grazing. They had come at last to the Land of Milk and Honey.

They did not go down into it, but turned towards the north, and followed a track along the side of the hill, where the grass was short and thick and good for the sheep. Shamashazir noticed a man ploughing a field just below them. 'What a queer sort of plough,' he thought; for it had no wheels. 'It must be very hard work for the oxen,' he said, pointing it out to Enoch. But Enoch had never seen a wheel on anything except a chariot, and he could not understand how a wheel could be fixed to a plough, or what good it would be.

When they sat down to their meal that night, the Ishakeen, who had also noticed the plough, said, 'The man that we saw ploughing this morning had come to his last furrow. And much land have I seen this day lying ready for the seed. If we do not go down into the villages at once, my husband, we shall be too late.'

The Ishak agreed that there was no time to be lost. 'I will send Enoch with Shamashazir tomorrow.'

The Ishakeen was shocked at the idea of her son going on such an expedition. He was too young and too precious to do trading with those accursed heathen.

'He is fourteen years and nearly a man,' said the Ishak. 'It is time that he learnt his duty. With Shamashazir, who is used to trading with all manner of men, he will learn well. Does not Shamashazir son of Teresh have knowledge about the price of wool, and the prices of corn and cheeses?'

Shamashazir smiled, thinking of his father and Gimil Mama sitting together in the warehouse. 'I have heard talk about wool,' he said. 'About corn I know only a little.' But he was eager to go and see these terrible savages. Enoch backed him up.

The Ishakeen was still uneasy. She tried hard to persuade her husband to change his mind. But the Ishak declared that no mother ever liked her son to grow up and do dangerous things. And the whole tribe agreed with him.

So the Ishakeen had to content herself with saying to the boys: 'See that you remember your prayers to the Great Spirit. And do not join in with the sacrifices of the corn people, for they are an abomination.'

The Ishak gave them most careful instructions about buying the corn: how to choose it, and how to examine the grain at the bottom of the sacks. 'For they will hide the bad grain at the bottom,' he said.

Eb and Sam, Shamashazir's friends, were chosen to go with them. Eb made a solemn vow before the Great Spirit to protect the Ishak's son with his life. Then they set off with three donkeys, saddled with baskets to bring back the grain in, and laden with fleeces, and cheeses made from goats' milk, to exchange for the corn.

The rest of the tribe went slowly towards the northern trade route, to get to it before Serag passed that way. They did not want to hurry their sheep.

It was hot in the plains among the ploughed fields and olive groves, and the boys took off their cloaks and put them in the donkeys' baskets. The donkeys, used to the mountain air, walked slowly in the dusty heat, and the boys felt in no mood to hurry.

But by the time that they had covered seven miles, Shamashazir's leg had begun to ache; and he was glad when at last the smoke from the village fire came in sight. The village itself was a large collection of one-roomed huts made of reed and plastered with mud. Round it was a low stone-and-earth wall, about the height of a man, which hid everything from their sight except the straw-thatched roofs of the circular huts.

When they reached the gate—an open gap—they saw that the whole village was decorated with flowers and berries and sheaves of corn; and they heard a noise of great excitement coming from within. Eb looked at Sam and raised his eyebrows ominously. 'The Feast of Sowing,' he said. 'You had better be quick with your buying and selling, young Ishakki. We don't want to get ourselves mixed up in *that*.'

Enoch looked a trifle anxious. His face and whole body became alert, and he walked with bent knees, crouching slightly and ready to spring to one side, as if he were hunting or being hunted. He and Shamashazir left the two men with the donkeys, in the shade of an olive-tree outside the village, and went up to the gate together; Enoch, still like some wild animal, half crouching. But Shamashazir walked with the calm dignity of a citizen of Ur.

The elders of the village were wearing long white linen robes, embroidered round the borders with scarlet and black. 'It must be a very rich village to buy so much cloth,' said Shamashazir, in Sumerian.

Enoch looked uneasily at him and whispered back, but in Akkadian: 'They may take you for some devil, if you talk in a strange language before we have exchanged words of peace.'

Shamashazir nodded and was silent.

Two of the white-robed elders were already coming to meet them. They asked the boys who they were and what their business was, speaking in a thick kind of dialect, which Shamashazir found difficult to understand. Enoch delivered his father's message about the corn, and explained that Shamashazir was a kinsman and a merchant from the City of Ur.

The elders were pleased. They felt honoured to have a visitor from so famous a city. For even in the Village of Kenan the city of Ur was known. They greeted both boys with ceremony and courtesy, which reassured Enoch. He straightened himself up, and followed after them into the open square in the centre of the village. There, the Ishak sat in front of his mud hut, on a wonderful wooden chair inlaid with silver and lapis lazuli.

The chair was so bright, and its workmanship so unexpected in the village of mud, that they both stared at it in wonder, not heeding at first the man who was sitting on it. The Ishak Moab was colourless; and his eyes were listless as if he had no joy in living. Enoch took an instant dislike to him. There was something fearful and guilty in the set of his face that repulsed the honour-loving Enoch. But Shamashazir, more used to scoundrels and liars and cowards, wondered what it was that made this tribal king cringe on his gorgeous throne.

With a nervous movement of his hand towards the seats of honour (two benches roughly hewn out of a tree with a stone axe), he invited them both to sit down; and offered them a meal and a night's rest. Enoch accepted with a bow—as was the custom of good manners. And they took their places, one on either side of the Ishak.

Talking rapidly, he began to apologize to Shamashazir for the meanness of his palace (which was nothing more than a mud hut, larger than those of the rest of the village). 'I have heard it said that in the City of Ur the King's palace is made of solid gold; and the houses of the meanest people are made of pottery.'

'The shrine of the Moon Dingir is made of gold. And the drains are made of pottery,' Shamashazir answered. 'But the houses are made of brick and wood.'

The Ishak had no idea what drains and bricks were; but went on impressively: 'I have been considering making myself a house with cut stone. It would be more difficult for thieves to break into, to steal my treasure.'

Shamashazir bowed. He had never seen a house of cut stone.

'But the stone is far away,' the Ishak Moab continued, looking towards the mountains, which were about two miles from the village as the crow flies. 'And my young men are too proud to carry stones. They say it is work for women and slaves. But to capture slaves, war is necessary.' And the Ishak shook his head, gave a deep sigh, and thinking he had done sufficient honour to his foreign guest, turned to Enoch and began talking to him about the crops and the weather: complaining how bad they had been, and how small the harvest was.

Shamashazir turned his attention to the rest of the village. On the ground, facing them, a semi-circle of cruel-faced elders listened intently to what the Ishak was saying.

The Ishak spoke with a heavy flatness in his voice. When he laughed, his laughter had a hollow ring, as if there were no humour in it; and the elders scowled. 'He is no leader of men,' Shamashazir thought, and wondered how he came to be the Ishak of such a fierce-looking, warlike tribe. There was no fear on the faces of the elders.

Then Shamashazir's attention was drawn towards a small boy of about seven years, who was sitting hugging his knees at the Ishak's feet, as still and solemn as a little old man. His only movement was to twist himself round now and again, to take a long look at Enoch while he was speaking. And then suddenly he turned a pair of dark, haunting eyes on to Shamashazir; and Shamashazir felt an inexplicable shudder of fear. He looked back into the little boy's face, curious to see why it had this effect. The pupils of the boy's eyes were dilated with a silent terror. But he seemed to decide that he liked Shamashazir; for, putting his hands to the ground, he shifted his position slightly, moving towards him as if he were moving towards a friend. Then he turned back to his former attitude of fixed attention, staring straight across the square.

Shamashazir looked in the same direction; but there was nothing visible more frightening than the faces of the elders—only the doorway of a large hut, an oblong of deep blackness in the sunbaked wall. It was a doorway like any other doorway, except that two men stood on guard, one on either side of it. It belonged to a hut like any other hut. But Shamashazir began to find his attention drawn more and more towards this particular doorway. Here and there a flake of mud had been chipped off the wall, revealing by the greyness of the reeds underneath, that the hut had not been built recently. Once or twice he thought he saw a faint movement in the blackness. There seemed to be somebody inside.

Then, suddenly, the little boy's back stiffened; and out of the doorway lunged an older boy. 'A bully! Of course!' And Shamashazir almost laughed at himself for feeling so concerned; for the older boy was no more than eleven years-by-the-sun. But his face was puffy and swollen and his eyes were bloodshot. He hovered outside the hut, then came stumbling towards them like a man who has been struck in the back with a knife. Shamashazir's hand gripped the hilt of his own knife; and he looked at Enoch, who was still talking to the Ishak. They both glanced up, and then went on with their conversation. Enoch turned slightly paler and the Ishak seemed to have become suddenly hoarse; but neither moved. And none of the watching elders stirred. Only the little boy watched every swaying movement with large, frightened eyes.

The older boy began to laugh, a wild, senseless laugh, and to roll his head round, babbling in a thick voice that Shamashazir could not understand. But Enoch could. For a moment his back curved into the hunter's crouching position; and his fingers twitched as if it were all he could do to keep his hand from the hilt of his knife. Then he looked at Shamashazir and pulled himself upright again.

The boy came forward, right up to the Ishak's knees, bringing with him a strong smell of wine. 'That explains his staggering,' thought Shamashazir. 'But why is the little boy afraid?' He would have brushed aside the incident as bullying; but lurching suddenly, the boy turned to Shamashazir and tried to fling his arms round his neck. Shamashazir pushed him off; and he fell to the ground, shaken with sobs, tears beginning to stream from his eyes.

The Ishak said, 'It is my son.' Then he added, as if some explanation were needed and this would be sufficient: 'At the new moon it is the Feast of the Corn Dingir.'

Not knowing what to answer, Shamashazir bowed; and then began to look round the village square for other signs of drunken feasting. Two women passed behind the huts, carrying earthenware pitchers on their heads, and speaking to each other in hushed and awed voices. A child followed, sucking a pomegranate and spitting out the pips. There seemed to be no one else about. He looked at the elders for signs of intoxication, but the circle of eyes met his, dark and watchful.

The Ishak turned back to Enoch and tried to continue his conversation, but his voice died away; and instead, he called for food to be brought in. Shamashazir noticed that Enoch's hands were clenched, and the muscles of his arms quivering slightly.

The little boy seemed to have taken a fancy to Shamashazir; for when they had eaten, and the Ishak had conducted them to a shady mulberry-tree to rest, the little boy followed. And when the Ishak left them, and they both lay down, he stayed behind, squatting on the ground a little beyond their feet.

Shamashazir asked him what his name was.

'Zepho,' he answered, and explained that he was the youngest son of the Ishak, and that Shaul was his brother. 'We are two,' he said, holding up two fingers and thoughtfully looking at them. 'Shaul says once there were all those.' And he held up the fingers of both hands. 'But after the Feast of the Corn Dingir they go. One goes, and one goes... Iran, and Agag, and when the full moon comes, Shaul is going. And at the next Feast it will be me, because I am the only one left. But that is not for a long time.' The litle boy's eyes grew round and his voice dropped to a whisper. 'They crown him like a king, and then they all bow down to him. And they worship him *as if he were the Dingir*!' He was silent, watching Shamashazir, who had sat up to hear better. And then he said almost inaudibly, giving a slight shudder, 'I do not like it. Nor does Shaul. We do not want to have honour like the men who go to battle.'

Shamashazir did not answer. He sat hugging his knees, trying to piece together what he had seen and heard, to make some kind of sense. The little boy, overcome by the heat and exhausted by his lonely terror, gradually toppled over on to the ground in a disturbed sleep.

Enoch lay beside his friend, face downwards, propped on his elbows, his forehead resting on his cupped fingers. He seemed deeply troubled.

'There is something evil going on in this village,' said Shamashazir. 'Something that I do not understand.'

Enoch looked at him sharply. But he said nothing.

'In Ur, the Feast of the Corn Dingir is a happy feast. The harvest has all been brought in, and the granaries in the Temple are full of corn. But here, in this village, the Ishak looks like a slave who has been caught stealing, and his son, nothing more than a boy, is crazy with drink.'

Suddenly Enoch sat up. 'Shamashazir of Ur,' he said. 'That boy is the sacrifice. Have you no mercy?'

Shamashazir's jaw dropped and his dark skin paled. 'The sacrifice, did you say? That boy we saw drunk? Is he to be *sacrificed*!'

'Have you not seen such sacrifices in Ur?'

'In Ur!' Shamashazir's astonished voice rose to a high squeak. 'In Ur! Ur is a city of enlightenment and new discoveries. We do not sacrifice boys in Ur—not since the Flood! There have been no human sacrifices since the Flood.'

It was Enoch's turn to look astonished. 'You grow corn in Ur and you worship dingirs and yet you . . .' He could not finish his sentence. Slowly he relaxed and dropped back into his former position, lying very still with his face covered by his hands. For a long time there was silence under the cool mulberry-tree. All this time he had been thinking of Shamashazir as a practiser of savage rites, from a heathen city of abomination. He, the Ishakki of Enoch, had made a mistake and was in the wrong. By the customs of Shamashazir's family he would be expected to apologize. He was fighting his pride. But it was Shamashazir who at last broke the silence. 'If you thought we sacrificed people in Ur,' he said, 'I can understand why you did not want to speak to me.'

'You are merciful, O my brother,' said Enoch. 'My sin was great.'

No more words passed between them. But from that moment, Enoch's liking for Shamashazir turned into the deepest admiration. He felt sure that Shamashazir had been saved from death and sent to them by the Great Spirit; and that every word he said must be listened to and obeyed.

After the midday rest they went back to their seats of honour, one on each side of the Ishak. And the young men of the village entertained them with wild dances, and songs about the history of the people of Kenan. The Ishak apologized for there being no women to take part in the dances; but they were all very busy grinding corn and making bread and preparing for the days of feasting. It was a great pity that so important a traveller as Shamashazir had come at such a moment. He would understand that nothing less than the Feast of the Corn Dingir would cause such a breach of hospitality. To all of which Shamashazir bowed politely. He was feeling rather sick at what he had seen and heard in the village, and wanted to be alone, away from all the noise and shouting of these savage men. He said that he would like to see the women baking. He would like to know if they used the same kind of ovens as in Ur.

The Ishak thought this was a rather curious request. But he asked one of the elders to take Shamashazir round to the women's quarters; while Enoch sat watching the dancing men, continuing from time to time with his bargaining.

In a large open compound behind the Ishak's hut there was a scene of great busyness. Women were gathered in groups, working intently and talking together in low voices. Some were grinding corn between two flat stones; some mixing flour in earthenware bowls. And some were watching the ovens—conical ovens put over the raked-out centres of glowing fires. Inside, thin, wet lumps of dough, looking more like pancakes than bread, were stuck to the hot sides of the cones; and fell to the ground when they were cooked. It was a long and hot job to bake enough loaves for three days' feasting. The women worked with an almost eerie quietness—saying as few words to one another as necessary. They took no notice at all of Shamashazir, or the elder. But now and again they glanced towards a small group, who were sitting idly in front of the largest hut in the compound, rhythmically rocking their bodies to and fro.

How different from the laughter and bustle that went on in the kitchens of Ur, thought Shamashazir, as his eyes were drawn in the direction of the idle group. In the middle sat a woman wearing a golden necklace. She alone sat still, among the swaying bodies of her companions; and her face was swollen with crying. Shamashazir felt sure that she must be the mother of Shaul and Zepho; and that the other women were trying to comfort her with their sympathy. For when there was a break in the din that came from the men's quarters, he could hear the soft crooning of a mournful dirge-of-farewell to the dead.

Suddenly the Ishakeen looked up towards Shamashazir, and started to her feet. At the same time he felt a small, bony hand clutching at his fingers, and looking down, he saw Zepho, who must have followed him again. The Ishakeen came towards them calling the boy by name, and holding out some kind of sweetmeat to entice him towards her.

But Zepho wouldn't move. He clung tightly to Shamashazir's hand, and hid his face in Shamashazir's skirt. He did not like to see his mother's tears. They made him even more afraid.

The elder, standing beside Shamashazir, tried to drive the woman away. 'For shame on you,' he cried, scowling at her angrily. 'You think only of yourself and your own sons. O young and foolish one! You know nothing of famine. When the Corn Dingir is angry, and the young corn is accursed and dies withered on the hot earth. When every mother is weeping for her children; and the bones . . .'

But the wretched woman would not let him finish. 'All this I have heard a thousand times,' she cried. 'My laughing Shaul! My little Zepho!'

'Have I not lost six sons, killed in battle, for the tribe? And I am but a cousin of the Ishak,' shouted the elder proudly.

But an old woman who was bending over an oven stood upright and intervened in a harsh, squeaky voice. 'Thy sons were men, O Agag, son of my sister. In the days gone by, when men were men, it was the Ishak himself who gave his life for his people. But now you have fallen so low, you take babes with their mothers' milk fresh on their lips. . . .'

'Be quiet, you old witch!' shouted the elder. 'The Ishak cannot be spared. Do we want to have a war between the whole tribe every year, to decide who is to be Ishak?'

All the other women began to agree that the elder was right. They said that the Ishak could not be spared, and that the mother of Shaul should be a proud woman. They would far sooner lose one of their many children than their husbands. It was her own fault for not having more sons.

The poor mother picked up Zepho and carried him away with her. He did not resist; he only looked helplessly back towards Shamashazir. And Shamashazir went away, walking round all the village with the elder, back to the dancing men and the Ishak.

Very soon after he had taken his place again, he noticed Zepho sitting at his feet. He had broken away and come back to his friend.

When the sun set, the Ishak led Enoch and Shamashazir to an empty hut, that they were to share with Eb and Sam for the night. Zepho followed them, and squatted outside the hut, playing in the sand with a stick.

Neither of the boys had any difficulty in remembering the promise he had made to the Ishakeen about their prayers. The Village of Kenan was so horrible, they both wanted the Great Spirit's help more than they had ever wanted it before. Enoch began a song that Shamashazir knew well; and the three others joined in. Zepho crept inside the door and stood up, listening.

'The Lord of all the Earth, even the most Mighty One, hath spoken . . .' they sang; and:

> '*I will take no goat's milk out of thy house*
> *And no young lamb out of thy flocks.*
> *Offer unto the Lord the sacrifice of thanksgiving*
> *And pay thy vows unto the most high.*'

From near by, somewhere, there came a cough. Shamashazir opened his eyes. It did not sound like a child's cough.

Three elders were standing outside the door, staring fiercely in at them. Enoch had seen them too. He did not like the look of their scowling faces, and began to pray: 'O Lord, give us Thy strength and guide our feet.'

But Shamashazir nudged him. 'Put something in they can understand,' he said in Sumerian.

Enoch had been thinking all the day of dancing warriors and the price of corn. He did not understand what Shamashazir meant. He hesitated and stopped.

Shamashazir began to remember snatches of song that Enoch's mother had taught him:

> '*The Lord sayeth,*
> *Every beast of the forest is Mine;*
> *And the cattle upon a thousand hills;*
> *All the fowls on the mountains,*
> *And the wild beasts of the field, are Mine.*'

And then Shamashazir dared to put in words of his own, made up partly from the songs of Ur:

> '*Even the children of men are Mine.*
> *They shall not be sacrificed;*
> *Even to the demons of imagination.*'

He heard Enoch draw a sharp breath, and turned round. Outside the door stood the Ishak Moab and his two wives—one of them Zepho's mother, come to fetch her son. But behind, with spears at the ready, were seven elders and two young warriors, moving towards them with long, silent strides. The two women suddenly saw what was happening; and ran into the doorway of the hut, screaming, making a barrier between the boys and the warriors—

who halted. For the mother of Shaul was a sacred person.

Then the Ishak leapt to the side of his wives, shouting: 'Will you bring another curse on the village by shedding the blood of strangers on the days of the Corn Feast?'

'The words that we have heard spoken tonight will surely bring a curse on us,' one of the elders growled. And the growl was echoed from throat to throat round the circle of huts.

The Ishak turned lamely to Shamashazir: 'I must ask you to speak no more to your god, within the walls of my village.'

Shamashazir bowed, and said that they had finished their prayers for that night.

Then the elders went away, casting glances of displeasure after the Ishak, who walked uneasily before them with bowed head.

Zepho's mother stood looking at Shamashazir as if she wanted to say something, then turned and called her little son to come to bed. But he refused to leave; and she had to carry him away kicking and crying.

'Poor creature,' said the wife who was left behind.

'He's her last. She can't go to sleep without him close beside her.' And then, sighing, she also went away, thinking of the loss of her own sons, still fresh in her memory.

Although Shamashazir lay down on his mat, he could not sleep. Living in the mountains he had grown unaccustomed to such heat as brooded over the hot plains. He lay awake, thinking about the two boys Shaul and Zepho, and the horrible sacrifice to the Corn Dingir that was to take place on the day after tomorrow. And there were noises in the night—noises of frogs and crickets and cicadas—and human noises. Shamashazir found himself again and again listening to them, and trying to make out what they were. Snores —yes, and a woman's sobbing—that was to be expected. Then a low mumbling of men's voices. He heard Enoch sit up suddenly; and he wondered if the men were plotting to kill them because of their prayers to the Great Spirit. He loosened his knife in its sheath, and moved over to Enoch, softly calling his name. He could hear that Eb and Sam were awake. Enoch crawled to the door of the hut, listening; and Shamashazir joined him.

The voices seemed to come from the hut opposite the Ishak's. The hut that Zepho had been watching so intently. Suddenly, there was a wild high scream—a boy's scream, which was quickly muffled. And the sobbing from the woman broke out in a fresh agony.

'It's Shaul!' said Shamashazir. 'The young Ishakki. What are they doing to him?'

'The sacrifice is not to take place until the day after tomorrow,' said Enoch. 'I made sure so that we could get away in good time. Listen!'

And both the boys listened. Enoch with his better understanding of the language could make out something of what the men were saying. 'They are only trying to make him drink the wine,' he said. 'And he won't.'

'Why not?' Shamashazir asked.

But Enoch could not answer.

Eb, who knew something of getting drunk, suggested: 'He's planning to escape.'

'I hope he does,' said Shamashazir.

'It's useless. They are tying him up; and they will keep him tied up,' said Enoch.

'If he wanted to escape,' said Eb thoughtfully, 'he would pretend to swallow the wine and feign drunkenness. But he is only a boy against men.'

Shamashazir squatted with his head on his knees and his hands over his ears. He couldn't bear to hear such piteous cries. He was thinking.

'Now they have tied him up,' said Enoch.

By the light of the stars they could see two young warriors coming out of the hut and taking up positions of sentry duty—one standing on one side of the doorway, one on the other. The white patches of their loin-cloths swayed dimly in the darkness as they came to a halt. They were followed by an elder dressed in white, who crossed the compound on the other side of the fire, and was lost among the shadowy shapes of the huts. The snores had ceased. And their place had been taken by whispering voices coming from every direction. But over and above them all, sounded the sobbing of the woman who was Shaul's mother, and the strangled cries of Shaul himself.

'We must get him away from here,' said Shamashazir suddenly, in Sumerian.

'What?'

'We must get him away from here. We must rescue him and

take him with us,' Shamashazir repeated, still in Sumerian.

'Get him away, did you say? *We* must?'

'Yes!' said Shamashazir.

Enoch was shocked. It was impossible. 'We could not do it,' he said.

But Shamashazir insisted that it must be done. He could not bear to think of Shaul's fate. He tried to think out a plan.

'It is foolishness,' said Enoch. 'When Shaul goes, they will kill the little boy Zepho. No one can break the laws of a tribe.'

Shamashazir's voice fell. 'I had not thought about Zepho.'

The whispering voices died away and the snores began again. Both the boys went back to their mat beds and lay down. Shamashazir heard Enoch's breath coming deeply and evenly, and knew that he had fallen asleep. But he himself continued to lie awake, listening to the sobbing of the mother, and thinking about the two boys. Shaul was quieter now. He seemed to have fallen into a doze. 'He must be feeling near death after all that wine,' Shamashazir thought. He put his hands over his ears and shut his eyes. But he could not sleep.

He could not stop thinking about Shaul. He could not help making plans to save him. And still the woman went on sobbing. Shamashazir could bear it no longer. He woke Enoch up. 'We've got to save him,' he said in Sumerian. 'The Lord of all the Earth has spoken to me.'

Immediately Enoch sat up and was all attention. 'The Lord of all the Earth?' he whispered. 'O Shamashazir, my brother, I will follow you to the death. But I wish that you had not spoken those words. For this is a very fearful thing to do. The evil spirits of the corn people are mighty in their own land. I can feel them all about me now, crowding in the darkness of the tent.'

'We must make plans,' said Shamashazir in Sumerian, and Enoch answered in the same language, so that not even Eb and Sam could understand what they said.

'We must get both boys away,' said Shamashazir.

'*Both* boys? Where?'

'To your father.'

'No!' said Enoch firmly. 'The people of Kenan will follow. They will kill every man in the tribe of Enoch. The tribe of Enoch is too small.'

'Oh,' said Shamashazir, crestfallen.

But Enoch had a better idea. 'They are afraid of mountains,' he said. 'If we go to the mountains, they will follow and they will get lost and quickly go back home.'

'Let's take them to the mountains then. But your father? How can we meet him again?' Shamashazir did not fancy the idea of their wandering on their own in that wild country.

'I will send Sam to Father with two donkeys, with a message that we will meet him by the Lake of the Kingfishers,' said Enoch.

'Can we make that journey with only Eb?' asked Shamashazir.

'It will be difficult,' said Enoch. 'If a lion follows the donkey.'

Both the friends lay in silence in the dark for some time, thinking of the dangers of the journey. Shamashazir felt his courage oozing away; but the sobbing broke out afresh.

They thought of a plan to rescue Shaul. But it was difficult to know how to get Zepho out of his mother's hut in the middle of the night. And both boys were silent for some time, racking their brains for a solution.

'I will make the owl-call,' said Enoch at last. 'We will tell the little boy to listen.'

'I thought of that,' said Shamashazir; 'but it will be very late. We can't start work on rescuing Shaul until the village is asleep. It will take some time to break into the mud hut. The little boy will never keep awake so long. Could we fetch him first?'

'We cannot fetch the little boy first,' said Enoch. 'They would discover he was gone, and they would look for him all over the village. We cannot take the little boy,' he repeated firmly.

'But we must,' said Shamashazir, hitting his fist into the palm of his hand. 'What good is it to take one without the other?'

'Take two boys, and they will find another to sacrifice.'

'Ah! But the Ishak has no more sons. They can't sacrifice another boy until they have chosen a new Ishak.'

'Oh!' said Enoch.

'If the Great Spirit says take the little boy,' went on Shamashazir, 'the Great Spirit will wake him.'

'He will tell the plan to his mother.'

But Shamashazir disagreed. He had been to school in a big city. He had known a lot of little boys, and understood their ways far better than Enoch did. The more he thought, the more he felt sure that Zepho was a boy of brains and courage. If he trusted him with a secret, he would not tell.

After that there was no more gainsaying Shamashazir. And the two boys finished off the details of their plan. For the signal, Enoch would make the noise of an owl, hooting three times, then pausing, and then hooting twice more. No one would take any notice, if the little boy got up and went outside the hut for a short while.

Shamashazir would have to find a meeting-place, near by, and outside the village wall. He would have all the morning, while Enoch was finishing his corn-buying with the Ishak.

Shamashazir listened. 'And then I will see how the land lies behind the back of the other hut,' he said. 'And find where the path to the mountains starts. We must know the way well, to get back in the dark.'

'Fire,' said Enoch. 'Fire?'

'Yes—make a fire in the mountains to show us to the path. Eb will watch the fire.'

And then they began to plan the food they would need on the journey. They would keep back one cheese—even if it meant buying less corn. Corn they had in plenty. Drinking-horns they carried. 'But I wish we had some of that good bread I saw the women baking,' said Shamashazir thoughtfully, wondering if he could manage to persuade one of the women to give them a few loaves. Hunting and fishing for so small a party was easy—except when they had to go over the higher mountains. But the bread would come in handy. Enoch agreed.

Shamashazir's mind returned to their greatest difficulty—Zepho. Not only must he be rescued; but he must be told something of their plans beforehand. When and how was this to be done? He sat cross-legged, wiggling his toes in the still warm dust of the hut floor, his head buried in his hands, deep in thought, while Enoch went on talking about his own arrangements:

'Sam will take two donkeys laden with corn to Father. We will look as if we are going with Sam; but we will go to the foothills. Then we will come back—looking like three men with one donkey —not four men with three donkeys. People in the village will see us and think: "One donkey—new men come to buy corn." We will light the fire. . . .'

When Enoch had thought out the last details of his plan, he lay down and went to sleep; and Shamashazir soon followed him. Now that he knew what they were going to do, neither groans from Shaul nor cries from his mother had the power to disturb his night's rest.

Shamashazir woke the next morning with a tense feeling of excitement at the difficult task they were to perform before the sun set again. Slowly he became aware that the noises of the night had given place to a great deal of talking and laughing. He must have overslept; for the hut was empty. He crawled to the door, and found Enoch watching the young girls of the village, who were busy decorating the outside of the hut with fresh flowers and wreaths of corn. In the very middle of the compound, a merry group was at work, putting the finishing touches to the huge straw image of the Corn Dingir that lay like a great felled tree-trunk on the ground.

But Shamashazir was not interested in all this gaiety. He nodded to Enoch; and then his eyes turned towards Shaul's hut. The wretched boy was sitting hunched up outside the doorway, biting his nails, sober now, with all the fight gone out of him, and a look of hopeless misery on his face.

Two different young men stood on guard. They were dressed in embroidered kilts, shorter and fuller than the skirts worn in Ur. Both had shining copper bands round their necks, and held their spears erect by their sides; the polished and sharpened blades of the spears gleamed in the sun.

From the Ishak's hut came another resplendent young warrior, walking slowly across the open space with head erect and muscles gleaming, carrying in his hands a bowl of steaming porridge. Like a dancer, he lowered himself with one supple movement on to both knees in front of Shaul, bowed his head three times to the ground, and presented the young Ishakki with the food. All the men, women, and children in the centre of the village stopped their work and their chatter and knelt down, chanting praises to the Corn Dingir. The warrior was followed by a young girl, with flowers in her hair and round her neck, who carried a silver cup full of wine, and who took her place, kneeling, beside him.

The ghost of a smile flitted across Shaul's face as, before all the kneeling people, he took the bowl of porridge from the young warrior and the cup of wine from the girl. But it was only the ghost of a smile. A moment later he was listlessly trying to swallow the porridge, while his eyes darted fearful looks from side to side, like a captured bird seeking a way of escape. The sight of him made

Shamashazir's courage well up strongly again.

When Eb and Sam had fed the donkeys, Enoch insisted, in spite of Eb's warning, that they should all go into the hut and begin their morning prayers. But they had hardly sung the first few words when they were interrupted by the Ishak. 'O Shamashazir of Ur, and Enoch son of Enoch,' he said. 'Let not the anger of your god fall on my head. But my people are afraid. They say it will bring ill luck on the harvest if another dingir is worshipped in the village today. For the Corn Dingir is on his way—coming to be our guest and to attend the feast.' He spoke reluctantly, with anxious glances round him, as if he felt the Corn Dingir might already be within earshot.

'We do not sing songs to any *dingir*, but to the Lord of all the Earth, who is the Lord of all the dingirs,' said Enoch proudly.

But the Ishak answered sadly: 'The Lord of all the Earth has put a curse on the tribe of Kenan. He has turned His face from us; because of the death of Abel the shepherd, by the hand of his brother Cain.'

'Tell your people that we are servants of the Lord of all the Earth; and his little finger is more terrible than the Corn Dingir in all his fury, and we have sworn to obey Him.'

'If you try to sing your songs in this village my people will kill you,' the Ishak answered.

Enoch's eyes blazed fury. 'It will be the worse for them if they do.' And he grasped the hilt of his knife. But before he could draw it, Eb had seized his arm.

'Young master!' he said. 'There is no command from the Lord of all the Earth that we should sing sacred songs in this stinking heathen hut. Outside the walls there is clean air to breathe. We can pray better under a roof of olive branches, made by the Lord of all the Earth Himself, than in this place, made by hands that are defiled with wickedness.'

Enoch looked at Shamashazir to see what he would say. He disliked being preached to by Eb.

Shamashazir saw at once what an opportunity this might be for finding out how the land lay round the village. He bowed politely to the Ishak. 'We have no wish to bring more curses on the heads of your people,' he said. 'Would it please you to lead us to some place outside, where we can pray to the Great Spirit without offending the Corn Dingir?'

The Ishak ordered one of the elders to take them to the middle of the biggest olive grove. 'Let them not go near the ploughed fields that are ready for sowing,' he said.

With a scowl, the elder beckoned them to follow him. Outside the gate he turned to the left, walking round the open clearing that surrounded the village wall. The two boys had a wonderful opportunity of observing the ground they were to cross that night. When they had walked about a quarter of the way round the village, the elder turned sharply to the right into the olive grove, took them about a hundred yards among the trees, and then left them.

'That man,' said Eb, watching his back disappearing down the way they had come, 'has the looks of a weasel after blood. The sooner your bargaining is over, and we can leave this place, young Ishakki, the happier I shall be.'

They sang the sacred song that began: 'The sacrifice of the Lord is a contrite heart.' It was a long song with many verses. And they sang it facing eastward towards the morning sun. The beautiful words helped to clear away the evil taste that their night in the village had left in their mouths; and Shamashazir felt that the Great Spirit was very near them.

When they had come to the end, and turned to go back, Enoch swore that someone was watching them. 'He's over there, to the left,' he said, waving his arm in that direction, and starting off towards the right.

'This isn't the way we came,' said Shamashazir.

'A hunter never returns the way that he came,' Enoch said quietly. Then he went on in Sumerian, 'We will find the little boy's hut now.'

Shamashazir nodded, and followed him through the olive trees, bearing to the right. They came to the open clearing on the other side of the village, opposite the women's quarters. 'Which way is the hut?' Enoch asked.

'There—with red flowers on the roof.'

'I see it,' said Enoch. And he began to look round at the trees that skirted the clearing, for a suitable one to act as a meeting-place. Already his practised eye had spotted marks on the bark of a tree that showed it had been climbed by children. He gave it only a quick glance, then turned round, and pointing to the village, began to describe the tree to Shamashazir, while standing with his back to it. When Shamashazir had picked it out, Enoch began to describe the bushes and stones round it; so that Shamashazir would notice them and make no mistake. 'You know the tree?' he asked in Sumerian.

Shamashazir grunted.

Enoch changed to Akkadian. 'We must go quickly back. We are being watched,' he said, and led the way round the open clearing, past the back of Shaul's hut to the village gate.

Sam and Eb dropped a litle behind the two boys. 'What are those two plotting together?' Eb muttered. 'I don't like it when they drop into foreign tongues.'

But Sam only smiled and shrugged his shoulders. 'Some boys' game,' he answered.

Enoch went to finish his bargain with the Ishak. And Shamashazir, hoping he might be able to speak to Zepho alone, said he would like to look at the ploughs and harness, and learn how they cultivated their corn. In Ur they made many ploughs, and much harness for oxen, which they often took on their caravans. He would like to see the type of harness that they used in Kenan, and what sort of furrows the ploughs cut in the soil; and if the soil was different from the soil of Ur.

The elders were, of course, flattered at so much interest from the son of the famous Teresh. And one of them offered to show him round. They set off to look at the ploughs first. Shamashazir noticed that Zepho was following, but at a distance.

The plough were made of wood and the share was hardened by charring in the fire. The elder explained that the oxen dragged the point through the earth, while two men walked behind to hold it in position.

'We make ploughs with wheels on them in Ur,' said Shamashazir.

The elder nodded his head wisely. He had once seen a potter's wheel, and he had heard that Pharaoh of Egypt had wheels on his chariots; he had never seen any other kind of wheel. So he nodded and asked if they found the wheels worked well.

Shamashazir said that they did. They ploughed a deeper furrow. But the ploughs in Ur were tipped with copper; and that made them sharper and made them wear better than those of wood.

The elder was not very pleased at having his ploughs criticized. He thought they were perfect. But Ur was a very rich and famous city, and the people who lived in it must know great magic. Were they not such friends with the Moon Dingir that he fed them himself, for the love of their King's daughter? All that Shamashazir said should be listened to and considered carefully. 'And how many steps can a ploughman walk in a day with a copper-tipped plough?' he asked.

Of course, Shamashazir did not know. 'In Ur the people who plough are Sumerian,' he answered. 'They are smaller and shorter than your people; and they would take more steps in a day. It would not be fair to compare them. . . . And our soil is lighter,' he added, as he bent down to pick up a handful. He had heard a slight rustle close behind them, and wanted to see what it was. Through the bottom twigs of a bush he caught sight of a pair of small legs. Zepho was creeping closer.

They went on to look at a pair of oxen, still at work, finishing the last furrows of a field before the festival. Two men walked behind, holding the branch of the tree that acted as a plough. They struggled hard to keep its pointed nose going straight in the earth; and beads of perspiration stood out on their foreheads and ran down their naked chests. 'A plough with wheels is easier to steer,' said Shamashazir. 'You could grow twice as much corn if you had a plough with wheels.'

The elder said nothing. And they walked in silence beside the ploughmen right out into the open field.

Zepho's footsteps padded behind them. Shamashazir stopped and looked round.

'Even the Ishak's son is curious like other boys,' the elder remarked, glad to be able to change the subject from ploughs. 'He is interested in the stranger from Ur, and the tales of that marvellous city.' He wished that Shamashazir would talk of something else. To think of coming from a city where thousands of people lived, and being interested only in ovens and ploughs. He wished that Zepho would come up and ask him some childish question, about soldiers, or chariots, or the magic clay tablets that spoke.

But Shamashazir had another plan. 'I have a young brother at home who is full of curiosity,' he said. 'But something he likes even better than asking questions'—and he spoke loudly and clearly so that the little boy would hear—'is riding on a donkey.'

Zepho's face creased into a grin.

'Ah!' said the elder, seizing on this wonderful opportunity of getting rid of Shamashazir, and taking a comfortable doze under a shady tree. 'It would be a great honour to the Village of Kenan, and to the Ishak, if Shamashazir of Ur would graciously allow the Ishak's youngest son to take a ride on one of his donkeys.'

'It would be a pleasure,' said Shamashazir, trying to hide his smile of satisfaction. And the elder led the way back to the trees where the three donkeys were hobbled.

Shamashazir explained to Eb and Sam what he was going to do. They had no objections, so long as he did not overtire the donkey; the beasts had a long way to go that night. Sam untied Jemimah, the gentlest of the three animals, spread a cloak over the pack-saddle, and lifted Zepho on to her back—where he sat with one foot in each pack-basket; for there were no stirrups.

With a sigh of relief, the elder sank to the ground under a shady tree, and gave himself up to the enjoyment of the pleasant morning. Sam showed Zepho how to hold the bridle, and make the donkey do what he wanted. Then he set off beside him along the clearing that went round the outside of the village wall. But Sam's company would upset all Shamashazir's plans. When they were out of earshot of the elder, he asked him to go back to Eb. Sam was not used to taking orders from anyone but his own Ishak's family. He looked at Shamashazir, scratching his head. Jemimah was his treasured pet; Shamashazir was a townsman. 'What! Let one of my donkeys out of my sight?' he said.

Shamashazir saw at once the reason for Sam's objection; but he was desperate. There was only one argument that bore any weight with the tribe of Enoch. 'The Great Spirit has given me a message for the little Ishakki of Kenan, which I must tell him alone,' he said.

Sam looked at him a long time, turning things over in his rather slow mind. Shamashazir was a stranger. How would the Great Spirit speak to a stranger? Those were his first thoughts. But then he remembered that Shamashazir came of Noah's line; and that he had been especially saved from certain death by the Great Spirit; and that he was a friend of Enoch's . . . 'Very well,' he said slowly, and went back thoughtfully to rejoin Eb under the trees.

But the most difficult part of Shamashazir's plan was still to come. How, in the name of Nannar, was he to explain to Zepho that he must leave his father and mother, and run away with them that very night? He looked at him jogging along on the donkey, behaving now like any ordinary boy, all the fear and dread gone out of his face. It made it more difficult than ever.

It was Jemimah that came to the rescue. Finding that her master had left her, she didn't see why she should go trotting along for a pair of strangers; and she stopped at a tasty patch of grass that grew under the shade of the olive-trees, put her head down and began to nibble.

Zepho laughed and patted her neck. 'She's hungry! She's eating grass!' Then he turned in his saddle and looked Shamashazir up and down as only a child can. 'You've hurt your leg,' he said.

Shamashazir thoughtfully dug his sandal into the dust. Here was his chance. 'I fell down a very high mountain . . . I would have been killed. But the Lord of all the Earth put out His Hand and saved me,' he said.

'What did he save you from?' Zepho asked.

'From being smashed to pieces like a broken pitcher, and from death.'

'Ah,' said Zepho, his large eyes growing still larger in wonderment.

Shamashazir went on: 'The Lord of all the Earth is mighty and can stretch out His hand to save whom He pleases.'

'Did you like being saved?'

'Yes,' said Shamashazir emphatically. 'It hurt at the time—most good things have to be paid for—but in the end it was grand.'

'Did it hurt very much? As much as a scorpion's sting?'

'Well,' said Shamashazir, not wanting to frighten the little boy too much, but at the same time trying to prepare him for the difficulties ahead—'I've never been stung by a scorpion. But I was frightened.'

'Were you as frightened as being sacrificed to the Corn Dingir?'

'No, I wasn't. It doesn't always hurt more than, say, leaving your father and mother.'

'Oh,' said Zepho.

Shamashazir saw that he was thinking; and pulled the donkey's head away from the grass she was eating, and made her walk on.

Presently Zepho took a deep breath and said, 'Would he save me?'

'Yes; but you must do exactly what I tell you.'

'I can,' said Zepho stolidly.

'It's difficult.'

'I can do it. Would I have to leave Father and Mother?'

'Yes, you would.' Shamashazir watched him, reluctant to give away any of their plans until he was sure of Zepho's courage.

The little boy was very quiet, thinking; then at last he said hesitatingly, 'Where would I have to go?'

Shamashazir smiled triumphantly. 'To the City of Ur.'

Zepho clenched his small fists and bit his lips. To him, the City of Ur was as remote and terrifying as the realm of the Corn Dingir. 'Will Iran and Agag be there?' he asked.

'Iran and Agag? Who are they?' said Shamashazir. Then he remembered that they were the names of two of Zepho's dead brothers. Zepho was confusing the City of Ur with the Land of the Underworld. To leave his parents and go away was as cold and lonely as the thought of death. 'Not Iran and Agag,' he said gently. 'They are dead. But your brother Shaul will be there, and so will I, and Jemimah the donkey will come with us.'

Zepho looked at Shamashazir and felt Jemimah's stubbly coat with his hand. She was snatching mouthfuls of grass and chewing them as she walked, with a pleasant crunching sound. She was good and safe and real, Zepho felt, and so was Shamashazir. No harm could befall him while he was with them. They were safer than his father and mother. He did not understand that Shamashazir and the donkey were at peace with the earth and its maker, whereas his father was torn with guilt and his mother frantic with grief. The guilt of his father hurt him and the grief of his mother frightened him. And to add to his troubles, the Corn Dingir was horrible—like the faces of the elders before a sacrifice. 'Shall we go now?' he asked.

'No,' said Shamashazir. 'We must wait until it is dark.'

Zepho did not like the dark. He puckered his forehead in a frown.

Shamashazir guessed that he was having doubts. 'He is thinking of his mother; he will tell her,' he thought. 'This is a secret of the Lord of all the Earth,' he said aloud. 'If you tell anyone, I shall be killed, and so shall my friend Enoch, and so will Shaul and you. Do you understand? You must not speak of it to your father, or your mother, or Shaul—or anyone except me or my friend Enoch.'

Zepho nodded; but his face was strained.

They were going past Sam and Eb and the elder again now. Shamashazir let the conversation drop. And they walked in silence, until they came in sight of the tree that Enoch had marked outside

76

the women's quarters; and Zepho heard his mother crying. The lines of strain in his small face deepened, so that it looked again like the face of a little old man.

'I will tell nobody,' he whispered, 'if the Lord of all the Earth will save me, and Shaul.'

Shamashazir stopped the donkey under the tree: 'Could you come out of your hut, and climb through the wall, and come here, to this tree—in the dark, and alone?'

Zepho thought of the dark, and the weird noises of the night and the tales of evil spirits. 'Yes ... I could come,' he said, shivering.

They went on, Shamashazir leading the donkey once more round the walls, and speaking all the time with his head bent to Zepho's ear. He repeated again: 'And you will speak of it to no one—not to any man, or woman, or animal, not to any of your cousins? To speak of this thing is death.'

Between each name that Shamashazir mentioned, Zepho nodded his head. Then he drew himself up very straight.

'I am the Ishak's son,' he said solemnly. 'I give you my word I will keep this secret.'

Shamashazir believed him. 'Now listen to what you must do,' he went on, glancing at Zepho's bare feet at the bottom of the pack-baskets. 'Have you any sandals?'

Zepho nodded.

'Has Shaul any?'

Zepho nodded again. 'I shall be wearing mine tomorrow at the feast of the Corn Dingir; because I am the Ishak's son.'

'Can you sleep with them under your mat tonight?'

'Yes. . . .'

'And Shaul's?'

Zepho thought Shaul's sandals would be in his hut. He would find them.

'No . . .' said Shamashazir. 'You mustn't go into Shaul's hut. It would be better to have some other sandals. Bring a pair of your mother's.'

'Put them under my mat?' Zepho inquired.

Shamashazir nodded. 'Tonight you must lie down on your mat, and you must pretend to go to sleep. But you must not sleep. You must keep awake for a *very long time*.'

'I will lie on my sandals.'

'And all the time you must listen for an owl.'

'I often hear an owl,' said Zepho. 'He goes "toowhit, toowhit".'

'This owl will go "toowhit, toowhit, toowhit." Then he will stop, and go "toowhit, toowhit".'

'I have never heard an owl do that.'

'It's my voice,' said Shamashazir apologetically. 'I'm no good at mimicking. But your owl will sound like an owl, except that he will go "toowhit" three times, and then two.'

Zepho nodded.

'Make sure he is the right owl. If he's the wrong one it may be death to us all. If you are not sure, wait a little, and he will make the same noise again.'

'Yes . . .' said Zepho, his eyes widening with the effort to remember.

Shamashazir went on explaining exactly what Zepho must do, until he felt sure that Zepho knew it all. They had come back to the wall behind the women's quarters. 'Can you find that tree in the dark?' he asked.

'Yes,' said Zepho. 'It is the tree we found the snake trying to climb.' And then he looked doubtfully towards the wall. It was built of mud, strengthened by stakes driven into the ground, and was about the height of a man's head—too high for Zepho to climb over. But every six or seven feet, a narrow gap, or crenelle, had been cut in the upper part, wide enough to fire arrows through—and low enough for a boy of seven to reach, and climb into, and to squeeze his body through. 'Sometimes there are scorpions,' he said. 'Judy put her hand into one of the holes. And a scorpion stung her. And she died.'

Shamashazir thought that they ought to examine the wall for scorpions. But the question was how to do it without arousing suspicion. He did not fancy putting his face close to one of those dark crenelles. He knew all about scorpions, their darting poisonous stings and their skulking habits. He wished he had a dog to smell them out. And then he suddenly thought of Jemimah. Donkeys were wonderfully wise beasts. He would try her and see what she would do to help them. He asked Zepho if he could make the donkey go over to the wall by himself; and he showed him which way to pull on the bridle to change her direction. Then he went to the olive-trees and began pulling up handfuls of grass.

Zepho managed his part well. And Jemimah came close up to

the wall, almost as if she had strayed there by herself. Shamashazir followed with his handful of grass, and stood near one of the crenelles—holding it out to Jemimah. She came towards him, daintily stretching out her neck for the food; and then stopped and backed.

'Oh!' said Shamashazir. 'She doesn't like it. A good thing we tried her. There must be something evil in the wall.' He moved on to the next crenelle, glancing into its cobwebby darkness as he passed. He could have sworn that he caught sight of two watching eyes that looked straight into his own, and suddenly withdrew. Someone inside the village was watching them. He stood motionless with the grass in his hand, wondering what had been overheard and how to avert suspicion. Then he felt a soft wet nuzzling. The donkey was eating the grass in his hand. She seemed to have no fear of the second crenelle. 'I don't think there is anything here,' said Shamashazir very loudly and clearly, pretending to be disappointed; while he dropped the grass on to the ground to mark the place. The watcher after all might be only an inquisitive child.

'I'll go and have a look in the other hole again . . .' he added. 'I have heard it said that, in Egypt, the scorpion is a dingir.'

'Don't,' said Zepho. 'Come away.'

But Shamashazir went up to the first crenelle, and keeping well away, pretended to peer into it. 'I can't see anything,' he said truthfully. 'But it was queer the way the donkey behaved.' He led Zepho some way round the clearing and under the trees, before he spoke again. 'We had better go back to the elder,' he said.

Eb was waiting impatiently for them to return. Enoch had already finished his bargaining with the Ishak; and was watching men from the village emptying earthen jars of corn into the baskets of the other two donkeys. He was longing to ask Shamashazir what luck he had had; but it was impossible with so many men coming and going. They had to pretend to talk of other things.

'This seems very good corn,' he began, as the elder took his leave of them and started to walk back to the gate of the village. 'What do you think of it?'

Shamashazir let some of it run through his hand. 'It seems to me excellent,' he said. 'I have been looking at ploughs. But afterwards I took the Ishak's son several times round the village on Jemimah. He is brave and quick to learn. He will make a good Ishak of his people.'

By which Enoch knew that Shamashazir had spoken to Zepho, and was pleased with the result. He told him he had bought enough corn to fill five baskets, and that they still had a cheese left for themselves.

'What about the bread?' said Shamashazir. 'I praised the cooking this morning, hoping that they would give us some to take with us.'

'They are bringing two dozen loaves. I gave them a honeycomb for it.'

At that moment two young girls came towards them, each carrying a pile of freshly baked loaves balanced on her head. They both smiled winningly at Shamashazir, and presented their loaves to Enoch. With the cheese they had left, the loaves completely filled the sixth basket.

'The Ishak gives to his friends with both hands!' said Shamashazir, politely bowing. 'When I go back to the great City of Ur, I shall remember the village of Kenan for ever.' And then he paused and added, 'For its pretty girls and its good bread.'

The girls went laughingly away.

When they had finished their packing and arrangements, they left the donkeys and Eb and Sam; and walked back to the village in order that Shamashazir might say good-bye to the Ishak. Glancing at Zepho, who was still following close behind, and speaking in Sumerian, Shamashazir asked if Enoch had had any opportunity of warning Shaul of their plans. But Enoch shook his head. 'He is too well guarded; and I was with the Ishak all the time.'

'If he is drunk, it won't matter,' said Shamashazir.

'He is very unhappy without wine. I think he will drink tonight. But better we speak to him,' and Enoch shook his head. He could see Sam and Eb refusing to help them, if Shaul had not even been warned.

In the centre of the village they found that the preparations for the feast were beginning to quicken up. All the young warriors, with the help of the children, were taking wood out into one of the fields for a bonfire. The women and girls were rolling out the last balls of dough ready to put in the oven. Brightly coloured carpets were being spread before the doors of the elders' huts. And in the very middle of the village square, the gigantic figure of the Corn Dingir was being set up. It was more than twice as tall as a man, and looked rather like a long, thin, straw guy.

Shamashazir, used to images, bowed as he went by this fantastic figure. But Enoch stalked past with his head erect and his eyes on fire; for to him it was a devil. Several of the elders noticed him and scowled. One pulled at the Ishak's robe to attract his attention. But he chose to ignore both Enoch and the elder, and remained thoughtfully unmoved in his chair of state, with his eyes only on Shaul. He hardly glanced at Enoch and Shamashazir as they approached him and bowed their farewells.

Shaul was crouched on the ground between his two guards with his head in his hands, gently rocking his body to and fro, softly moaning to himself. But when he suddenly looked up and saw Zepho, he called out to him in a peevish voice, wanting to know where he had been all this time, and what he had been doing.

Zepho reluctantly halted, keeping his eyes on Shamashazir, who watched him anxiously, wondering what he was going to answer. 'I've been riding a donkey,' he began nervously.

'A donkey!' shouted Shaul. 'I want to ride a donkey.'

The elders groaned—for the last requests of the Ishakki had to be obeyed, and they wanted to get rid of their guests. But the two boys looked at each other significantly; for here was their chance.

Back under the trees, Enoch quickly told Sam to take the baskets off the biggest and strongest donkey—which also happened to be the most capricious and difficult to manage. Then Shaul was helped into the saddle; and his two guards seized the bridle. But Enoch held up his hand and said, 'Wait! For this donkey will not go with strangers.'

'The Ishakki cannot ride without his guards,' shouted the elders. 'These worshippers of the Great Spirit are not to be trusted. The donkey might run away with the Ishakki into the mountains.' And they began to argue about what had best be done: some saying that the guards had better go in front and line the path, for the donkey could not go very fast; and others suggesting that one of Enoch's servants should take one side, and two guards walk on the other side.

Then the Ishak raised his hand and said, 'Peace!' And slowly the hubbub died away. 'There are not many more hours in which I shall see my son alive. And the days that I shall be a father to my sons are numbered. Therefore I, his father, will take the bridle of the Ishakki. And I will run beside him, that I may see the last smile of pleasure on his face. Let Shamashazir of Ur take the other bridle.

For it is not right that the Ishak of Kenan should go in harness with a serving-man.'

Eb was annoyed at being called a serving-man, and looked as if he would spit on the ground. But he pulled himself up in time, remembering that he must not endanger the life of his young Ishakki by such a gesture of contempt. The good-natured Sam was only worried about the way 'all those heathen' might treat his donkey. He hung on to the bridle, until Shamashazir gently took it from his hand, and signed for him to stand back. In spite of the Ishak, there might be a chance of speaking to Shaul. But when Shamashazir saw the way the warriors spread themselves along the open space that surrounded the wall, he realized there was little hope.

They walked round the village first. And then Shaul said that he wanted to go faster; and Shamashazir tugged at his bridle. But the donkey objected, and suddenly stuck his heels into the ground and would not move. Sam came running out of the crowd ahead, calling to him. Then the donkey pricked up his ears and went at such a pace that both Shamashazir and the Ishak were left behind. The Ishak was not used to running; and Shamashazir was hampered by his injured leg. Then it was that Enoch, as swift as an arrow, darted out of the crowd and seized the capricious donkey.

The Ishak suddenly stopped and began searching the ground, saying: 'I have lost my ring.'

The Ishak's ring was a ring of state. No man could be Ishak without it. It was a calamity to lose it. All the watching warriors, who heard him, ran up to him and fell on their hands and knees, searching the ground round his footprints. For a few moments Enoch was alone with Shaul. 'Tonight we will come and save you,' he said quietly into his ear, slowing the donkey to a walk.

Shaul looked at him, startled.

'Drink the wine tonight and you will be saved.'

But Shaul only looked bewildered.

'Don't you want to escape?' said Enoch angrily. 'Drink the wine, so that they won't tie you up. . . .' But Shaul still looked at him dumbly. Enoch was going to speak again; but fortunately, he turned in time to see the Ishak standing just behind him with the ring in his hand. He glanced towards Enoch, and then raising his hand, shouted that the ring was found.

One of the warriors was chosen to take the Ishak's place. But

Shaul did not seem to want to go on any more. One of the guards helped him off the donkey. And while it was being resaddled, the Ishak came up to Enoch and thanked him for his prompt action. 'Enoch son of Enoch is to be trusted to act wisely and well,' he said, bowing to Enoch and looking at his son. 'The tribe of Enoch will have a good Ishak when the time comes.'

Enoch bowed back and they said good-bye; and set out on the first stage of their journey without any further hindrances.

Zepho followed the strangers to the gate of the village; and watched them set off down the path that led to the north, until it took a bend and they were out of sight behind some tall cypress-trees. Then he ran back round the outside of the village wall, to look again at the place where he was to meet Enoch that night. He must make sure that he remembered the-gap-that-had-no-scorpion. He found the tree where they had seen the snake. But when he crossed over the clearing to the wall, he could not find the grass that Shamashazir had dropped there. It had all been blown away. There were bits of it sticking to the stones lying about, and bits scattered on the earth; but no tidy pile to mark the-gap-that-had-no-scorpion.

But young as Zepho was, he was not dismayed. He began at once to examine the tracks of the donkeys in the dust. It was the second crenelle—the one on the left. He squatted down on his haunches, like the men when they examined the trail of a bear. He was so absorbed with the marks in the dust that he did not notice his father, approaching from among the olive-trees, until he was quite near. He looked up guiltily, for he knew that he was not allowed outside the village walls alone. But surprisingly his father was not angry. He stooped down and picked up his little son, swung him up on to his back, and began walking out towards the open fields.

Zepho could feel his heart beating so violently that he was sure his father must feel it too. But he said nothing until they were well outside the village, and right away from the olive-trees. Then the Ishak put him down and remarked: 'You had a ride on the donkey, too?'

'Yes,' said Zepho. 'He trotted and he galloped; but most of the time he walked.'

'And did Shamashazir of Ur hold the bridle all the time?'

'Most of the time he did; but sometimes one of the donkey men did. And sometimes I made him go by myself.'

'Ah . . .' said the Ishak. 'And Shamashazir of Ur, what did he say to you?'

Zepho looked anxiously up at his father. 'A secret,' he whispered.

'A secret?' The Ishak nodded, but he did not ask what the secret was. 'Secrets are not to be told,' he said.

There was silence for a few moments. Zepho was longing to tell his father everything. He bit his tongue to stop himself from speaking. His father seemed so kind and understanding. They were in the middle of the Corn Dingir's fields, yet the Corn Dingir was forgotten.

'Shamashazir of Ur is a good man?' said Zepho, asking a question.

His father did not answer for some time. Then he said, 'Ur is a great city.' And they went back to the village.

But instead of going into the gate, they turned off to the right, and walked round outside the walls to where the Ishak had found Zepho.

'There are scorpions in that wall,' said the Ishak. 'They live in the crenelles through which the warriors fire their arrows.'

Zepho's heart stood still. He was afraid to say anything, and his legs trembled.

'Are you afraid of scorpions, my son? Oh yes, of course! You were there when Judy was bitten. Come now, you had better go back to your mother.' Then the Ishak took his little son up to the wall, and put him down in front of one of the crenelles. 'Come, get through that hole,' he said. 'It is perfectly safe.'

Trembling, Zepho climbed through, while the Ishak turned away and walked back to the gate through the olive-trees.

8 THE BEACON

When Enoch and Shamashazir left the village, they turned north-wards, and started to go back the way they had come, through the ploughed fields, olive groves and vineyards of Kenan; as if they were setting out to catch up the tribe of Enoch on the northern trade route. But when they had gone about a couple of miles, and there were no more signs of men at work on the land, they began to explain their plans to Eb and Sam.

For some time Eb listened. Then he jerked his head back with a snort. 'Ha!' he said. 'You are talking just a lot of boys' nonsense. In the days when the tribe was great, your grandfather would have set fire to the whole village and burned them alive.'

'We are not a great tribe,' said Enoch, 'and my father's ways are not the ways of my grandfather.'

'Then leave the hornets' nest in peace. We don't want them all on our trail like a pack of hunting dogs.'

'They won't be,' said Enoch. 'Shamashazir son of Teresh and I have carefully thought out every detail. One of you is to take a message to my father, to warn him to turn at once into the mountains and to meet us by the Lake of the Kingfishers. And we will go this way, over the rocky pass.'

'I will do no such thing,' said Eb. 'Your father would have my life.'

With great dignity Enoch drew himself up to his full height (which was still much less than Eb's). His eyes flashed, and he said, 'Who is the servant and who is the master, Eb son of Perez? You are to obey me as you have sworn to obey the Ishak; or one day I shall remember your disobedience.'

Eb shrugged his shoulders and his eyes turned away from Enoch's face. 'How do you think you will break into that mud hut without any water?' he asked.

There was a silence. Enoch did not know much about mud walls.

'We can take water,' said Shamashazir.

'Ah!' said Enoch. 'Shamashazir knows about such things, for the City of Ur is made of clay bricks, which are made of mud. He has told me.'

'Perhaps!' said Eb. 'But does Shamashazir of the city know how to move silently through long grass at night? And has not Shamashazir a broken leg? He will kick a stone in the ground, or stumble over a tussock of grass, and he will climb the wall with the noise of a horse. You will both be discovered. And I shall have to carry the news of your death to your father.'

Enoch was silent.

'And the boy Zepho,' Eb went on. 'He sleeps with his mother. She will miss him before you can reach the first vineyard; and you will be hampered by your heavy burden.'

Shamashazir couldn't help admitting to himself that all this was perfectly true.

But Enoch said very quietly, 'The Great Spirit has spoken to Shamashazir son of Teresh. And when the Great Spirit speaks He must be obeyed, even though it means death.'

There was a silence. Then Eb stopped the donkeys.... 'Let Sam take the corn to your father, and warn him to escape into the hills. I will stay and see that this thing is properly done. But as I swore to guard you with my life, O Enoch son of Enoch, it will be I who will come down with you into the village to break into this hut; and Shamashazir son of Teresh who will stay on the hill to keep the fire burning that shall guide us back.'

'What do you say, Shamashazir?' Enoch asked. 'Is this fair?'

Shamashazir was bitterly disappointed not to be able to come with Enoch. But he realized that his clumsiness and his injured leg might wreck the whole plan; so he could do nothing but say: 'Yes, it is fair.'

When they had gone another mile towards the north, in the direction of the flock, they parted with Sam and with two donkeys laden with corn. They had come three miles from the Village of Kenan. There would be four more to the place where they had left the tribe of Enoch. They reckoned it would have moved on another eight or nine miles. Sam would have about twelve or thirteen to travel with his heavily laden little beasts. But he thought he could get there before dusk; if all went well.

The other three turned off into the hills on their right, where they lit a fire in a sheltered valley, and sat down to wait until sunset. They found a wild vine growing against a hot southern wall of rock. And Shamashazir said he thought the grapes looked ripe. So they picked and ate them to add to their food. Then they rested, thankful, after their sleepless night, to lie down in that peaceful valley under a clear sky.

Enoch and Eb took it in turns to keep watch, while Shamashazir slept under the cool shelter of a rock, or lay thinking of all the feelings and events that had brought them to this destination. Rabbits played on the hill; and a lizard sunned itself on the hot stone. Corn dingirs and ritual sacrifices and the tragedy of Kenan seemed very far away—like a bad dream. How much more sensible it would be to turn back and follow the tribe of Enoch. Enoch, his friend, believed him to have heard the commands of the Great Spirit; but was that really true? What good was it going to do the tribe of Kenan, to rescue just two of its victims and leave all the rest to suffer? And Enoch might not come out alive—none of them might. Twice he opened his mouth to confess that he had only imagined the Great Spirit's commands, and that they had better go after Sam; but twice something stopped the words from being uttered.

When the afternoon began to cool off, Eb got up and said they would need more food than bread and cheese the next day; he would go and catch a few rabbits. The skins would do to carry the water that they wanted to soften the clay of the Ishakki's hut. And he slithered away through the grass.

Enoch and Shamashazir sat by the fire, keeping watch over the donkey, as they had watched over the sheep. And Enoch told Shamashazir the story of Cain and Abel—how Cain was branded as a murderer by the Lord of all the Earth, and how every man's hand was against him. But Shamashazir hardly heard what he said.

He was still thinking of his responsibility for Enoch's life.

Eb came back with three rabbits. And they started on the last stage of their journey—three miles along the side of the hills, southward, until the Village of Kenan came in sight again. And then on a little farther, until they had drawn level with it at the place they had chosen for the beacon.

They set to work at once collecting firewood, which they made into a pile ready for the night. Then they sat down. And Eb and Enoch picked out the best path to follow through the vineyards and olive groves that lay at their feet. They wanted to avoid leaving footprints on the newly ploughed earth of the fields; but it did not seem possible to go the whole way without crossing any ploughed land.

When they had finally settled the way and committed it to memory, Eb said that it would be foolish for them to sleep all night on the open hill, in full view of the village. They had better find a more sheltered camping-place on the eastern slope. So they followed a goat-track, round behind the crest of the hill, to a platform of rock which ran along the side of a shallow gorge. 'At the head of this gorge there are caves,' said Eb. 'Do you remember?'

Enoch nodded. 'We can find this platform tonight by the light of our torches,' he said. 'And we shall be safe if they try to follow us across the valley. Tomorrow we can go along the ledge at the top of the gorge to the caves, and hide in them all day.'

'Two men can defend the caves against a whole tribe,' said Eb.

They took their baskets of food off the donkey, and hid them among heavy stones on the ledge; and then they collected a small pile of rotten wood and goats' dung for their fire. For rotten wood and goats' dung would not blaze too high or make a smoke. Their preparations finished, they sat down and watched the tide of shadowy darkness slowly rising over the mountains towards the higher peaks, waiting for the cover of night to hide their movements.

As the sun went down, so Shamashazir's memory seemed to come to life again. And he seemed to be back in the Village of Kenan, feeling all that Shaul was feeling and hearing the sobs of the Ishakeen. The note of hushed excitement in Enoch's and Eb's voices stirred his courage.

'It is time to eat,' said Eb at last. He took Jemimah by the bridle and led her back over the hill, to the place where they had left their wood for the beacon. The others followed through the gathering dusk.

Eb lit the fire in the usual way, by striking a piece of flint and a piece of iron-stone together, and letting the sparks fall on a handful of dried grass. Then, by the light of the fire, he skinned two of the rabbits with great skill and care, keeping their skins undamaged; and they roasted the backs and legs on spits of wood.

When they had eaten a good meal, Eb and Enoch bound up the legs and necks of each of the rabbit-skins with threads of their own long hair, twisted round and round, and took them to a near-by spring to fill with water. Eb scooped up water with his drinking-horn, while Enoch held a flaming pine branch to give him light.

Then they gave final instructions to Shamashazir. 'Keep Jemimah to the windward side of the fire,' said Enoch. 'Then her scent will be blown into the smoke and lost. But if you hear anything that sounds like a lion coming too close, wave a flaming branch in its face.'

'Or throw hot embers at it,' said Eb.

Shamashazir replied, 'Yes,' as calmly as he could.

'If you watch the donkey carefully,' Eb went on, 'you can *see* if there is a lion about. Her hair will rise up on end all down her back; and she will stamp her feet.'

'May the Great Spirit keep you in His care,' said Enoch. Then he and Eb took off their sandals. And armed with their knives, the skins of water, a cloak to wrap round Shaul to prevent him from struggling, and Shamashazir's skirt to use as a gag, they slipped silently away into the darkness.

Shamashazir whispered, 'Good-bye,' his teeth chattering slightly.

There was no path downwards from the mountains into the plain. And at first they had to make their way over very uneven grass, and stones, by the dim light of the stars. Sometimes the hill-side seemed to disappear in darkness before them. And Enoch, who was the smallest and lightest, had to go first, using the cloak as a rope to hold on to; while Eb crouched low, throwing all his weight into the pull. They knew that there was no steep precipice before them; but there were many sudden drops from the rocks that might have resulted in a sprained ankle or a broken leg.

As they came down to the level, the going became easier. Most of the smaller stones had been removed and built into rough walls, dividing the fields from the vineyards, which were planted in straight rows running north and south, east and west. By taking a bearing on a star, they could walk straight forward, almost without fear of stumbling against an unseen obstacle. For the stone walls showed dimly pale against the darker earth and vines. They moved swiftly on tiptoe, with slightly bent knees, like wild animals ready to spring; and their feet made no sound on the hard-baked earth. They were happy to be in action at last. And they both felt sorry for Shamashazir, left behind to watch by the fire.

The first vineyard ended with another rough low wall, made of loose stones, which had to be carefully climbed. And then they were in the darkness of an olive grove, feeling their way between the trees, which had been planted higgledy-piggledy. They slowed their pace, keeping their eyes on the patches of starlit sky appearing between the leaves and branches, and doubling in and out. It was difficult to keep in the right direction. And when they at last found themselves at the edge of an open field, they had to take a fresh bearing from the stars before they could be certain which way to go. The field was newly ploughed and the earth was soft. It would be unwise to leave footsteps across it. So they turned to the left and skirted the edge, walking through the tufted grass until their feet felt the hard-beaten earth of a path.

'This path will lead us to the main gate,' said Enoch.

They followed it a little way, as silently as two shadows, until the pointed thatch roofs of the village were clearly silhouetted against the sky in front of them. Then they turned to the right, leaving the path, and skirted the edge of the belt of olive-trees, where they had prayed that morning. On their left was the open clearing that surrounded the village. But they kept under the shadow of the trees, gliding from shadow to shadow as silently as dew falls on the grass—listening intently for the sound of anyone stirring. Eb said that the people of the corn country moved like oxen. It would be easy to hear if there was anyone about outside the walls.

When they stopped to listen, they could hear the distant sounds of a woman's sobbing and an old man's snoring—every time getting nearer and louder. And they were guided by the voice of Shaul moaning in his sleep. When they thought they must be directly opposite his hut, they slowed down their pace and reconnoitred. Enoch had noticed one or two little bushes of broom, growing in the open space between them and the village walls, which would give them cover if anyone was watching. So they hovered a moment under the trees, looking for a place where the broom swayed gently in the soft breeze and they could cross that starlit open stretch. And then, like two shadows among the dancing shadows of the broom, they flitted over and were close under the wall.

The crenelles in the rampart were far too narrow for a man to squeeze through. So Enoch, who was the lightest, climbed over and let himself slowly down on the other side. He landed on a handful of dead leaves, which rustled slightly even under his careful feet. He signalled Eb to move along a little, and found a place where the earth was clear of rubbish, where he could drop down soundlessly.

The back of Shaul's hut was only a few feet away. Softly, they touched its warm sunbaked mud with their hands, feeling for the ridges of the upright posts, which Shamashazir had said would be inside the clay, and would be about the length of a forearm apart. Without speaking, Enoch moved Eb's hand to a spot about the level of his shoulder from the ground. Eb took out his knife, and began to drill a tiny hole; from time to time filling it with spittle to soften the mud. A foot to the right, Enoch began to drill another hole. They worked with the points of their knives, thrusting downwards, so that the holes, when they got larger, could be filled with the water they carried.

Shamashazir had explained that the huts were made on a circle of long thin sticks, stuck into the ground, and tied together in a bunch at the top. Between the sticks, rushes were woven in and out like a basket; and the whole was covered in clay or mud. If the rushes were new it would be very difficult to cut through the wall. But he had noticed that the rushes looked grey; and he thought they would crumble away when the clay was melted.

When Enoch had bored about an inch deep, his knife suddenly slid forward with a slight rustle into a soft substance. The rushes! He took off his drinking-horn, and very slowly trickled water into the hole, letting it overflow down the outside of the hut; giving it time to soak into the clay before he began working downwards again with his knife. Eb did the same, softening the clay with water, and making a long, thin groove. When their drinking-horns were empty, they pricked a tiny hole in each rabbit-skin, and used the water they had carried in them, slowly squeezing it, drop by drop, into the wet grooves—always working downwards—until the grooves were both about three feet long. Then they began to cut across, prising out small bits of clay, and stooping down to lay them soundlessly on the ground. They could feel the rushes inside. They were soft, and broke with a slight rustle when they poked their fingers into them. Behind the rushes there was more clay. But they must deal with that later. The outside layer was coming away more easily, in larger chunks, sometimes bringing bits of rush away, making a sound like a mouse tearing up paper. Enoch was certain that the noise could be heard inside the hut. And he prayed that Shaul was drunk and asleep.

When they had removed all the loose clay they could from the outside, they each took a skin again and squeezed out a jet of water, hoping it would go through the rushes, and soften up the inside clay. Then the truly difficult work of breaking through began. It was impossible to do it without noise. The rushes crackled and rustled, and the wall gave way in unexpectedly large chunks. One piece fell inside the hut with such a thud that they both stopped work and gripped each other's hands. It was an unspoken signal, for they dared not even whisper. Silently, each wiped the clay off his knife on his leg. And they stood back-to-back, waiting for what might happen. They could hear Shaul breathing heavily inside the hut. Enoch turned and swiftly hung the cloak that they carried over the hole—to block out the starlight, in case one of the sentries looked in to see what was the matter. But there was no sound of anyone stirring near the door. They both felt certain that the sentries suspected the truth, and were creeping up on them with their spears. Silently, without the rustle of a leaf, they slipped back to the wall of the village, and stood in its shadow, watching. But nothing happened.

'I can't understand it!' Eb whispered. 'What are those sentries doing? I don't like it! I'm going to see.'

Enoch tried to persuade him to wait. But he remained obdurate. 'I can't go on working with the feeling that they are creeping about in the shadows. I could stick my knife through the ribs of one of them without making a sound.'

But Enoch said there was no sense in that. There were two sentries; they were tall men armed with spears—and he himself was only a lad, and too small to deal with the second without the risk of making a noise. They had better stay where they were. If nothing happened they could go on.

Eb shook his head. 'I suppose you are right. But I don't like it.

I'm going to have a look.' In the end, Enoch let him go, watching him disappear into the darkness while he waited under the shadow of the wall. It was not long before he felt a light touch on his shoulder, and Eb whispered triumphantly in his ear: 'They are dead asleep ... like drunkards ... the fools.'

'Wondrous are the ways of the Lord of all the Earth,' Enoch said. And they went back to the hut, working at the hole until it was big enough for Enoch to climb through easily.

They could hear where Shaul lay breathing heavily and still moaning. They listened for some time to make sure that there was no one else sleeping with him. But neither of them could hear any other sound. Enoch thrust his knife into its sheath, and taking Shamashazir's skirt in his hands, slipped through the hole they had made. Inside the hut, he dropped to his hands and knees; and feeling his way with the tips of his fingers, he crawled across the floor; until he was so near to Shaul that the fumes of wine from the boy's breath blew into his face.

Softly he moved his hand forward, until the fingers felt Shaul's shoulders—up towards his throat and chin they crept. And then, down came his other hand, with Shamashazir's skirt, over Shaul's mouth. Quickly, the agile Enoch whipped Shaul into a sitting position, whispering all the time in his ear: 'Keep still. We've come to save you. We've come to save you. Keep still.'

For a moment Shaul was too benumbed with sleep to do anything but moan and gurgle, while Enoch tied the skirt into position with Shamashazir's linen belt. Then he stood upright; and, keeping a firm grip on Shaul's arms lest he started to struggle, raised him to his feet and carried him to the hole they had made; where the strong arms of Eb were waiting to pull him through. There was a slight rustle of falling dust, as Shaul's body brushed against the broken edges of the hut; and then the boy was hoisted on to Eb's broad shoulders like a sack. Enoch followed silently—stepping after him, then slipping through the trees and over the outer walls of the village—flitting across the clearing into the shelter of the olive grove, where they were hidden from sight. But Shaul was moaning and grunting and struggling. And although he was gagged, and his head wrapped in the cloak, small sounds carried far on that silent night.

They groped their way expertly among the tree-trunks, Enoch going ahead, and Eb following the faint gleam on the white underneath of the rabbit-skins, which hung from Enoch's belt down the middle of his back. Several hundred paces inside the olive grove they put Shaul down and tried to pacify him. 'Quiet, lad!' Eb whispered. 'We are trying to take you to safety. The Great Spirit has sent Enoch son of Enoch to save you from death.'

Shaul was too drunk to take much in, but he seemed to understand something, for he stopped struggling and let them wrap him up more securely, although he kept on moaning in a way that made them still afraid of being heard. Enoch made the hunting shriek of a laughing hyena to cover up the sounds; and they started off again —but now bearing to the right, towards the path that led from the village gate. There was danger in it. But once they were on that path Eb could go without Enoch's guidance. He would be able to run at the slow trot of the hunting shepherds, and get Shaul to safety, in less than half the time it would take to stumble over the rough ground of the vineyards and ploughed fields.

Enoch turned and twisted among the olive-trees, keeping his eyes on a constellation of stars, that he calculated to be in the right direction; and feeling with his sensitive feet for any change in the ground that would show they had reached the path.

Suddenly the darkness of the trees was cut by a straight line of starry sky; and he turned sharply to the left towards the hills. On the hard surface of the path their tracks would be more difficult to follow. Eb said that when he got farther on, if all was quiet behind him, he would do a little doubling back; and lay a few false trails, to give them more time in the morning. 'Those heathen will get to the mountains, and find our camping-place, while we are climbing along the face of the cliff in front of them. They'll be close on our heels all the way,' he said rather gloomily.

The olive-trees that grew along the side of the path came suddenly to an end. And they saw the beacon, like a red star fallen from the sky, glowing in front of them. Eb put Shaul down, and began to take Shamashazir's skirt off his head; but the boy flopped to the ground and lay helpless at their feet. 'What's the matter?' Enoch said. 'Have we suffocated him with all that cloth over his face?'

Eb bent down and felt the boy's heart. 'He's alive. . . .'

They eased the gag out of Shaul's mouth; and Eb laid him across his shoulders again, saying that the fresh air would soon revive him; and that he could go on alone now. Enoch had better do what he had to do quickly. 'And may the Lord of all the Earth be close to you this night, O Enoch son of Enoch,' he said fervently. He hated parting from his young Ishakki, whom he had promised to defend with his life. He watched him go back down the path, and disappear into the olive-trees on the right. And then he strode off in the opposite direction, towards the light of the beacon on the hill, while Enoch set out to do the most dangerous part of their night's work.

They had taken a long time rescuing Shaul. It must be very late. Could so young a boy as Zepho keep awake, listening? Enoch asked himself, as he moved like a shadow through the olive-trees, working round in a great circle towards the women's quarters, to avoid the village, and straining his ears for the faint crackle of a twig, or any sign that would warn him that men were waiting for him in the olive grove.

He came at last to the clearing, a little to the east of the meeting-place, and stood and listened. The village was quiet—much too quiet. There was not even the sound of the Ishakeen's sobs to be heard. But he put his hands to his mouth and gave the signal of the owl. From where he stood he would see when Zepho, or anyone else, crossed the open clearing ahead. He waited a little, but there was no sign of a shadow moving, nor rustle of sound near the wall. He gave the signal again; and then, silently as moonlight on water, he glided towards the tree of meeting. Not a twig snapped, not a leaf rustled, not a tuft of grass sighed where his feet touched the earth. And all the time he was listening—listening. Zepho might be at the meeting-place already. It was impossible to pick out the tree in the dark; it was much like all the others. But he had marked it by the silhouette of the village roofs against the sky. And as he moved he watched them fall into the right pattern. He had reached the meeting-place.

He listened for sounds of breathing or a faint movement among the grasses—but all was silent, all was still. He made the owl signal again and waited—watching the clearing between him and the village. A light breeze stirred the broom bushes and one seemed to take the shape of a boy. But it remained fixed to its place. 'He has fallen asleep,' he thought. 'Or he is afraid to come.' Again he gave the owl signal. The leaves of the olive-trees softly rustled overhead. Shamashazir saw a face watching him through a crenelle, he remembered. Enoch moved away from the tree of meeting, still keeping his eyes on the open space that Zepho was to cross. Some of those clumsy warriors might come in answer to his call. For some moments he hovered, moving from tree to tree; but listening for any sound of breathing that might give his enemies away, or tell him that Zepho had crossed at the wrong place, and was waiting under another tree.

Then, suddenly, the silence was broken by a woman's screaming. 'They've discovered!' he thought. And swift as a hare, he turned and fled, dodging the staggered trunks of the olive-trees. He heard a man shout. The screams stopped. And then the pounding of his heart, as he ran, seemed to drown all further sounds.

Shamashazir, left alone on the hill-side with Jemimah, sat with his knees drawn up and teeth still chattering, trying to listen for some sound of the retreating feet of Enoch and Eb. But they were as skilled at moving over strange ground in the dark as they were at moving over familiar ground in the daylight. Not the crack of a twig nor the clink of a stone reached his ears. They seemed to have vanished off the face of the earth; and he was suddenly alone. Between him and his home stretched the White Mountains of terror and a journey of several moons. Between him and his friends lay the unseen fields of the Corn Dingir; and beyond them the Sea at the End of the World. No wonder his teeth chattered. He clenched his jaw to try to stop them, for the noise hindered his concentration; and he tried again to pray to the Great Spirit. But it was the Corn Dingir who moved in the darkness below him; and the mountain dingirs who whispered in the hills behind him. 'Eb would never be afraid like this,' he said to himself, 'nor would Enoch my friend. They depend on me. I must not forget the work that I am to do. I must not use my store of wood too soon; and I must keep a proper account of the time.'

He began to wonder how he could judge the passing of the hours; time always went so slowly when one waited in suspense. There was no moon to cast a shadow; but at the Senior School in Ur he had learnt something of the movement of the stars. He got up and went over to the wood pile, and carefully selected two straight sticks of unequal length, with which to take a sight. But the grass was too thick to drive their blunt ends through it into the earth. He struggled with them till he broke one, and then, remembering how Sam put a point on his fishing-spears, he knelt by the fire and thrust the butts into the flames till they began to burn. He pulled them out flaming, doused them in the grass, and knocked off the charred wood, as he had seen Sam do. Deciding that the star Gag-si-Sa (Sirius) was in the best position for his purpose, he chose a thin patch in the turf and drove the longer stick easily into the ground. Then, crouching on his knees, he found by trial and error the right distance for the two sticks to be apart, carefully selected his point in line, and drove the shorter gently into the earth, testing its height with his eye, until the two heads met on the star Gag-si-Sa.

Reassured now as to the passing of time, he settled himself down more securely to wait, sitting wih his elbows on his knees and his chin in his hands. The flames of the fire flickered lazily beside him. The smallest branch seemed to take an age to burn. He tried to follow in his mind the steps of Enoch and Eb: now they had got to the fields and olive groves; now they had reached the walls of the village; now they had started work. He got up and took another sight from his two sticks. The star had moved slightly.

'If they are discovered, the Kenanites will surely light torches,' he thought. But he was not sure if the lights would show so far. He strained his eyes and ears, trying to detect a tiny glow in the darkness or hear a distant shout. But all was silent, except for the croaking of frogs in a distant pond, the soft purr and crackle of the flames, and the gentle sound of Jemimah munching grass.

From time to time he got up and took another observation. Gag-si-Sa was steadily moving. He drove other sticks into the ground to show the different points it reached. They must have broken into the hut by now; it was time to pile up the beacon, he thankfully decided. And first dragging a large branch off the wood pile, he began to drop handfuls of dry heather on to the flames, so that they leaped up high, crackling and hissing. Backwards and forwards to the wood pile he went, heaping the fuel higher and higher, thinking of Eb coming safely on the return journey and Enoch fetching the little boy, completely absorbed in his work. He had forgotten all about Jemimah. But he was suddenly startled out of his thoughts by hearing her scrambling to her feet. He looked behind him. She was standing with her ears cocked towards the mountains to the north, intently listening.

Shamashazir, thinking immediately of lions, seized a burning branch, and holding it above his head, went towards the little donkey, trying to see by its fitful light if her hair was standing up on end. She backed away from him in terror.

Lighted twigs were falling on the long grass, setting it afire. He tried to stamp them out with his sandals; but the flames scorched his feet. He hastily threw the branch back on to the fire; and seizing the turfs that they had cut to make the hearth, threw them on the burning grass; and the flames fizzled out.

Shamashazir was learning his lesson. He selected two well-burnt stumps of wood, without any twigs and branches, and holding them above his head went out into the darkness to mount guard beyond Jemimah. She was still sniffing the air, with her ears well forward, flicking her tail excitedly. He had his hands full. He must not let the flames of the beacon die down. He must not lose the donkey. He hoped that he would be able to hold out until Eb returned.

Leaving Jemimah unguarded again, he piled more fuel on the fire. And taking out two more burning brands, he began to walk backwards and forwards in front of her, peering into the darkness for any sign of two green eyes catching the light of the flames.

Then, suddenly, Jemimah gave a tremendous bray that echoed all round the hills. Shamashazir dropped one of the torches; but it was burning low, and the impact of its fall into the cool dewy grass put it out. He ran back to seize a fresh brand. Jemimah swung her head towards him and the flames lit up the bright glow of her eyes —two burning, ghostly eyes shining in the darkness, as though some evil spirit had taken control of the friendly little donkey. With trembling hands he stooped to the fire. She shifted her feet, slightly altering her stand, so that her head pointed more to the east of the mountains behind them. Shamashazir strained his eyes towards the dark ridge of rock silhouetted clearly against the starlit sky. There was a movement along the rugged edge—something rounded was appearing and disappearing on the skyline—surely too small for a lion or a bear? He breathed a sigh of relief and tried to make out what it was. It had no horns. It could not be a goat. The skyline dipped for a space. The creature moved on; and he clearly saw the head and shoulders of a man! Quickly he threw the two torches back into the flames, and dropped on to his hands and knees.

He had already learnt enough from Enoch to be surprised at a man showing himself against the skyline. 'It can't be one of the hill tribes, or a man used to the mountains,' he thought. 'It must be a Kenanite. And there must be more than one of them.' He began to crawl in a circle away from the betraying light of the fire so that they should not know his whereabouts. For a long time he lay still with beating heart and eyes fixed on the black line of rock against the sky for any further movement. The flames began to die down. The fire was becoming useless as a beacon. 'Better let it die,' he thought. 'If Eb can't see the fire he will guess that something is wrong. It will stop him walking into a trap. He will go back to Enoch and they will go another way into the mountains. But how am I to find them again?'

Suddenly Jemimah let forth another colossal bray, which echoed like the roar of a lion through the silence.

'Jemimah!' he thought. 'If I let her loose she will lead me to them. He began to crawl round the fire to where the little donkey was tensely straining at the rope that held her. With fumbling hands he untied the knot. There was a rattle of scrambling hooves on stones. And, before he could grab her halter, Jemimah was away into the darknes. His link with Enoch and Eb was lost. But he could still hear the steady thud of her hooves.

For which direction was she heading? He listened. North, it seemed. But where was the northern star? Right round to the left. Surely Jemimah was heading straight for the mountains! Unless his ears deceived him she was going towards the ridge where he had seen the figure of the man. The Corn Dingir! The Corn Dingir had come to wile away their donkey. 'And to lead Enoch and Eb astray as well,' he thought, looking at the embers of the beacon, which he had allowed to die down to nothing more than a glowing patch of ashes in the grass. Quickly, almost frantically, calling out loud to the Great Spirit for help, he began to pile on more brushwood, in small handfuls, and then larger branches, until the flames leaped up high again, hissing and crackling in a great blast of heat, that made him step backwards to get away from it.

Then, out of the darkness, he heard a voice calling his name:

'O Shamashazir of Ur, bring a torch from your fire, to light up the pits and crevices that the evil spirits have dug in the rocks of their ill-famed mountain. I have been crawling on my hands and knees since sunset, for fear of walking through those demon-possessed cornfields of Kenan.'

'Sam!' shouted Shamashazir. 'How did you get here?' He seized a fresh brand of flaming wood, and began to climb up the rocks towards Sam's voice. Now and again he could hear Jemimah's hooves and Sam talking to her—calling her the 'light of his eyes and the delight of his heart'.

When at last Shamashazir met them, Sam was walking upright

with his hand on Jemimah's saddle, letting her guide him along the easiest way. Shamashazir laughed with joy to see them.

'Ah,' said Sam to Jemimah. 'O sweetness of my soul, if I had had you with me all the time to be my guide, my hands would not be bleeding, nor my legs covered in bruises.'

He had walked nearly twenty six miles since they had parted that morning; but the last part of the journey had been the worst. Most of the way had been through olive groves and vineyards. But when he got near to the Village of Kenan he had taken to the hills. He threw himself down on the ground near the fire, and swallowed the water which Shamashazir offered him, in one gulp.

'What did the Ishak say?' Shamashazir asked.

'He said nothing but that he would be at the Lake of the Kingfishers. But I could see by the way he looked he was not pleased. Then the Ishakeen came up and scolded him for sending you. And he still said nothing; until the Ishakeen asked how you could take two boys and one donkey through the mountains to the Lake of the Kingfishers, and only one man with any sense in his head. And then he said to me, "Go back O Samuel, friend of the beasts. Go back the way you came. And if my son comes out of this heathen village alive, go along with him to the Lake of the Kingfishers."— And so here I am,' added Sam.

It wasn't long after this that they heard the cry of a corncrake below them. 'That'll be Eb. One of them is back safely,' said Sam. He put his hands to his mouth and made an answering call.

A few moments later, Eb loomed up out of the darkness with the limp body of Shaul slung over his shoulders. He let the boy slide to the ground, where he fell in a heap, moaning; and then he gave Sam a hearty slap across the shoulders. 'There's none save Enoch son of Enoch I'd be better pleased to see,' he declared.

But Shamashazir was curious about Shaul. He bent over him, staring into his pale face and glazed eyes.

'He's all right,' said Eb. 'He's been sick. Give him some water.' And he tossed a rabbit-skin bottle over to Shamashazir, which he had filled at the Frog Spring on the way.

Shamashazir squeezed a little water into Shaul's mouth. Then he went and sat with the others round the fire. And they talked of what they had each done, and what they would do next; until Sam said that he was hungry. He had come fourteen miles since he had last eaten—'and that wasn't much.'

'We've nothing here,' said Eb. 'We left all the food on the other side of the hill.'

'Well,' said Sam, rubbing his stomach and getting to his feet, 'the sooner we get there the better.'

'I am not moving from this place till I see Enoch son of Enoch safe again. Shamashazir of Ur will have to take you.'

But Shamashazir was not sure that he would be able to lead the way back in the darkness. He hesitated. '*I* will stay by the fire and wait for Enoch,' he said.

But Eb wouldn't hear of it. He had made his vow to his Ishak; and every minute that Enoch was out of his sight was an agony to him. If Shamashazir could not find the way, then Sam would have to wait.

They sat silent for a few minutes, listening and waiting, but no signal from Enoch broke into the murmurs of the night. At last Sam said that if he did not go, he would fall asleep; and that if Shamashazir could not lead the way, perhaps Jemimah could. 'I'd as soon trust her as yourself, Eb.'

Eb snorted and stood up. Together the two men sat the half-conscious body of Shaul on the back of the patient Jemimah. And, with Sam walking beside her—with one arm round the boy and the other hand patting the donkey's neck, explaining to her that he wanted his food—they set off over the hill. Shamashazir followed behind, carrying a torch to light the path. And Eb sat down by the fire again to keep his watch alone.

After Zepho had been pushed through the narrow crenelle in the village wall by his father, he found himself behind the mud huts of the women's quarters. He did not run directly back to his mother, but stood feeling the dusty earth with his toes, looking at the dark slit through which he had just come—the crenelle that had no scorpion. And he wondered how he would find it again at night.

Burrowing in the hot dust, his right foot discovered something hard and sharp; and he stooped down to dig it out with his fingers. It was a triangular piece of broken pitcher, as large as his hand. He picked it up, examined it, and pushed it gently into the bottom of the crenelle, so that a point stuck out. He could see it easily now; but could he find it in the dark? He took a few steps away, shut his eyes, and began to feel along the wall with his hands. But as he came to the crenelle he gave the piece of pottery a slight jar and knocked it inwards. It didn't stick out nearly far enough. Something bigger was needed. Zepho went through all his possessions in his mind, until he remembered that, hanging on a twig that stuck out from a post in his mother's hut, was a worn-out basket. 'That basket would fit tightly in the hole and stick out so that you knocked it,' he said to himself; and he ran off to fetch it. There was no one in the hut. And by poking at the basket with one of his sandals, which were lying on the floor ready for the celebrations the next day, he easily got it down.

But on his way back he ran into his mother—she had been anxiously looking for him. She stooped down, seized him, basket, sandal and all, and hugged him tight, calling him her little honey and her lamb, while Zepho struggled to get free.

'I looked among the olive-trees, and in the fields, and you were not there. I thought those two strangers from the Mountains of the Wicked Dingirs had taken you away with them. Where have you been all this time?'

'I've been with Father,' Zepho said, when at last she let him go. And he started to walk off; but she called him back.

'It's dinner-time. Come and eat a little food. Just a little. I've found some special dried raisins for you. And there's honey.'

'I'll come presently. I've got something important to do first. It's *very* important.' He looked up at her excitedly; and his eyes were bright and fearless.

She noticed that a change had come over him; but she did not ask the reason. She was too thankful to see him happy again. 'Run along then,' she said, 'and do your important business. But be quick with it, or all the raisins will be eaten.'

The basket fitted into the hole firmly, and stuck out— 'so that if you ran close to the wall in the dark, you'd bump into it,' Zepho said to himself with satisfaction. It had taken hardly a moment to put it into place. He replaced his sandal in the hut; and soon he was beside his mother among the ovens in the women's quarters— pleased with his morning's work, and lolling up against her happily while he gobbled his food; for she was his mother, and he might never see her again.

No one among the women could help noticing the tremendous change in Zepho since the morning. But they put it down to his ride on the donkey. 'It took his mind off,' his stepmother remarked from the depth of her own experience. And they picked out titbits to encourage him to eat.

After dinner, Zepho could not keep away from his basket in the wall. He found a long stick which would do for a spear, and took his stand under the shade of a tree at the back of the hut, standing very straight with his head well back and the stick at his side, like one of the guards before Shaul's door. But he had had little sleep each night for the last quarter of a moon; and the afternoon was hot and drowsy. His knees began to give awkward twitches and jerks, and his head seemed to want to fall forward on his chest. It was no good trying to stand up any longer. He laid the stick down, and squatted beside it on the ground, with his arms round his knees—and before he knew it, he was asleep. He was very tired, and he slept peacefully and deeply well into the late afternoon.

He woke up bewildered to find himself again beside his mother, among the conical ovens in the women's quarters. She had picked him up and carried him there while he slept. His head lay on her soft thigh; and the tips of her fingers gently fondled his smooth black hair. When she saw that he was awake she pressed food on him—which he refused. He got up and moved about restlessly for a few moments; until he saw an opportunity of slipping away. He didn't want to be followed. With sidelong glances at the women, he set off first towards the men's compound, where his father's mud palace and Shaul's hut stood. The men were all sitting round the fire eating, with their backs towards him. He slipped by unnoticed and made his way to the crenelle. His basket was still there!

He squatted down in front of it to wait for nightfall. But the brassy sun seemed hardly to move in the hot sky. He soon got tired of doing nothing, and began marking out fields and vine-yards, and building village walls in the dust, telling himself a story about a boy who ran away and half talking to himself; while bit by bit the shadows lengthened. And he suddenly looked up and saw that his father was standing over him.

'Bedtime, my son,' the Ishak said rather sadly.

Zepho stood up and stretched, giving a glance at the basket in the wall as he did so. His father swung him up on to his shoulder; and once more the little boy felt himself surrounded by the love that only fathers can give, and once more he longed to tell him his secret.

'Let us go and look at the ovens,' said the Ishak. 'Maybe the women have left some pieces of bread in them.'

All the children loved pieces of bread hot from the ovens. And Zepho suddenly realized that he had eaten no supper and that he was hungry. He grinned and nodded. And they went into the women's quarters, where the baking fires had gone out. But the conical ovens still stood in their places, like a village of giant, bottomless flower-pots turned upside-down. From the height of his father's shoulder, Zepho could look down into them without getting his face scorched by the heat from the remains of the glowing charcoal, which lay round the outside. When he had spotted part of a broken loaf left behind (for the loaves were thin and flat like large soft biscuits), his father bent down and reached for it with his long arm. And Zepho, on his perch, began almost happily to munch hot spiced bread made with eggs and milk.

Then the Ishak kissed his little son goodnight and let him slide down to the ground. And Zepho thought that it would be the last time that he would ever see his father again. An uncomfortable lump seemed to rise in his throat. His lips trembled; and his eyes began to fill with tears like a baby's. But he pulled himself together, remembering that he was the Ishak's son, stood up straight, and said, 'When I am grown up I shall come back and be Ishak. And I shall fight the Corn Dingir.'

His father gave a start which made Zepho wonder if he had given away his secret. But then he smiled. That was all right. He often smiled in the days before they had shut Shaul up in his hut. Then he placed his hand gently on the little boy's head and bending down, murmured very quietly in his ear—such words that would have made the elders cry 'Sacrilege!' if they had overheard them. 'May the Great Spirit of Shamashazir of Ur and of Enoch son of Enoch bless you, my son,' he said.

Zepho looked up at him, round-eyed. 'Mother does not like Shamashazir and Enoch,' he thought. 'But Father does, and so do I.' But he said nothing. And when he had run round the back of the women's quarters, to take one last look at the basket in the wall, he went into his mother's hut and began his preparations.

First he took a pair of her old sandals, which lay on the floor in a corner, and his own sandals, that had been cleaned with bees-wax and olive oil for the feast the next day, and put them under his little rush mat. 'They will be very uncomfortable to lie on,' he thought. 'But they will stop me from going to sleep.' Then he fetched out his old stone knife, and a broken arrowhead that might be useful, and put them with the sandals. Then he lay down and pretended to go to sleep.

But he was so excited he could not lie still. His mother had not come into the hut yet. She was outside in the cool of the evening listening to Shaul's cries, and moaning softly to herself. It was dark in the hut; and she could not see if he was asleep or awake. It was quite safe to sit up. Gradually, as the other noises of the village died away, the shouts and drunken laughter from Shaul's hut seemed to grow louder. It was better to hear him shouting and singing than screaming as he had done the night before.

Then, as the air become chilly, Zepho heard his mother move to come in; and he quickly lay down and curled himself up on his mat. He felt her come near and bend over him. She took him in her arms and kissed him and cried over him, as he hated being kissed and cried over. Then she lay down on her mat beside him with her hand touching his shoulder. He got up, and drew his mat (with all that lay under it) to the open doorway, where he could hear the cry of the owl when it came. But it was a long time coming. He lay on his stomach with his head out of the door, listening and listening. And there was no sound of an owl. Only Shaul was making a noise. It would not be easy to hear an owl with his brother making such a noise. If only Shaul would be quiet . . .

Sometimes he was quiet for a little, then he started off again. . . . It was no use listening for an owl while Shaul was making that noise—or for a donkey either. But all the same a donkey was there. It had corn sprouting out of its ears; and he was sitting on its back. And Shamashazir of Ur was there, running beside him. And the donkey was going faster and faster. Shamashazir kept telling him to get off. He couldn't get off. The donkey wouldn't stop. And then it started to gallop straight into a blazing fire. Zepho— terrified—jumped off its back and fell on the ground with a tremendous thud.

He woke up trembling with fear, his heart beating furiously and his teeth chattering. He began to whimper for his mother. But she, exhausted by her grief, had fallen into a deep and troubled sleep. The village was very quiet. There was no donkey with straw in his ears and no flaming fire. . . . There was silence. Even Shaul was silent. Zepho remembered that he was supposed to be listening for an owl. . . . But he couldn't hear it. He got up from his mat, his legs still trembling, and went into the cool night air outside the hut, and listened again.

It was very quiet. Not a sound came from Shaul. Had Shaul gone, leaving him behind? Shamashazir of Ur had said he mustn't go to sleep. But Shamashazir of Ur had come into his dream and woken him up. He took the stone knife and the arrow-head in his hand, and clutching all four sandals to his chest, ran behind the huts, his bare feet silently padding the cool dust. It was so dark under the trees that he bumped into the wall before he expected and nearly dropped the sandals. Feeling his way along it with one elbow and one foot, he began to creep cautiously round. He passed by one—two—then three empty crenelles; and then suddenly received a sharp jab in his bare ribs that made him jump and nearly cry out. The scorpion!

But no, it was not a scorpion. It was the basket. And it was where he had left it. He dug his toes into a niche in the wall, climbed up, squeezed through; and climbed down on the other side, still clutching the four sandals, which kept slipping out of his arms. Then he hurried across the open clearing and began to look for the olive-tree where he was to meet Enoch. It was to the left, he thought. But he had walked some way with his father when they found the hole that had no scorpion. He was not sure if he could find the tree. But it was a special tree. He would know the feel of its trunk. But how could he feel anything, with these horrible sandals slipping out of his arms all the time? He sat down and put on his own sandals, groping about in the dark. Then he took up the other two (he could carry them in one hand), and went on with his search, feeling the trunks of the trees with his free hand.

A thin one. 'No, that's not it'—a fat one—a tree with a low branch that they climbed into—'It's the next one.' And it was the next one. He sat down under it, and waited, listening for sounds of anyone moving. But there were no sounds—except for the chirruping of a cricket, and the leaves of the olive-trees gently moving overhead. He called very softly: 'Enoch son of Enoch, friend of Shamashazir of Ur, are you there?' But no one answered.

A deep choking sob that hurt rose up in his throat. *They had gone without him!* They had left him alone in the dark at the mercy of the cruel Corn Dingir. He clenched his little fists hard, to try to choke back his tears; and then suddenly realized that he had lost his stone knife *and* his broken arrow-head when he put on his sandals. For a moment a great wave of despair rolled over him— but only for a moment; for Zepho was a little boy with the courage of a king. It wasn't any good sitting there, waiting in the dark for Enoch. He would never come. He got up, brushed his tears away, and walked slowly out into the clearing, looking longingly towards the hills where he knew that Shamashazir and Enoch and Shaul would be—the hills of the evil dingirs, who were afraid of the Lord of all the Earth. What had his father said? 'May the Great Spirit of Shamashazir of Ur and Enoch son of Enoch bless you, my son.' Zepho took a deep breath and filled out his chest with courage.

Over his head a canopy of stars gazed coldly down at him. 'Just like the roof of a huge hut,' he thought, as he looked up at them in wonder. For he had never been out so late at night before and had never seen such a clear sweep of stars. They reached right down to the earth—right down to the hills where Shamashazir was. And *one* was so low that it seemed to have dropped out of the sky altogether. It was redder and duller than the rest, warmer and more friendly—like a fire. And it seemed to blink at Zepho as if it were talking to him. 'It is the star of Shamashazir,' he said suddenly to himself. 'And it is calling me to come.'

Clutching one of his mother's sandals in each hand, he began to tiptoe softly along the open clearing, round the outside of the village wall, towards the main gateway. Past the back of the elders' huts he went, then past the empty hut where Shamashazir and Enoch had slept the night before—and the huts of the young warriors—tiptoeing all the time; on past Shaul's hut—then the huts of more young warriors—until at last he came to the gate of the village, and found what he wanted: the path which led to the spring by the mountains. And he turned his back on his home, and his mother and father, and set off to follow the path out into the unknown darkness. He was very small. He was only seven—a tiny, moving creature swallowed up in the night—and his heart was thumping violently. But it was the heart of a lion. And he went steadily on towards the star of Shamashazir.

Through the olive groves he went, past the silent olive-trees that loomed with a heavy blackness out of the darkness. Often they rose up in front of him like towering giants and hid the star of Shamashazir from sight; and he was frightened. But he went on, and the star of Shamashazir came into view again, only to disappear once more behind another tree.

Things rustled in the grass by his side, and once a headless white bird flew silently across his path. An owl hooted in a tree close by, sending shivers of terror down his back. It did not hoot the owl signal of Enoch, friend of Shamashazir.

The olive-trees came to an end in time; and the open fields of the Corn Dingir were spread out before him. A strange whiteness seemed to hang over them—a moving, living thing without shape or substance, heaving and dancing over the fields. Zepho wondered if the Corn Dingir could see in the dark. He crouched down among some young broom bushes, longing to run quickly to the other side, but afraid he might make a noise and attract the Corn Dingir's attention. He began to walk slowly and carefully, with trembling knees and chattering teeth, step by step towards the star of Shamashazir. Half-way across he began to breathe more freely. It seemed that the Corn Dingir slept at night like men; or that he could not see in the dark.

Ahead of him the star of Shamashazir burned brighter and clearer. 'Shamashazir is there waiting for me,' Zepho thought, and it gave him courage again. He hurried on to the end of the fields less cautiously. There were vineyards ahead—vineyards of the Wine Dingir. And the Wine Dingir was jolly and less cruel. He felt safer. He began to run through the rows of the vines, until his legs ached and he had to drop back to a walk.

There were rustlings among the vine leaves, and mysterious noises. And far away a bellow came from the hills in front. 'A lion!' thought Zepho. And he stopped still in his tracks, ready to run back. But now between him and the village lay the fields of the Corn Dingir. He could *never* cross them again. . . . Better to go and meet the lion. . . . Besides, the star of Shamashazir was burning even more brightly than before. It seemed to him to leap up higher like a fire, as if in answer to his fear. He could hear the frogs croaking—and knew he must be coming near the spring where the oxen drank, and the path ended. He had often been to the spring before, but never any farther; for beyond that the grass was wild and rough and the country of the terrible mountain dingirs began—but the mountain dingirs were friends of Shamashazir.

The croaking of the frogs grew louder and nearer with every step, until it seemed to surround him; and the path lost itself in the rough dried mud made by the trampling of cattle that had come down to the spring to drink. For a moment he was afraid to go any farther. But when he looked back and saw nothing but blackness behind him, he was even more afraid. Ahead of him the star of Shamashazir seemed to call to him to go on. He stumbled over the rough mud, fell, and picked himself up again; then crouched down, testing the ground ahead of him with his hands, like a monkey. But he was soon over the dried mud, and could feel well-cropped grass under his feet. This was much better; and he went forward faster.

Suddenly a mountain dingir, all covered in thorns, stretched out his pointed fingers and scratched Zepho's leg painfully. He could feel the wet blood trickling down. He began to whimper like a child who wants its mother. 'I am the friend of Shamashazir of Ur, and the Lord of all the Earth. Don't you dare scratch me,' he cried through his tears, struggling on. He could see the shadowy forms of the dingirs moving through the darkness, black and jagged, looming over him like cruel rocks. The ground was sloping uphill; and the grass was getting longer and growing in tussocks that nearly tripped him up if he tried to go fast. He found himself getting out of breath and panting as if he had been running. 'The dingirs are squeezing all the breath out of me,' he thought; but he went on, holding his mother's sandals out in front of him as a protection. Then his hands ran into something soft, that gave way as he touched it and lightly tickled his arms with a clammy, delicate touch, but which did not hurt him. 'I'm sorry,' he said. 'I am a friend of Shamashazir and the Lord of all the Earth. I did not mean to bump into you; but I can't see in the dark.' The creature gave no answer, and Zepho struggled on.

The ground became steeper. But the star of Shamashazir was very red—as red as a fire. And it rose and fell, getting larger and smaller like a fire. He hit his toe against a sharp rock and fell down, giving a cry of pain. It hurt so much he felt sure he would never be able to walk again. But slowly the pain lessened; and he rubbed his foot with his hand until he could stand up and put his foot to the ground. Then, limping at first and giving an occasional whimper to keep himself company, he struggled on.

Now, when he looked up, he could see the dark line of the mountains against the starlit sky—jagged and awesome. But the star of Shamashazir lay on the earth, between him and the mountain peaks; and it was more like a fire than ever.

The ground had become steep and stony. This must be the mountains. But how hard they were for an exhausted little boy to climb in the dark. He toiled on, still keeping tight hold of his mother's sandals. It was so steep, he had to bend forward and balance himself with his hands. . . . He couldn't see the star of Shamashazir. He climbed up several feet, on all fours. And then he stood up again and looked for it. But the star of Shamashazir had gone.

A great blackness seemed to have risen up in front of him— a sharp, cruel, jagged shape like the gigantic tusk of a wild boar. And Zepho could imagine a pair of wicked pig's eyes watching him. He began to whimper again. Where was he to go now? If he couldn't see the star of Shamashazir, he would be lost. And who would protect him from the dingir in front? He stepped back to get away from it, but his feet landed, with a jerk that upset his balance, on a heap of little stones that went rattling down the hill behind him. Crying out in terror, he made a grab at the rock in front. Then suddenly the darkness was filled with voices calling his name: 'Zepho! Zepho!'

They called in strange cadences carrying far, and echoing softly against the mountains in a way that Zepho had never heard before —some near, some far away and faint—all calling his name: 'Zepho.' Quite beautiful they were, and had a friendly lilt about them that brought back some of Zepho's courage. And he shouted with all his breath: 'O Shamashazir of Ur help me! Help me, O Lord of all the Earth, who saved Shamashazir from death! Come and help me.'

Then one voice called much nearer: 'Ze-e-e-ph-o. It is I, Enoch son of Enoch. Stay where you are. Don't move. The mountains are dangerous in the dark.'

'Enoch son of Enoch, the friend of Shamashazir!' Zepho didn't stop to wonder how he got there, but regardless of the warning, began to feel his way back, knocking down a stone as he moved.

Enoch heard it, for he shouted again louder and nearer: 'Stay where you are. There is a cleft in the rock beside you.'

Zepho wasn't sure what a 'cleft in the rock' was. But this time he obeyed and stood still, until Enoch called to him again to know where he was.

'I am here,' said Zepho 'Close to the great tooth of the mountain dingir that has swallowed up the star of Shamashazir.' Then he turned round to look at it once more to see if the mountain dingir had come any nearer. The great tooth had disappeared. The star of Shamashazir burnt as brightly as before. Enoch son of Enoch must have driven it away. He was coming nearer now. Zepho could hear his footsteps on the rocks.

'How did you get here?' Enoch asked in a not-too-pleased voice.

'I came by myself.'

'Why didn't you wait under the tree as Shamashazir told you?'

'You went without me,' Zepho sobbed.

'You went too soon,' said Enoch. 'You should have waited. But I suppose you fell asleep?'

'Y-e-s,' said Zepho, with a shuddering sob.

'How did you find your way?'

'I followed the star of Shamashazir.'

Enoch understood at once what the star of Shamashazir was, and spoke more kindly. He told Zepho to get on his back, helping him up. Zepho clung tightly, trembling, as Enoch moved cautiously over the uneven ground; and he watched the star of Shamashazir through his tears. It was glowing like a small fire. Every step Enoch took seemed to make it larger, until dancing flames came out of it, and smoke came out of it, and there was a man standing by it. When he saw the man, Enoch gave a queer high call, like the call of an evil spirit in the night. And the man answered him with the same high-pitched call. Then he took a burning brand out of the fire, and holding it over his head, came to meet them. Zepho could see that it was not Shamashazir, but one of the shepherds who had looked after the donkeys. When they came up to the man with the torch Enoch put him on the ground and said that he could walk. And they climbed up to the fire together by its light. Then the man went down on one knee and held the torch up to Enoch's face. 'O Ishakki of my people, is all well with thee?' he said.

'All is well,' Enoch answered. 'Have you seen any lights in the village?'

'I have seen no lights, and no sounds have I heard.'

'Where is the boy?'

'He is here . . . at the camping-place, and Sam has come. Your father sent him.'

'Sam? That is great news.'

Then the man Eb handed Enoch his torch, and stooped down and took another burning brand out of the fire. 'Take one, too,' he said to Zepho.

Zepho bent down as he was told, holding the burning brand as far away from him as he could. And the man Eb poured a skin of water over the glowing embers, so that they hissed and sizzled like a bundle of snakes; and the fire, the star of Shamashazir, turned black. They were left holding their torches in darkness. And all around lay the country of the mountain dingirs—and no Shamashazir? Zepho could see Eb moving about, bent over the ground in the flickering, uncertain light, lifting up pieces of turf and covering up all marks of the fire. When he had finished, the man Eb took Zepho's torch in one hand, and lifted Zepho himself under his arm, in a most uncomfortable manner, with his head and legs hanging loosely down. And they set off into the darkness to find Shamashazir.

Sam was right. Jemimah led them safely to their camping-place. They laid Shaul on the rocky ledge, and lit a small, glowing fire, made of sheep's dung, dried leaves and turf, with Shamashazir's torch. Then Sam helped himself to one of the loaves they had brought from Kenan, and a piece of cheese, while Shamashazir took the same torch—now flaming anew from the fire, and examined Shaul.

The boy's eyes were open; but he stared at Shamashazir unknowingly. 'You are quite safe now,' said Shamashazir, remembering his own experiences in the cave. 'You are still alive. You're not going to be killed. You are coming to Ur with us.' Then he remembered that Shaul had probably never heard of Ur. It was difficult to explain to a boy who stared at him with such a vacant look. There wasn't much more that he could say, except: 'Everything is all right.' 'And that,' said Shamashazir to himself, 'is what the Ishak Moab would have said to his son, before they sacrificed him to the Corn Dingir.' The little brother was the only one who could explain. Enoch was long in coming. . . . Shamashazir left Shaul, and went back to the fire and to Sam's comfortable chat.

'You can't tell him anything,' said Sam. 'Best to sit and talk of donkeys. There's nothing like talk of beasts to make a man or a boy feel at home among friends, and . . . alive.' And Sam began, Shamashazir tried to listen; but all the time he was thinking of Enoch and Zepho; and Shaul was moaning. But when Shamashazir looked at him again, his eyes were closed and he was breathing evenly. Sam's voice died away in the middle of a sentence. Shamashazir looked round to see what was the matter. Sam had his head on one side, listening. Suddenly he gave the curlew's high whistle; and from the distance came an answering call.

'Enoch son of Enoch is here!' exclaimed Sam. 'And he has the little boy with him!'

Shamashazir was so relieved that he laughed outright.

Sam picked out a torch, and went to meet them, casting before him a flickering light along the path.

Eb was carrying Zepho under one arm, the boy's head and legs dangling limply. He put the bewildered child feet downwards on the rock. For a moment Zepho swayed slightly, then he cried: 'Shamashazir.'

'Here,' said Sam, gently pushing a piece of bread into his hands, 'eat this. Get something inside your stomach and then go to sleep. We start before dawn, and that won't be long now.'

Satisfied that he had found Shamashazir, Zepho did as he was told, nestling down between his brother and his protector, chewing his bread, and feeling safer than he had done for many days. And very soon he was in a deep, untroubled sleep.

When Eb, who had been keeping the last watch, woke them up, Enoch and Zepho were on their feet at once; but it took a moment for the sense of danger to penetrate the fumes of sleep in Shamashazir's head, and he sat up rubbing his eyes.

'Wake the other boy, and give them food and water,' said Eb, 'while we see to the donkey.'

Shaul was bewildered and confused. His head was throbbing. He thought he was still in the Village of Kenan, and cried to be left to sleep.

'Wake up, wake up!' shouted Zepho. 'We are running away from the Corn Dingir with Shamashazir. We are going to Ur. . . . And if you don't wake up, the Corn Dingir will come after us and catch us.'

Shaul sat up and rubbed his eyes. But as he did so, the whole of the starry heavens seemed to whirl round and turn upside-down; and he fell back, groaning.

'Give him this herb to chew,' said Sam urgently. 'I found it in the lands to the north and thought we might need it.'

Shamashazir gave Shaul the herb and some water. Then he and Zepho swallowed as much bread and cheese as they could cram into their excited stomachs.

Zepho chattered to his brother about Ur: 'They have wheels and copper chips on their ploughs, and boats on the water. And they never sacrifice boys to the dingirs—never! It's the wheels and the copper on the ploughs that make the corn grow. I heard Shamashazir of Ur say so to Agag.'

By now it was light enough to see the colour of one another's faces, and the stars were disappearing.

Shaul, who was gradually beginning to understand where he was, and what was expected of him, said he would try to eat. But the bread tasted like sawdust; and he managed to swallow only a mouthful or two. Then Enoch handed him a pair of sandals and told him to put them on; and he fumbled with the ties in the dim light. They did not fit properly. They were too small. 'I don't know how I'm going to walk in these,' he said. 'I don't know how I'm going to walk at all . . .' and his voice sounded shaky with tears.

Eb came and helped him rather impatiently. And when he had got the sandals on, Eb hoisted him roughly to his feet, and putting a supporting arm round his waist, said, 'Right, we are ready.'

Sam led the way with the donkey round the side of a grassy hillock. Enoch followed him with Zepho, helping him over difficult rocks; and then came Shamashazir, limping slightly with his stiff leg; and last of all, Eb with Shaul.

The way was easy at first; which made it possible to start while the light was still uncertain. But as the tip of the sun appeared over the mountains to the east, they turned towards it; and scrambled along a narrow goat-track that ran half-way up the side of a rocky cliff. It was narrow, and it was rough, and the sun was in their eyes. Below them the cliff dropped down to a dry gully of bare boulders. In normal circumstances Shamashazir could never have walked along it with his bad leg, but the thought of their pursuers made him forget the danger of the mountains; and he prayed that he would not slip. 'Those men from the village won't like this at all,' he said to himself, and the thought gave him courage.

When Enoch had heard a woman screaming in the Village of Kenan, he had been quite right in guessing that it was Zepho's mother, discovering her son's disappearance. . . .

She had been woken by the doleful hooting of an owl, and the feeling that she was alone in the hut. She had sat up and reached for her son's mat, which he had moved near the doorway. But the mat was empty. Zepho's mat was often empty for a few moments during the night. He had gone outside; he would be back as usual in a moment, she had told herself. But her mother's heart would not believe it. Zepho was not just outside the hut. She felt that a long distance divided her from her youngest son. In a few days he would be her only son. She had run out of the hut to look for him among the trees inside the wall, where he had been playing. But he wasn't there. She had run back to the hut, moaning, to feel if he had gone back to his mat. He wasn't there. And she had run screaming out into the middle of the ovens of the women's quarters.

It was then that Enoch, who had made the noise like an owl, had turned and run. He ran so hard that his thumping heart drowned all the tumult that happened afterwards. Or he thought it did.

For at the back of the Ishak's hut, which opened on to the women's quarters, a man was seated, watching; and he had suddenly leapt up and seized the screaming woman. A hand was laid over her mouth; a strong arm held her round her shoulders. Words were whispered into her ear which silenced her, while he shouted out (for anyone awake in the village to hear): 'Come when I tell you, woman! Am I not your lord and master?' It was her husband, Moab the Ishak, who held her. But it was the secret words that he whispered into her ear that stopped her screams, and made her walk quietly beside him to the door of his hut.

He had lied—anything to stop her screaming. He had said, 'Zepho is with me.... He came to me because he was afraid of your tears. And he is sleeping in the darkness of my hut.'

The moment she stepped inside she knew it wasn't true. She said she did not believe him, and that she must feel her son for herself.

'You will wake him up,' said the Ishak, keeping a firm hold on her. 'Surely you have no mercy in your grief.' The Ishakeen moaned.

Then the Ishak forced her to sit down beside him on his sleeping-mat. 'Listen!' he said. 'I will tell you a story and you can judge for yourself.'

The Ishakeen moaned again and laid her head on his shoulder. And the Ishak began in a low, murmuring voice:

'There was once a widow who had one son. And the son ran away from her to serve the king of a far country. But she was so stricken with grief at losing him that she called upon all the dingirs of the earth and the water and the air, to bring her only son back to her. And in the end, the Dingir of the Moon answered her prayer, and said, "I have taken a liking to your son. I have a mind to make him into a great man and the father of many people. But to do this he will have to live most of his life in a far city; and you will not see him again until you are an old woman." And the woman wept, and said, "Have pity on me, O great Dingir of the Moon, and let me hold my son in my arms just once more while he is young." And the Moon Dingir answered: "I am moved to pity. You can have your son back tomorrow—but he will die at the end of a year." '

'And what did the widow answer?' said the Ishakeen.

'She had her son back. And he died.'

'She should not have done that. She should have let him go,' said the Ishakeen, again feeling for her husband's hand.

'Because you have answered like a woman of wisdom, I will tell you what I this day have seen—it was on the face of Shamashazir of Ur that I first saw light. I knew that he was a friend of the Lord of all the Earth, and had no fear of the Corn Dingir. To him the Corn Dingir was nothing but a thing of straw, and a slave. And I saw a great pity on his face for our son Shaul and our son Zepho.'

'So when I had finished speaking with Enoch son of Enoch, I went to the gate that leads into the fields, to speak with Shamashazir of Ur, to learn more of this Lord of all the Earth. But he had our son Zepho on a donkey, and was leading him round the village. "That is strange," I said to myself. "For what reason does so great a chief take a child on a donkey?" And I listened. I heard them going round the walls of the village, and I strolled among the huts on the inside of the wall, looking at the preparations for the feast. And I heard their voices going towards the women's quarters. So I also wandered towards the women's quarters, to see the bread that was made for the feast.'

'I saw you,' said the Ishakeen. 'You went behind my hut.'

'I heard them speaking about scorpions in the wall!' said the Ishak, lowering his voice to a whisper.

'Why?' the Ishakeen asked.

'They were looking for a gap in the wall, where there were *no* scorpions! And I said to myself, "Why does so great a chief as Shamashazir of Ur look for a gap in the wall with no scorpions in it?" And I understood. For a moment Shamashazir looked into my eyes through a crenelle; and I understood.' The Ishak was silent, thinking. Then he said, 'I also saw that Enoch son of Enoch uttered secret words to our son Shaul, while I was searching for my ring. But these words I could not hear. But by reason of these words that I could not hear, I put sleeping herbs into the cups of the sentries that guard our son Shaul; and I have sat before my hut listening to all the noises of the night, and watching for what might take place.'

'And what happened?' the Ishakeen asked.

'When the sun had set, a fire appeared, shining upon the lower slopes of the mountains.'

'That is nothing!' said the Ishakeen, disappointed. 'Fires are often lit on the mountains when the shepherds go by.'

'Shaul has been very quiet for a long time now . . .'

'That also is nothing, O Moab, my lord . . .'

'I saw our son Zepho leave your hut . . . and go towards the hole in the wall where I had shown him no scorpions hid.'

'Oh!' said the Ishakeen.

'Then afterwards, some time afterwards, I heard the call of an owl.'

'That is nothing—there are many owls.'

'Not many owls that hoot once, twice, three times, and then wait and hoot twice more.'

'I heard that owl,' said the Ishakeen.

'And after that you came out of your hut, screaming.'

'I pray to the Corn Dingir that you are right.'

'Hush . . . don't pray to the Corn Dingir. We have defied him; and he will have no mercy on us. Better to pray to the Lord of all the Earth, who is the friend of Shamashazir of Ur and Enoch son of Enoch.'

And then the Ishak knelt down, as he had seen Shamashazir and Enoch kneel down; and he pulled his wife on to the floor beside him, and they both prayed:

'O Lord of all the Earth, we are the children of Cain and less than the dust in your sight; but nevertheless, take our sons into your keeping, and free them from the curse that is upon the village.'

Then they got up and went to the other door of the Ishak's hut—that faced the men's quarters of the village. And they listened; but they could hear no sound at all coming from Shaul's hut. Over on the right, one of the elders was snoring. A couple of bullfrogs were croaking at the village well, and under the trees the crickets were chirruping. The Ishak pointed out a small red star that glowed low down on the far-away hill-side.

Then they lay down on mats in the Ishak's hut and tried to sleep. But it was impossible. The Ishakeen was longing for the morning, when she could find out for certain if her son Shaul had gone. And Moab her husband was thinking what he could best do, to delay the tribe from following the boys into the mountains. A new Ishak would have to be chosen. And quickly, for the corn could not be sown until the son of the Ishak had been sacrificed. The old Ishak foresaw trouble for the tribe—perhaps starvation and famine. But his own sons would be safe. 'The people of Ur serve the Moon Dingir,' he thought. 'And their corn is good. And the King's son sleeps peacefully in his bed at nights. But it is not good for a tribe to desert the dingirs of its fathers.'

By the time the sun had risen, all was shouting and confusion within the walls of Kenan. It did not take the elders long to see that the escape had been made through the hole in Shaul's hut. But the ground round the village was so covered with footprints that it was not easy to discover at once in which direction the kidnappers had gone. They would have to make a cast, and pick up the tracks where they left the trodden paths. But the Ishak was not there to give the order for the cast to be made. He was asleep with his wife; and it was death to go in and disturb him. The elders had to be content to stand outside and shout . . . until one of them said, 'Perhaps the Ishak also is gone.'

At that, one of the young warriors volunteered to go into the royal hut to see. But an elder who was cousin to the Ishak and an heir to the throne, prevented him. 'There is another son,' he said. 'Let him be found.' This cousin was cunning. He knew that the moment the last son of Moab had been killed, a new Ishak would have to be chosen; and he had great hopes that it might be himself. He had at least twenty sons, some of them too old to sacrifice. He would willingly let a few of them die for the tribe, in order that he might have the honour and glory of being Ishak.

But one of the sons, Irad, a boy a little younger than Shamas-hazir, was standing next to him when he spoke. He was a clever boy. He guessed what might happen to him or his younger brother. He did not wish his father to be the new Ishak. He saw at once that it was important to wake the old Ishak; and to look for Shaul—if he wasn't dead. He went into the royal hut.

'Who dares to disturb me?' came Ishak's voice, commandingly, from the darkness.

'Fire!' cried Irad, and ran out again, hoping the Ishak had not seen who he was.

Now the Ishak knew that if anyone came into his hut and shouted 'Fire!' it was his duty to go at once to command his people. He had to come out. He stepped to the doorway. 'What is this?' he said. 'Where is the fire? What is all this noise about?'

'Shaul your son has been stolen or killed in the night, and his body carried away—and today is the day of the sacrifice to the Corn Dingir.'

'I have another son,' said the Ishak calmly.

There was a moment's silence. Then the crowd began to shout: 'Where is Zepho, the young Ishakki? Find him.' And they began a search all through the village for Zepho. They searched in all the huts; they looked up into all the trees and down into all the ovens; but he was not there. Then they said perhaps his mother had hidden him or he had run away into the vineyards. So they began to look for him outside the village walls. This was exactly what the Ishak hoped they would do; for their footsteps would destroy any trace of a telltale trail.

By the time they had found Eb's footprints, going through the soft earth of one of the vineyards, Shamashazir's party were well along the cliff path, but not yet out of sight of the camping-place; and they could be seen by pursuers coming over the hills.

The warrior who had found Eb's tracks called a halt in the search, in order not to spoil the footprints, and went straight back to the Ishak to tell him. Even he could see, by the way Eb had dug his heels into the ground, that he was carrying something heavy and was walking with difficulty. While he was explaining his theory to the Ishak, another man came in to say that he had found Zepho's trail beyond the spring; and that it led to the mountains.

As the Ishak Moab did not want to be killed for helping his sons to escape, he had to order a party of warriors to follow the tracks. They were both leading towards the same place. He knew his men were afraid of the mountains. The fugitives had had a good chance to escape; and he had made his own plans. But first he warned the search-party to be careful; for he had heard a lion in the night. This was not true; but the Ishak was not the kind of man to bother about the truth on such an occasion.

The warriors set out on their search, waving their spears above their heads; and running with great lolloping strides which made the distance between the village and the mountains look insignificant. They set out in two parties and met on the hill. They found where the beacon-fire had been, and then the tracks to the camping-place. . . . And from there they looked down into a deep gully, and saw a group of tiny figures disappear round a rocky buttress. There was no need to do any more stalking. They could run straight on—as straight as the uneven going would allow.

Meanwhile, the Ishak Moab went back into his hut. He put on his sandals, picked up his richly embroidered cloak, put some food in a wallet, and then addressed his people. 'Without my sons,' he said, 'I am no longer Ishak, but Moab son of Moab, as I was born. I shall go forth and look for my sons; and without them I shall not return.' Then he took off the bracelets of gold, which the Ishaks of Kenan always wore round their arms, and laid them on the royal chair, kissed his younger wife, telling her to remember his words, and went, following the group of warriors who had gone on ahead, and whom he could see in the distance, climbing the hill. But he still wore the Ishak's ring on the first finger of his left hand.

The elders of the village sat down in a circle round the fire, to discuss what they should do if the boys were not found; for the sowing of the corn was urgent. They might have to choose a new Ishak. It would be best to decide who it should be now, while they were waiting.

The young lads of fourteen and under, sons of the elders, sat outside the circle and listened. . . . One of them might have to act as a sacrifice that very day. But not one of them thought it would be himself—that is to say—not until the votes of the elders seemed to be going in favour of his father. But the talk of the elders seemed to centre first on one cousin and then on another—talking, talking, never deciding. Until at last, Irad, the most resourceful of the young lads watching, got up and went away. Three times they had mentioned his father as if he were going to be chosen; and then another name had been mentioned. He could not bear to listen to them any longer. He thought he would be happier up in the mountains helping to look for Shaul and Zepho. 'If I go out to the mountains,' he thought, 'at least I shall be safe for tonight.'

'He thinks it's going to be *his* father,' the other boys murmured among themselves when he had gone. 'I shouldn't be surprised if it was.'

Silently Irad's younger brother got up from the group and went to look for him. He found him among the food that was being prepared for the feast. Both boys helped themselves when no one was looking their way. They hid two or three flat loaves under their skirts; and each took a handful of raisins. Then they set off to follow the trail of the warriors to the mountains.

But hardly had they got half-way across the plain when they were joined by six more of the lads. 'It was terrible,' they said, 'sitting and listening to those old men talk, talk, talk.' It would be better to do something. If only they could find Shaul and Zepho they would be safe. For in two years' time they would be too old to sacrifice. When they got to the foot of the hills they could see the figure of the Ishak Moab like a small dot high up ahead of them.

Shamashazir and Enoch had seen the party of warriors come over on the crest of the hill. But they knew they had only a few steps to go before they would be out of sight, hidden by a shoulder of rock. And then, Eb said, he was sure they would not be far from the caves.

Looking back and seeing the pursuers, had acted like a tonic on Shaul. He asked for his bread, which they had put with the food in the donkey's basket, and said that he could walk by himself. This was a great help to them all; for it freed Eb to give a hand to Shamashazir when he needed it; and they could get along more quickly.

Safely round the shoulder, and for a moment out of sight of their pursuers, they halted to take their bearings. The rock-filled gully below them stretched away to the foot of another cliff. Eb said he was sure it was the cliff where the caves were. So they pushed on hopefully along the goat-track, until they found a place where there had been a fall of rock, and they could scramble down into the gully. The boulders of the gully were worn smooth by water; for it had once been the bed of a river. Some of them were loosely poised on one another, and tipped dangerously when the boys stepped on them. Eb warned Shaul and Zepho to be very careful. 'We don't want any broken legs or ankles,' he said. And he himself walked beside Shamashazir, giving him a hand over the most treacherous parts, and testing each boulder before he would let him step on it. Shamashazir would have little chance of saving himself if one of the boulders slipped.

They had not gone very far along the gully, when Enoch, who was used to walking over this kind of treacherous ground and had gone ahead with Sam and the donkey, called back to say that the entrance to the caves was in sight. And he and Sam began to press on as fast as they could, balancing on the uncertain boulders with the sureness of goats.

'They are leaving us behind,' said Shamashazir, anxiously trying to go faster. But Eb checked him.

'There's no hurry. We always send a party of scouts ahead to make sure there are no lions or bears in the caves.'

'What if there are?'

For a moment Eb said nothing.

But Shaul, who was just ahead of them, began to drop back. He was listening for the reply. Neither Shamashazir nor Eb noticed him; they were too intent on the boulders, and the problem ahead.

'We'd have to go on,' said Eb at last. 'Better to meet a hungry lion than to fall into the hands of those savages behind us.'

Shaul heard what he said. He stopped and looked back, trembling. Lions! Bears! On the towering hill behind he thought he could see the ledge where they had spent the night—not so very far away. The following tribesmen were still hidden by the shoulder of rock; but they would soon be coming round it. They were the young warriors of his own tribe and they would come quickly. He waited for Shamashazir to catch up and to pass him; and followed slowly, hanging back, keeping just behind Shamashazir, moving silently as a boy knows how to move.

Then suddenly, when he saw the opportunity, he turned, and ran frantically over the rough boulders back towards the tribesmen that he knew—who seemed less terrible than the wild animals of the mountains. But the quick ears of Eb heard the sudden scurry. He let go of Shamashazir's hand and was after Shaul like a mountain goat. 'I'll not let you go like that, you young good-for-nothing wine-skin,' he muttered between his teeth. 'And all the trouble we've taken for you!'

Shaul was still weak and no match for the agile Eb. He was caught in a few strides, picked up, and slung over Eb's broad shoulders. But as he found himself lifted off his feet, he screamed with all the power left in his lungs. And he went on screaming, as Eb, leaving Shamashazir to fend for himself, strode over the remaining boulders towards the dark entrance of the caverns. He went on screaming until the underground earthy air of the caves blew cool on his bare arms, and the high vault of the roof yawned over his head; and his screaming voice boomed and echoed through the maze of caves, like the bellow of a dying dingir; and he stopped dead in terror of his own voice.

Eb put him gently down, keeping a firm hold on him. And they watched Shamashazir coming over the last rocks of the gully, helped by Enoch. Shaul was surprised that Eb neither scolded him nor hit him. The man stood silent, watching Shamashazir with a tenseness which Shaul could feel in the fingers that clutched his arm. His silence was more terrifying than a blow; for Shaul realized that Eb, the bold and sure, was afraid. But as the figures of Shamashazir and Enoch came through the light of the entrance into the gloom, and stood beside them, Eb loosened his grip and Shaul felt his whole body relax.

Shamashazir was out of breath. 'Why did you let him scream like that?' he panted. 'They will know we are in the cave.'

'You do not know these people of the plains,' Eb answered. 'They will know exactly what we wish them to know.'

They did not go far into the cave, but kept near the entrance; from where they could see the warriors, and not be seen.

Shamashazir had hardly got his breath before they appeared round a shoulder of rock, moving rather hesitantly along the gully, talking to one another a great deal, and pointing to signs on the path.

'They are already afraid. Look at them,' said Eb, putting his arm round Shaul and laughing. 'Shaul, my lad, you've managed to curdle the blood in their veins like the battle cries of the armies of Jericho. It won't take very long to fill their hearts with such a dread of the mountain dingirs that they will be falling over one another to get away from here. . . .' Eb was laughing; but Shamashazir noticed that he kept his hand on Shaul's shoulder, to make sure that the boy did not suddenly run out of the cave.

Shamashazir thought he was making light of their danger, and felt for the hilt of his knife, loosening it in its sheath, to make sure that it was still there and ready for use. Farther back in the cave he could hear Sam's voice talking and talking to the donkey Jemimah.

The warriors came nearer. Near enough for them to hear the words that they spoke to one another. Shamashazir felt Zepho's small hand slip into his. He held it tight. And they watched in silence, broken only by the steady rise and fall of Sam's voice behind them. 'What is Sam doing?' he whispered to Enoch, who had come up beside him and taken hold of Zepho's other hand.

'Wait, and you will see a mighty magic,' said Enoch. And then he softly made the sound of a far-away donkey's bray.

A great roaring bellow suddenly filled the cave. It seemed to come at them in every direction, in shattering waves of sound. Shamashazir drew back against the wall, and Zepho clung to him, terrified. But in the dim light he could just see Enoch's face. There was a smile on it; and he stood quite unmoved, holding tightly to Zepho. He nodded reassuringly to Shamashazir—it was impossible to speak—and then he looked out towards the cave entrance. Shamashazir followed his glance. The warriors outside were in a panic, falling backwards, scrambling and stumbling over the rough stones in their hurry to escape.

The bellowing died down. But the warriors did not stop.

'You wouldn't think one harmless little donkey calling to her mate could do so much damage, would you?' said Eb, his eyes shining with laughter.

It was a pity those inside the cave could not watch the warriors out of sight round the cliff, scrambling up on to the goat-track. There they clung, backs against the rock, with lowered spears, edging their way cautiously step by step along the narrow ledge.

Then suddenly the man at the farther end, nearest home, turned round and began to run. His panic spread from one man to another, until the whole line of them were fleeing along the rocky ledge, stumbling over the uneven ground, and catching hold of one another in terror, to save themselves from falling into the gully below.

Back in the cave, Eb was saying. 'That scream the young wild-cat made caught them between the eyes. They'll go back and tell the Ishak they saw us eaten by lions!'

Sam, chuckling quietly to himself, brought them food; and they sat well inside the mouth of the cave, eating and talking. Shaul's appetite was coming back with the excitement; and he began to be less afraid of his saviours.

After they had eaten, they lay down and slept well into the afternoon, while Sam kept watch; for they were exceedingly tired.

Zepho was the first to wake. Before Sam could realize what he was doing, and without thinking, he had jumped up and run out into the bright sunlight. 'Hi! You there! Come back!' Sam shouted after him.

Zepho turned and came in at once. But Eb and Enoch were on their feet with their hands to their knives, as if they had never been to sleep.

Sam waved them back. 'It is only the child,' he said. 'He ran out of the cave.'

'Oh!' said Eb. 'Then we must go on at once.'

They saddled Jemimah, woke up Saul, and started out.

High above them, a man, well hidden behind a rock, watched them go until they were out of sight; then he leapt out of his hiding-place and went rather clumsily, half walking, half running, following the direction they had taken into the heart of the mountains.

Their way lay upwards now, through a forest, to a high ridge. But the slope was not steep, and the ground was soft and even. At first the two smaller boys were excited to be under the cool quietness of the trees. They had never seen anything like the great tall trunks that rose so high over their heads; and the coolness and altitude seemed to quicken their spirits. But they very soon grew tired. And before they were half-way through, Shaul could hardly drag one leg after the other; and Zepho had to be given a ride on Jemimah. Shamashazir asked why they couldn't stop then and there, and sleep in the forest. They seemed to have come miles from their pursuers. But both Eb and Enoch shook their heads and said no.

Enoch had the feeling that they were still followed by something; though he was not sure if it was man or beast. And Eb agreed that it would be safer to camp in the bar rock higher up. Once they had got there, they could sleep in peace without fear of lions, who dislike the cold, and keep to the valleys.

'But we shall have to carry wood,' said Shamashazir. 'How are we going to do that?'

'We shall sleep without a fire tonight,' Eb answered. 'The smoke might act as a beacon to our pursuers.'

Sam thought that Eb was being too cautious. No one from a corn-growing village would dare to spend the night in the mountains. But Eb said that he had not seen the Ishak among the band of warriors. There was no doubt another party was somewhere behind, still looking for them. It would be better to sleep on the high rocks. The trees would give too much cover to their pursuers. So they tramped wearily on. Eb and Sam took it in turns to carry Zepho. And they put Shaul on the donkey's back. Shamashazir was thankful that they had Sam with them; for Shaul looked utterly spent, and his own leg was aching. When they at last saw the trees thinning out ahead of them. Shamashazir suggested they should make a fire before they left the forest, and cook the last rabbit that they had with them. He did not fancy eating it raw, as the shepherds often did. 'If anyone sees the smoke coming up through the trees, it will deceive them into thinking we are camping here for the night,' he said.

Eb thought this an excellent idea. A little food would put heart into the boys. They quickly gathered armfuls of cedar-cones, strips of bark, and a few dead branches.

Zepho, whose strength seemed to return at the mention of food, helped them, scuttling about and picking up cedar-cones as fast as any man. He had never seen such curious things before. And he shouted with joy every time he found one that was a little larger than the others. But Shaul lay still on the ground, his head resting on his arm, caring for nothing. Sam carried the firestones, the sharp flint and the hard iron. And Zepho watched the sparks flying when he struck them together, dancing round them and standing on his head with delight. He had never seen fire made that way before. In the village a sacred flame was kept burning day and night. It never went out; and it never had to be relit. He had never seen so tiny a flame as the one that suddenly kindled in the handful of dried grasses Sam had laid on the ground. But it was not tiny for long. Sam fed it with cedar-needles and small twigs, and last of all, the cedar-cones, one at a time; then handfuls of them until they were glowing hot and red.

Then the two men and Shamashazir and Enoch speared the limbs and back of the rabbit on the ends of their knives; and held them over the flames, until the flesh began to sizzle and to give out a delicious smell that made even Shaul sit up and take notice. There wasn't much more than a mouthful for each of them. But it was more tasty than bread and cheese—all they had eaten that day, except for a few bilberries that the boys had picked coming through the forest.

'Tomorrow I shall do some hunting,' said Sam, throwing the bone of the leg that he had been eating into the ashes of the fire. He cleaned his knife in the earth, put it back in its sheath, and stood up. They all got to their feet to finish the last stage of their journey; for the shadows were deep over the valleys, and the rocks ahead of them were turning to gold. They covered the hot ashes with earth, to make sure no flames spreading through the cedar-needles started a forest-fire; and began the last steep climb over the bare rocks.

They found the dim traces of some sort of path that had been trodden out by goats. But it zigzagged over the rock so steeply that Shamashazir was constantly needing help, and Zepho was going on his hands and knees. The soft leather of Shaul's sandals was cut, and his feet were bleeding; but he did not complain. He hardly seemed to notice anything, but trudged on wearily without speaking.

Higher and higher they went. And higher and higher the gloomy shadows crept up the mountains. Shamashazir began to wonder if they would ever get to a level place, where they could camp before the darkness caught them. He could see that Eb was uneasily measuring the distance that they still had to travel. He had not calculated for the tiredness and slowness of the children. He began to speak harshly to them, urging them to go faster, even threatening to hit Shaul if he did not make an effort. Zepho needed no threats; he struggled bravely on, silent tears streaming down his face.

They found a place that was as sheltered as possible, behind some rocks, laid the two sheepskins on the ground, and huddled together as close as they could under the two cloaks; while Enoch kept the first watch.

But in spite of the sheepskin, the ground was hard and cold to lie on. Shamashazir and the two boys slept uneasily, and woke up in the night with their teeth chattering, to hear the low voices of Enoch and Eb talking to each other as they changed watch. Zepho sat up suddenly, letting a blast of even colder air chill Shamashazir's back. 'Look! Look! It's the Lord of all the Earth!' he cried excitedly.

Shamashazir's stiff and shivering limbs suddenly became supple with new life; and in one movement he had flung himself up into a sitting position, with his legs crossed in front of him and his hands crossed on his chest, in the Sumerian attitude of prayer, quite forgetting that the tribe of Enoch prayed to the Great Spirit on their knees. He held his eyes tightly shut, not daring to look. Enoch and Eb had stopped talking. 'What is it, young Zepho?' he heard Eb say in a calm, matter-of-fact voice. 'I suppose you've never seen anything like that before?'

Shamashazir opened his eyes. The rocks all round them were sparkling and shining with frost under a full moon. Their beauty was breathtaking. 'Thou art clothed in honour and majesty,' said Shamashazir to himself, remembering an ancient hymn to Nannar, Dingir of the Moon. Then he noticed how he was sitting. 'Is it Nannar?' he asked himself. 'Or is Zepho right, and is it the Great Spirit?' Was it the Earth that was so beautiful; or was it the moon? Where did the beauty come from? Was the Great Spirit present—perhaps talking to Nannar . . .? His reverie was interrupted by a piece of bread hitting his cheek and falling on the rock. Shaul and Zepho were both munching beside him, shivering.

'It is too cold to sleep,' said Shamashazir to Eb. 'And too beautiful,' he added. 'If you can't trust me to keep watch by myself, you can't stop me sitting up with you.'

'Me too,' said Zepho, and was echoed by Shaul.

Eb was quite ready to have a little company during the night. He was leaning against the two pack-baskets, pushed up against the rock to make a warm back for the watcher. Shamashazir and the two boys brought their cloaks and sheepskins and sat down beside him, huddled together with their knees up under their chins, and their backs against the baskets.

For a short time they listened and watched in silence. Then Zepho began to ask questions about Ur; and Shamashazir began to talk. He talked about Nannar and the feast of the Moon Dingir; and how the Ziggurat was like a very small mountain covered with trees; and how the priests walked up the steps, carrying food for the Moon Dingir, in a long procession that zigzagged up the side . . . until he felt Zepho slump against him.

'The boys have gone to sleep,' said Eb.

Shamashazir stopped talking. The moon was higher in the sky, almost directly over their heads; and the tops of the snow-clad mountains seemed below them. Looking down on the distant peaks, Shamashazir felt as if he hung in darkness, half-way between the moon and the earth. Strange thoughts began to take possession of him. The moon was light; the earth was light; and the sky in between was dark. Did the light come from the moon to the earth as a lamp lights a room? Or did it go from the earth to the moon? While he was wondering, a cloud which had been making a small, light patch in the sky, darkened and covered the moon. The rocks round him immediately vanished in blackness. The light was coming from the moon! 'It comes secretly through the darkness,' said Shamashazir to himself, 'not like the light of the sun which lightens the whole sky. The Lord of all the Earth must have made the Moon Dingir in His own image. For He comes to earth unseen, until He shines in the heart of some man—or woman. And you can see His light in their faces, like the face of Enoch's mother. And sometimes I see it in the face of Sam.' And he began to think of people in Ur whose faces had struck him, and to wonder if the Lord of all the Earth had spoken to them. 'There is Mushinti the wife of the Image Maker . . . and Naramea the Magistrate . . . and perhaps even Gimil Mama.' Then he began to wonder why he was counting people in Ur, trying to remember faces: his sister Dinah's arch and secret smile, Naychor's nervous, anxious face, Sarah's beam of friendliness, and Haran's look of complete innocence. He fell forward—and woke up.

The moonlight was paling, and far down on the horizon the distant peaks, looking like sea shells on the shore of the Great River, were catching the rays of the rising sun.

When, a few moments later, the first rays hit the rocks above them, they woke the rest of the party; and climbed up into the light to sing their morning song to the Great Spirit. It was now suddenly warm—in spite of the wind that was still blowing. Their voices echoed round the mountain peaks and valleys like a choir of fifty.

They could see now that they had been sleeping on the top of a great flat plateau. And when they had eaten their bread and cheese, they set out to find a way down on the other side, Zepho skipping about with excitement, and Shaul at last beginning to take an interest in his surroundings. They seemed to be walking through a world that did not belong to this earth at all, and where the Corn Dingir held no power. Even Enoch said that he had lost the feeling of being followed—which was not surprising, because no one in the valley below them could see up on to the middle of the ridge where they stood.

It took them some time to find a path down on the other side that was not too steep. And by the time they had reached the few scattered pines that marked the beginning of the next forest, it was midday and time to eat. But Sam said Jemimah must have water, and that they must go farther down until they found a stream where she could have a good drink.

So they went on into the dark coolness of the trees; and the hungry and thirsty boys had to be content with picking and eating bilberries as they walked. They found a stream bubbling out of a mossy basin of rock not very far down; and Sam let Jemimah drink a little. But not much, as the water was ice cold. Shaul and Zepho gasped and shuddered when they put their lips to it.

Enoch and Eb left them to collect fir-cones, and to help Sam light a fire, while they went to look for fish. They speared three and brought them back to be cooked on hot stones. Zepho was so hungry that he thought they would never be done. He bent over the stones with his head almost in the fire, longing to prod the fish with a stick; but Sam kept a sharp eye on him. Three fish were not much more than a mouthful among six hungry people; but they helped eke out the bread and cheese. And Shaul thought he had never tasted anything so good. The horrible after-taste of the wine in his mouth was wearing off; and he was beginning to realize that he was free again. He had already forgotten the cold wind and the shivering night that they had spent on the top of the plateau.

After they had eaten all that Eb had allowed them, Sam stretched himself out contentedly on the thick, soft carpet of pine-needles, and said he hoped that that night they would be allowed to sleep in a place where there was plenty of food and water, and no wind. And Enoch agreed. There was no hurry to press on, now that they were so far into the mountains, he said. And then he sat silent a little, with his head slightly tilted, listening.

'Hear anything?' asked Eb.

'No . . . o . . . o. But I still have the feeling we're being followed.'

'Must be a lion,' said Sam.

'No . . . o,' said Enoch. 'It's no kind of beast.' And he looked at Shaul thoughtfully.

'Couldn't be a man,' said Sam, glancing uneasily about him. 'One of those plainsmen would never get so far into the mountains.'

'It comes of meddling with those heathen dingirs,' Eb murmured under his breath—but loud enough for Shaul to hear.

They stopped for the night at an open clearing at the bottom of the valley, where there was a stream and plenty of fresh grass for Jemimah.

Enoch thought it looked a good place for food. He would go fishing and Sam could go rabbiting; while the rest of them collected wood. 'We shall need four fires round the camp tonight,' he said.

Eb sighed. Collecting wood was a job for women and boys. He looked regretfully at Enoch's fishing-spear, and then bent his great shoulders to his task, moving slowly and rather clumsily among the bushes. But Shamashazir worked hard in spite of his leg. Year after year he had gone out into the fields round Ur, to help with the corn harvests and date picking, with half the men and boys from the city. Magistrates and schoolboys, soldiers and merchants, turned out into the fields at those times. And when the corn was all safely stored in the Temple granaries, they finished up with feasting. So he worked with enthusiasm, thinking of the bright fires, and the good food that was coming; and for a time the two smaller boys worked beside him.

The cedar-cones had given place to pine-cones which lay thick on the ground. Zepho scooped them up in handfuls and made them into a pyramid; while Shaul went farther into the forest, looking for dead branches. But it seemed to Zepho that it took an awful lot of pine-cones to make a pile. Shaul was getting on much faster. He decided to give up the cones and follow his brother, treading his way through the bilberry bushes. He could feel the soft berries crushing under his feet. It seemed a pity to waste all that juicy fruit—and he was feeling so thirsty. He stooped down and began to pick the berries, cramming them into his mouth in handfuls. Somehow the pine-cones were forgotten. And Shaul came and squatted beside him.

The trouble with bilberries is that—like so many other pleasant fruits—they always seem to grow bigger and thicker and riper on the next bush. So it was with Shaul and Zepho. Once they started eating, they kept finding more and better fruit a little farther on. And instead of returning to their wood-collecting, they began to stray farther and farther from the camp.

It was shady, and warm, and very pleasant, crawling among the bilberries. It was the first time for many days that the two had found themselves alone together. There was something very comforting to Shaul in his little brother's presence. It took him back to the happy days when he had played 'Shepherds and Corn-growers' with the other boys of the village, and had never thought about the Corn Dingir. He remembered how they had all shouted and laughed and fought together. He was a boy then. Now he was an old, old man (at least he felt like one), and Zepho was almost a stranger.

It was some time before either of them said anything much. They had to get used to each other again. In silence they searched among the tiny leaves for the hidden berries, trampling on the springy stems, until a mosquito settled on Zepho's nose, and, with juice-stained hands, he brushed it off, leaving a purple mark across his face. Shaul laughed.

'What's funny?' said Zepho.

'Your nose! Look at your hands! They're purple.'

Zepho looked at his purple fingers and carefully smeared them on the other side of his nose.

'You silly jack-sparrow,' said Shaul, and suddenly rolled him over on to the soft carpet of conifer-needles.

Zepho giggled like a puppy. And then he lay on his back gazing up at the patches of sky that appeared through the trees above his head. 'What's a city, Shaul?' he asked. 'Have you ever seen one?'

'I've seen Jericho. That's a city.'

'Is it a city like Ur?'

'Well, it's full of enemies. You have to be careful in Jericho. Ur is different; it is full of friends.'

'But what's it look like?'

'It has walls.'

'Like in the vineyards?'

'No, high walls that go up over your head.'

'Like trees?'

'No, not like trees.'

'Like mountains?'

'Like cliffs, but smoother—quite smooth.'

'What, like ivory?'

'No, not like ivory. Like pitchers.'

'High up above your head and smooth like pitchers.'

'What do they have inside?'

'People—hundreds and hundreds of people. And they all have different faces.'

'Phew! And will they put us in these pitchers?'

'They are not pitchers, they are houses.'

'Houses. Do they have houses too?'

'Yes, but they are not like our houses.'

'Then they can't be houses.'

'They are houses. But they are different.'

'Oh,' said Zepho. 'Cities are very funny places. But these moun-tains are nice. And the rabbit is nice to eat. And so is the fish. And so are the berries.' And he suddenly turned round and began crawling off into the bushes at top speed after some more bilberries. He had not gone more than two yards when he stopped dead.

'Shaul!' he said. 'There's a man!'

'Where?'

'He's gone now. I saw his legs.'

'Sam's or Eb's, you silly,' said Shaul; but he sounded very uneasy.

'No, they weren't! They weren't Sam's or Eb's.' Zepho lowered his voice to a whisper. 'Do you think they were the ... *Corn Dingir's*?'

The Corn Dingir! Shaul dropped the berry he held in his hand, on its way to his mouth, got up, and began to make his way clumsily back towards the camp; Zepho followed.

Now and then they stopped to argue about the way, afraid they might be lost, and afraid to shout to the men. Every now and then they heard what they thought must be Shamashazir dropping wood on the pile, and knew they were going in the right direction. They were thankful at last to see the lights of the fires through the trees; and then to find Sam busily cooking fish and rabbit, and parching corn on hot stones. Shamashazir had thrown himself flat on his back, and was gazing up at the branches of the pine-trees, enjoying the savoury smell. Eb and Enoch were still bringing in the wood.

Shaul sat down next to Shamashazir. He felt that Shamashazir had the most power to protect him. But he said nothing—until Enoch stopped with the last armful of wood, and looking anxiously towards the place where the boys had been playing, murmured to Eb that he had that feeling they were being followed.

'Zepho saw a man's legs,' said Shaul cautiously.

'Oh!' exclaimed Shamashazir.

'Where?' Enoch asked.

And Shaul, with Zepho's help, explained where they had been.

'Did you go in that direction, Eb?' Enoch asked.

Eb shook his head.

'They weren't his legs. His are hairy legs. These legs were smooth like proper legs.'

'Shamashazir's legs are smooth,' said Sam.

Zepho looked at Shamashazir's legs. 'They are too dark,' he said. 'Shaul and I have proper legs.'

There was an uneasy silence. Then Eb said, 'Not all the men of the mountains have hairy legs.' But this was small comfort.

'Last night,' said Enoch, 'it was dark before we sung our evening song to the Lord of all the Earth.'

'Ah!' said Eb. 'Maybe He was tired of waiting so long after sunset; and never heard our prayer.'

'He knew that we feared the treacherous stones of the mountain, in the dark, more than His displeasure.'

'Is it the Corn Dingir?' Zepho asked. Nobody answered him. They finished their cooking; but a gloom had settled down over them. They had no heart for eating. They sat round the cooking-fire, waiting and watching for the setting sun to tell them that the hour of prayer had come. Then Enoch rose silently, and beckoned the others to follow him to a little outcrop of rocks that rose up among the trees. And there they sang:

> *'Hear O Thou Shepherd of Thy people,*
> *Thou that leadest us like sheep,*
> *Stir up Thy strength and come and help us,*
> *For we are in danger because of our sins.'*

When they had finished, the last line was taken up by an echo:

> *'For we are in danger because of our sins.'*

It was a far-away echo, thin and clear, and like no other echo that any of them had ever heard before. And they were afraid; and bowed their heads to the ground in silence. And so they stayed for a long time, until Shamashazir said in almost a whisper, 'I have heard the voices that speak in these mountains.'

'Ssst,' said Enoch, and began to chant in a slightly unsteady voice a prayer of defence against evil spirits:

> *'My flesh and my heart faileth,*
> *For they that forsake Thee shall perish.*
> *Be Thou our judge, O Lord,*
> *For we have walked innocently, doing Thy will.'*

And then they sang the usual prayer for forgiveness. There was no further echo. And in time, enough courage returned to them to go back to their fire, where their food was waiting for them.

Enoch led the way, stepping carefully in the dark; as always, alert; but now in the slightly crouching position, ready to spring to one side, which Shamashazir knew meant fear. Suddenly he stopped, crouching lower. And Shamashazir saw over his back—rising out of the smoke of the four fires, red like the spirit of fire—the head and shoulders of a man, that flickered and shimmered in the moving light. In an instant Shamashazir had dropped down behind his friend. Sam, farther back, seeing that something was wrong, made the two boys crouch among the rocks.

Then Enoch made a slight sign with his hand to Eb, and slipped to the left, hiding behind a huge boulder. Shamashazir and Eb joined him, leaving the boys with Sam.

'It is the Ishak of Kenan,' Shamashazir whispered.

Eb shook his head. 'That was no *man*.'

'But I saw his face.'

'Hisst! The Ishak of a heathen tribe takes the face of his god. That was no man's voice that wailed for mercy while we prayed, but an evil spirit trembling before the name of the Lord.' And then he thumped the palm of his hand with his fist. 'I ask you: how could a man of the plains follow us that distance through the mountains?'

But Shamashazir did not answer.

And Enoch was silent. The training of a long line of Ishaks forbade him to show doubt, even in front of his friends; and he felt doubt. For what evil spirit would dare to stand within the four fires of a servant of the Great Spirit. He screwed up his eyes wisely, debating in his own mind. 'Look again and see if he is still there,' he said to Eb.

Eb hesitated before moving away. He was afraid of no man— but heathen gods! They sent a shudder up his spine and a cold feeling to the pit of his stomach. He had no confidence in his own righteousness to protect him, nor in his young Ishakki's. 'He is still there,' he said, returning. 'He has been sent by the Lord of all the Earth to punish you and Shamashazir for your foolishness. You had best send the boys back to him and let us go.'

'Never!' said Enoch, all his fighting spirit roused.

But Shamashazir was also having doubts. 'Let me look at him

again,' he said. Cautiously he crawled round the boulder. The *thing* was still there. But it had moved a little away from the fire and seemed to be listening. Its features were in shadow and difficult to see. But its body had lost its flickering light. There was nothing ghostly or unearthly about it.

Enoch joined his friend. 'Surely it is a man,' whispered Shamashazir.

Enoch gazed long, sensitively assessing the turn of the *thing's* head and line of the muscles in its back. 'Y-e-s,' he said reluctantly; for he could not help feeling doubt that the Ishak had come so far into the mountains. Then, suddenly, doubt was gone, his body went tense like a pointing dog's; and motioning Shamashazir to keep silent, he moved a little away, crouching with his head close to the ground.

'What is it?' Shamashazir whispered after a short interval.

'Men moving higher up the mountains. He must have left his warriors behind and come alone to deceive us. . . . I could get him with a sling-stone.'

'No!' said Shamashazir firmly. Though he did not know why he said it.

'Why not? You are not afraid? The men on the hill will never be there in time to catch *me*.'

'He is a man. What good will it do?'

'He has Jemimah and all our stores. And if we kill *him*, all his warriors will go home.' Enoch crouched, waiting for Shamashazir's answer.

It was slow in coming: 'Why should they? He is only a tool in their hands.'

'He is the Ishak.'

'He is a father. It is not he who wants to sacrifice his own sons.'

'But our food,' Enoch insisted, 'and my father's donkey. He is better dead.'

'No!' said Shamashazir again, urgently, unable to think of further argument.

Enoch turned and looked him straight in the eye. It was a battle of wills in the semi-darkness . . . life or death for the Ishak Moab. Shamashazir remembered how Enoch had defied his father; and now his eyes blazed with hate for the man Moab and all he stood for. To pit against Enoch's fire, Shamashazir had only a certain pity, and a certain reverence for all men, beginning to flicker like a small flame behind his natural boy's fighting spirit. But now his fighting spirit was growing stronger. It was on Enoch's side, and Enoch's eyes were calling it. The Ishak was evil, nothing but a devil and a worshipper of devils. Shamashazir felt himself beginning to weaken. Passionately he prayed for help. It was as if the Ishak heard him; for immediately he began to shout.

'O Shamashazir of Ur and Enoch son of Enoch, I come in peace,' he cried. 'Take me with you as your servant wherever you take my two sons; for I am no longer the Ishak of my people, but a man without a god and without a tribe. For this reason I have lain down my sword and my spear and followed you alone into the mountains of the evil dingirs.'

'He lies,' said Enoch, 'when he says he comes alone. He does not know the cunning keenness of our ears . . . I could tell the man was treacherous when I talked to him.'

Shamashazir could not deny that the Ishak was treacherous. He had noticed the shiftiness of his eyes as he sat on his throne. And yet now he knew he heard the ring of truth in his voice. 'Why does he sit in the light of the fires where we can so easily kill him, if he comes to recapture the boys?' he asked. Enoch had no answer to that. Shamashazir went on: 'Can't Sam go down and get Jemimah and our food?'

Reluctantly Enoch agreed. But it had better be Eb. He had his own reasons. He called him softly, telling him to fetch the donkey.

'Let me first find some good stones for my sling,' said Eb, feeling about on the ground.

The battle for the Ishak's life had begun again. 'If you kill him,' said Shamashazir angrily, 'you are nothing but fools and murderers. A man comes to you with peace in his hand; and you see a demon. A father comes looking for his sons; and you see a wild beast that has to be slain.'

'You do not hear what I hear, O Shamashazir of Ur,' said Eb. 'There are men on the mountain-side.'

'I know it. But there are wild tribes in the mountains,' Shamashazir retorted.

'They make too much noise.'

'They have drunk wine.'

Eb did not mind being called a murderer, but he could not stand being called a fool. It was possible that Shamashazir was right, and the noise came from drunken tribesmen. In fact, when he came to think of it, it was more likely than that the warriors from Kenan had ventured so far. 'It is true,' he said, quoting an old saying, 'that fear will drive a man to the foot of a mountain, but only love will take him over the peak. I will take my knife from its sheath, but no stone for my sling. And I will bring back the donkey, O Shamashazir of Ur. But you have taken our lives in your hands. Let the guilt of spilling our blood be on your head.' And he was gone, feeling his way over the rough ground.

In the deepening darkness, Enoch and Shamashazir could not see him go. But they sat together and watched every movement of the Ishak down by the fire. There was no need now to hide behind the boulder; for the night screened them. And Sam joined them with the two boys, complaining that Zepho was struggling to get to his father. 'Speak to him, O Shamashazir son of Noah. I can do nothing to make him keep still.'

'You promised me you would do exactly what you were told,' said Shamashazir sternly to the little boy.

'It was what *you* told me, not him,' said Zepho, contritely hanging his head.

'I tell you to be quiet!'

'But it is *Father*,' said Zepho, with a sob.

'I know it is.'

'They won't let me go.'

'Of course not.'

'Why . . .?'

There was no answer to Zepho's insistent questioning. And he was quiet for a little time, trying to puzzle it out.

Sam and Enoch were listening to the noises from the hill, which were now getting louder, so that even Shamashazir could hear them plainly. And the Ishak, too, they thought, seemed to be listening— rather apprehensively, Shamashazir pointed out.

'From where they are,' said Sam, 'they must see the fires. And yet they are moving down the hill and not trying to hide their presence.'

'The Ishak is afraid,' said Shamashazir. 'Is he running away?'

'Ah . . .' said Sam. 'That well may be. He acts like a hunted man. We shall see in a moment; he will move out of the light.'

No sooner had he spoken, when the Ishak dropped on to his hands and knees and disappeared into the darkness in their direction. They were very quiet for some time, listening for sounds of cracking twigs. Then they saw Jemimah vanish from beside the fires, and knew that Eb had reached her. Was the Ishak afraid of Eb, after all? He might have keener ears than they expected, or the gift of knowing when a foe was near. Somewhere between them was the clink of stone on stone.

'He's coming this way,' said Enoch, 'walking upright. Where are the boys?' But they had both vanished. Even Enoch had not noticed them go; he had been so intent on what was happening in front of them.

A few moments later they heard Zepho's pattering footsteps going down the hill.

'Shall I get him?' asked Sam. But before either Enoch or Shamashazir could decide on an answer, they heard Zepho's voice calling to his father, and the Ishak answering softly: 'Hisst, my son! Do not leave Shamashazir of Ur and Enoch son of Enoch, for the forest is full of foes.'

'Ah . . .' said Sam. 'So Sh . . .'

But Enoch silenced him before he could say that Shamashazir was right. Zepho had dropped his voice. Enoch was straining to hear what he said.

'They would not let me go. They are up the hill. I ran to you, Father. But I cannot see where you are.'

'There is only one boy moving,' said Enoch. 'I can hear no sound of Shaul.'

Then from lower down, came the clip-clop of Jemimah's hooves.

'We must go,' said Shamashazir. 'For Eb will bump into the Ishak and kill him in the dark.'

'He has heard what we have heard and seen what we have seen,' Enoch answered. 'But if you are afraid, I will give him the cry of "Peace", and he will understand.' And a night hawk's cry rang out from close beside Shamashazir.

So the listeners waited, while all three people on the hill drew closer to one another. Zepho was talking to his father continually, groping his way towards him. And the Ishak was answering back, his voice getting lower and lower as he drew near his little son. Then they heard Zepho cry: 'Father!' and break into stiff, childish sobs.

'There is no real evil in the Ishak Moab's heart,' said Sam.

Enoch was silent. The Ishak Moab was weak, which he despised; and the Ishak Moab was a heathen, which was evil. He brushed the Ishak Moab aside as unworthy of consideration. The noises from the other hill behind the fires were demanding his attention. All this time they had been coming nearer, twigs snapping, stones falling, and the continuous murmur of voices. Enoch listened intently, puzzled by something. 'They are not the voices of warriors, drunk or sober,' he said. Shamashazir breathed a sigh of relief. Enoch went on: 'I can hear boys' voices among them, two ... three ... four ...'

Suddenly there was a high-pitched wail: 'He's gone! They've all gone ...' For a moment the movements stopped. Then a lad's half-broken voice shouted something about 'fires', and the cracking of sticks and the talking began again, louder and more urgent.

'It's a party of boys who have escaped from battle,' said Sam thoughtfully, remembering another battle and the boys who escaped it. Enoch agreed with him. All the deeper voices, now they had come closer, were hardly broken. They decided to go down the hill to meet the Ishak and Eb—Enoch calling to him with the curlew's call, to tell him they were coming. But as the shouts and cries above them increased, and continued to confirm the belief that they came from a party of boys who were hungry and lost, Shamashazir, with Enoch's permission, began to shout to Shaul and Zepho that they were going back to the fire; and that all was safe.

'Shaul! Zepho!' he shouted. 'We are going back to the fire, to eat. It is I, Shamashazir, calling.'

But no sooner were his words launched on the clear air, when cries of excitement came echoing back, cries which resolved themselves clearly into heard words: 'O father of thy people! Have mercy upon us; we are hungry!'

They could see that Eb had already got back to the fire with Jemimah. He left her there and came to meet them with two torches, which lit up the silhouette of the Ishak, carrying Zepho. Then the cries on the hill became louder: 'O father of thy people! We are cold—and the mountain is dark.' Eb left one torch with the Ishak Moab, and came on towards them with the other, greeting Shamashazir with almost as much respect as he used for the Ishak Enoch. For a moment Shamashazir glowed with pride. Then he remembered how he had been on the point of giving way, and letting the Ishak Moab be killed. There was nothing to be proud of. 'It is by the grace of the Lord of the Earth,' he said. But no one quite understood what he meant.

Eb, with his torch, led the way back to the fires, where they found the Ishak Moab waiting for them on his knees, with his head bowed to the ground. 'Let it be known I come in peace, asking for mercy,' he said.

Enoch did not answer at once. So Shamashazir told the Ishak to rise up and share their food. Gratefully he got up, looking about him.

'Where is Shaul?' said Eb. 'I thought he was with the little one.'

Zepho shook his head. No, he had come alone. 'I thought he stayed with you. He was shivering. And I heard stones rattling in his mouth.'

'The young fool,' muttered Sam. But the Ishak stood silently peering into the darkness and listening.

Then they all began to call Shaul. But there was no answer to their call, except from the boys above.

'That's Irad's voice! I can hear Irad! Father, that's Irad!' Zepho shouted suddenly.

'Irad?'

'Yes. He's up there with the boys. And there's Mesha too ... Irad and Mesha. They are both up there.'

The Ishak listened with a new interest. Yes. The voices were familiar; and what he had not noticed before, they spoke with the perfect accents of Kenanites. Irad was the son of his cousin. One of the cousins who might be the new Ishak. He picked out other boys ... boys escaping from the Corn Dingir. The Ishak realized it with a shock; as if the whole tribe were deserting the gods of their fathers. But a few moments later it appeared there were only eight of them. The eight who, unknown, had followed him from the village. One by one they came in sight of the fire, limping, hollow-eyed and bedraggled, and threw themselves on the ground in its warmth, face downwards, panting and calling for water and food. Sam gave them water. And Enoch, when he had consulted Shamashazir, said they could finish up the cheese and have a handful of corn each. It was husky and uncooked. But the boys chewed it gratefully.

When the last and eighth straggler had come in, the Ishak, still listening, asked: 'Are there no more?' He was half hoping that Shaul might be among them. But Irad sat up and counted eight.

'No,' he said. 'We are all here.'

'You got across those mountains on your own,' said Sam. 'You did well.'

'What made you come?' Shamashazir asked.

Irad pointed and shrugged his shoulders. 'I wasn't going to be made a sacrifice of,' he said defiantly. 'And those others . . . they were afraid to go back by themselves. So they had to come where I wanted them.'

The Ishak was anxious about Shaul. He wanted to go and look for him. But he realized that if the boy was afraid, he would only run farther away. He wanted to call him, but knew that his son would never trust him. 'Call him, O Shamashazir of Ur,' he said. 'He will believe in you;' and his voice had the fall of a man's whose spirit is broken.

So Shamashazir shouted: 'Shaul! Shaul! Come back to the fire and eat. There is nothing to fear.'

But only the brooding silence of the mountains answered his call. Then Enoch called, with the yodelling shepherd call that echoed all round the hills. But Shamashazir thought that would frighten Shaul still more. He was not used to the sound, and Shamashazir remembered how he had felt when he first heard it in the mountains, with the stories of the mountain voices.

'Better make the fires up and trust to hunger and the smell of roast rabbit to bring him back,' said Sam, throwing on light pine branches that crackled and flared and hissed. 'There's nothing more we can do.'

There was nothing more. They sat down in a circle round the most windward of the fires and waited for their food. Zepho snuggled up happily beside his father as if he had never been parted from him. He had lost the look of an old, old man and smiled happily to himself like any ordinary boy, now and again looking up at his father to make sure he was actually there and that he was not dreaming some happy dream. 'Are we really in the forest, Father, with Shamashazir of Ur and Enoch son of Enoch?' he asked.

Then when they had finished eating, Shamashazir said, 'Let the Ishak Moab tell his story.' For they were all eager to hear what had happened in the village after Shaul's escape.

The Ishak was silent for a little, collecting his thoughts, and listening for a sound in the undergrowth that might be made by his son. Then he began to speak with the low, trembling voice of an old man, or a man who is lost:

'Before the days of Cain, there was no ploughing or sowing of corn. It grew like a wild plant among the grasses of a far country, and the women and children of the tribe went searching for it, and gathered each precious ear in their hands, and put it in a basket. In those days the people of the earth all worshipped the Great Spirit. But when any man died, they put a handful of corn into a bowl made of unbaked clay beside him; and buried him in the ground.'

'We put corn beside our dead in Ur, for them to eat on their journey to the Underworld,' said Shamashazir.

The Ishak looked at him, surprised. 'And does the corn sprout out of the graves, rich and green?'

'No,' said Shamashazir. 'No corn sprouts out of the graves. It disappears; and we know that the dead have eaten it.'

The Ishak looked puzzled. 'In my country the corn sprouts out of the graves; and it is always better than any corn that is sown in the fields. By that we know that the Corn Dingir has accepted the dead man, and is giving us his thanks.'

It was Shamashazir's turn to look puzzled; but the Ishak went on:

'All men worshipped the Great Spirit in those days. The Corn Dingir was nothing more than an elf of the open hills, who planted corn among the grasses, for the women to find when they went searching for food. They knew nothing of ploughing or sowing, nor how plants grew from seeds. It was Cain the curious, the father of my people, who discovered the great secret of corn sowing.

'He chose a spot where the earth was bare of weeds. And he dug a hole with the shoulder-bone of an ox, and buried a handful. And he watched over it, until it came up with a small blade of green, and until it grew tall. But the corn that Cain planted was weak and thin, and the ears were small; not like the rich corn that grew on the graves of the dead. And Cain took a torch from the fire, and went out on to the hills at midnight to look for the corn elf. And it is said that he sat down under an oak-tree; and the corn elf called out of the darkness in a high, wailing voice: "Alas, and alas, I am but a poor wailing elf for lack of blood. If I had the blood of men in my veins, I should become a mighty dingir; and I would feed my servants with harvests of rich corn that would make them mighty."

'Then Cain went back to his father's house and began looking for a man whom he could kill for the corn elf. But no stranger came that way, and he met no man out hunting. And he grew sullen.

But as he sat brooding, his brother Abel, who was a shepherd, came in with a lamb across his shoulders. And he laughed at Cain, and said, "Why are you so silent, O grower of the corn that shrivels up in the sun?" And Cain rose up from his seat on the ground in a passion of jealousy and hurled a great stone at the head of his brother; so that Abel fell to the ground dead. And Cain carried his body away and buried him secretly in the ground. And all around, and all over his grave, he spread the seeds of the corn. And the corn grew green and rich.

'But when his father found out what he had done, he put his curse on him and his sons, for ever and ever, saying that they were murderers. And he drove him away from the tribe, and forbade him to worship the Great Spirit; because of the blood that was on his hands. And Cain filled a basket with corn seeds, and went away sorrowfully to a new country with his sons and his daughters and his wives. And when they had built huts to live in, Cain commanded his sons to kill him, because of the curse that was on his head; and to sow corn in the earth where they buried his body.

'And they did so. And the corn grew richer and greener than any corn that they had seen before. And they knew that the words of Cain were wise words. But because of the curse on their heads which forbade them to serve the Great Spirit, they served the Corn Dingir. And every year one man gave himself as a sacrifice for the people.'

And then the Ishak went on to tell them what had happened in the village on the night of Shaul's escape; and how he had drugged the sentries and silenced his wife; and how, in the morning, he had decided to come into the mountains to look for his sons. 'For,' he said, 'without them I am no longer Ishak. I am nothing.'

Shamashazir only half heard the last part of the Ishak's story. He was thinking about the legend of Cain. He had heard the story of Cain and Abel before, but a different version. He felt very thankful that the corn grew so well in the fields of Ur without the sacrifice of human blood; and he wondered why.

His thoughts were broken into by Eb: 'So it was you who sent those two sentries to sleep, O Moab of Kenan. Without you, our plans would have failed, and Enoch son of Enoch, and I, his unfaithful servant, would have been dead. And there would have been mourning in the tribe of Enoch. I thank you from the bottom of my heart, for I promised the Ishak of Enoch to defend his son with my life.' He looked at Enoch as he spoke. Enoch looked at Shamashazir.

'I also thank you, O Ishak Moab,' said Shamashazir.

Enoch rose self-consciously from his place. It hurt his pride to think that he owed his life to a man with the curse of Cain on his head. But he was not going to seem ungracious in the eyes of Shamashazir by not giving thanks where thanks were due. So he bowed stiffly, and said, 'Accept my thanks, O Ishak,' and then sat down again.

Zepho had fallen asleep, leaning against his father's side. The Ishak laid him gently down on the ground, and then asked Eb if he had seen or heard any sign of Shaul while they had been talking. Eb shook his head. But Enoch said he did not think he was very far away. He could feel his presence; although there was no sound or sign of him.

They lay down to sleep—except Eb, who kept the first watch, and the Ishak Moab, who, although he lay down, could not go to sleep for thinking of his son.

Shaul had not gone far. He was too frightened of the strange silence; and could not put it out of his head that the Corn Dingir might be lurking about among the trees. When they had left their hiding-place in the rocks, he had crept after them at a distance, to be within sound of their voices. He had lain trembling in some bushes all through his father's story, wondering what they could be saying. 'Offering them gold to send me back,' he thought.

Then the talking stopped, and there was silence over the whole forest—a fearful silence that made Shaul long for the company of men and the comfort of fire-light. He began to creep nearer and nearer, feeling with his hands in the darkness, and silently sliding his knees forward through the bilberry bushes, until he could see the flames of the fires through the trees. From time to time Eb called him again: 'Shaul! The ants'll be eating your fish.'

And Shaul began to feel hungry, desperately hungry. He decided he would creep near enough to see where the fish was, and wait until Eb's back was turned to it. And then he would creep in and seize it.

Eb had begun to talk softly, as if he knew that the boy was approaching: 'Don't you fear the lions, lad? At night they leave their dens and go on the prowl, looking for some poor beast to eat. It's not safe for a boy of your age to be out in the forest alone in the dark. It'd be better to sit by a fire with good men who have said their prayers.' Above the hiss of the flames, and the gentle munching of Jemimah eating grass, he heard a rustle in the dead leaves. He went on talking, as if to himself: 'It takes a skilful man to bore a hole in a mud hut in the dark without making a noise. And I am a hunter and a shepherd, not a builder of cities. And yet the sentries that guarded the Young Ishakki never stirred. We went round the hut and found them asleep. I thought their sleep was put on them by the Lord of all the Earth. But it was your father, the Ishak Moab. He put herbs in their drink for the love of his son. He is a man who has no courage and yet some courage . . . a man . . .'

He let his voice die away to silence. He could hear Shaul moving quite plainly now. A moment later his head appeared among the bilberry bushes in the circle of light. Eb could see him from the corner of his eye. He could also see that the Ishak, who was lying down, had not gone to sleep. He went on talking, never showing by a muscle of his face that he had seen Shaul. He knew that the slightest move would send the boy scuttling off into the forest again; and that the Ishak's eyes were open; and that the boy was making a noise. He began to speak in riddles, hoping that the Ishak would understand and keep still; and that the boy would not guess his presence was known. 'If a man wants a sparrow to sit on his hand he'd better keep as still as a tree,' he said thoughtfully. 'At least that was the way my mother taught it to me. My father said it was a dove. But I don't see that it matters, dove or sparrow, so long as you keep still.'

He saw Shaul's hand stretch towards the fish, which they had laid out on a flat stone to tempt him. But the Ishak chose just that moment to turn his head. He seemed to suspect that his son was near, and was unable to control his impatience. Shaul's hand shot back without taking the fish, and Eb heard him crashing through the bushes. The Ishak started to his feet.

'Sit down,' Eb commanded. 'You shouldn't have moved your head. I had him all but hooked.'

The Ishak lay down again, mumbling to himself, 'I am a broken man, and my son does not trust me.'

The light-sleeping Sam, woken by the disturbance, looked at him with kindly eyes as if he were a beast in pain. 'Has the boy not come back yet?' he asked.

'He's not far away,' Eb answered. 'I saw him put out his hand for the fish.'

'He's a young fool of a boy to be afraid. He's not got much sense in his head, that boy, not half the sense of his young brother. If he gets himself picked up by a lion, after all we have done for him, it will serve him right. I've no use for that sort of a boy.'

'He is my son,' said the Ishak. 'He's still crazed with fear.' And he sat up again, unable to lie down and wait.

'Let him listen again to the story you told us,' said Sam, hoping to keep the Ishak's mind occupied, as well as enticing the boy.

Eb grunted his agreement. So the Ishak began again to tell the story of how he had shown Zepho a hole in the wall where there was no scorpion, and how he had put herbs in the sentries' drink, and how he had silenced his wife when she had wanted to rouse the village. By the time he had finished, Shaul was standing up among the bilberry bushes visible by the light of the fire. His eyes were fixed on his father, and he was listening intently.

Eb stretched out his hand for the leg of rabbit and threw it to him, saying: 'Here! Catch!' And when Shaul had picked it up from the ground, Eb, whose back was now turned to him again as if he were not interested in whether he came or went, said, 'Come and sit down and eat your food by the light of the fire. If you eat food in the dark you'll find yourself swallowing ants, and things that you didn't mean to.'

Like a dog with its tail between its legs, Shaul crept into the circle of fires. The Ishak murmured, 'My son, you are safe,' and held out his arms to him.

But Shaul sat down near Sam, as far from his father as he could get, and finished up the rabbit and the fish they had put out for him, without saying a word. Then he wiped his hands on the grass and muttered, 'I'm thirsty.' And Eb gave him a drink from one of the skin water-bottles. It tasted even more horrible than the day before; and Shaul drank only a sip.

Eb tossed him a handful of raisins. 'Here! Take these and go to sleep,' he said. And Shaul curled up on the ground beside Sam, still as far away from his father as he could get.

In the morning, Zepho was glad to see that Shaul had come back, for he and Shamashazir and the eight cousins had slept soundly through all the rustlings and noises of the night. But he was much more excited—and danced up and down with joy—to find that his father was still with them, and had not been spirited away by the dingirs. 'Are you coming with us all the way to Ur, Father? To be slaves of Shamashazir?' he cried.

His father bowed his head. A slave! .... And he the Ishak of his people. An honourable man would kill himself.

But Shamashazir, used to reading men's thoughts, understood his shame at the word 'slave', and said, 'In Ur, a slave can buy goods and send them on a trading journey; and when he has sufficient goods he can buy his freedom.'

The Ishak looked at Shamashazir, eager-faced, and thought: 'Shamashazir of Ur is good. The people of Ur must be good, if even a slave can own property and trade with it to buy his freedom. It would be better to be a slave of the people of the Lord of all the Earth than an Ishak of the children of Kenan the accursed.'

'So be it,' he said to Shamashazir. 'I am a man of no account. Yet it will be better to be a door-keeper in a house of the Great Spirit than an Ishak to the Corn Dingir. If you will take my sons to be your servants, I also will be your servant, until my sons are of age and I can buy their freedom.' He put his hand into the bosom of his robe and felt for a small bundle wrapped in cloth and tied round his neck (in which he had put a few gold valuables left to him by his father), to make sure that it was still safe.

But the sun was lighting up the peaks of the mountains above them. 'We go to pray,' said Enoch. He motioned the Ishak to stay by the fire with the sleeping boys and his two sons.

The Ishak bowed his head and sat down. Shaul glanced at him distastefully, and went over to talk to Jemimah. Zepho sat by his father, watching the others out of sight. Then he said, 'Won't any god have us, Father!' 'None.'

'I can do without a god while I have you, Father.' He lay back.

As they went up through the trees, Shamashazir turned back to look at the eleven round the fire. 'To be a man without a god and without a tribe must be a terrible thing,' he thought. 'I should always be afraid.' They sang:

> 'He maketh my feet like harts' feet
> And setteth me up on high.
> He is the defender of all who put their trust in Him.'

The Ishak could hear the beautiful words drifting through the trees; but they gave him no comfort, for he knew they were not for him.

12 WILD MEN OF THE MOUNTAINS

With fifteen mouths to feed, they would have to spend much more
time in hunting and fishing; and the journey would take longer.
The boys would earn their keep collecting wood for the fires at
night; and there would be far less danger from wild beasts; but the
food was a serious handicap. If they went too slowly, Enoch was
afraid his father would get to the Lake of Kingfishers and give up
waiting for them. 'There's not much grazing for the sheep there,' he
thought.

'If only we had a copper pot,' said Shamashazir, gazing thoughtfully at Jemimah's baskets . . . 'Then we could parch the corn and

eat that.'

'Eat the tribe's winter store,' said Eb in a shocked voice. 'Give the food of the children of the Lord to the accursed!'

'There are granaries in Ur,' Shamashazir answered. 'Serag my cousin will have corn in his pack-saddles. If only we could find a copper-smith in these mountains and get a copper pot. We must get back in time or we shall miss my cousin Serag.'

'We shall get back,' said Eb. 'Do you think I would let this pagan rabble stop me? There are many convenient *cliffs* in these mountains, for those who lag behind with hunger.' He got to his feet and stretched, then picked up his fishing-spear and went off to the stream.

Sam followed him a moment later. 'The grass has been eaten short over there,' he remarked to Enoch, with a tilt of his head towards the southern slope of the valley, and set off in that direction, to hunt for rabbits.

Shamashazir looked at the still sleeping boys. He imagined them weak with hunger, being pushed over the cliff so as not to delay the party; and his civilized stomach felt sick. 'I wish we could find copper-smiths,' he muttered between his teeth.

Enoch, who had seen old people and sick children left behind to die before, was surprised at the look of distress on his friend's face. But he loved and admired Shamashazir. When he got up to follow Sam, he felt as urgently as Shamashazir the need to find a copper-smith.

When the hunters came back with the fish and game that they had caught, Enoch mentioned the subject of copper-smiths again, asking Eb and Sam if they had come across a tribe anywhere in these mountains.

'I've seen smoke,' said Sam.

'Where?'

But he could not remember.

Then Eb said that he'd seen smoke, too, and picking up a stick, began drawing maps in the ashes with it, arguing with Sam as to where the smoke would be. In the end they both agreed that if they went a little out of their way to the south they would probably come upon it the next day. 'We shall lose another day,' he said.

But Enoch thought that it was worth it, if they could buy a copper pot.

Eb woke up the eight cousins, who got up stretching and yawning, and groaning over their stiff knees and sore feet.

They ate the food silently and guiltily; all except Irad, who thought of nothing except having something in his stomach. It wasn't until they started on their journey, when they could hang back out of sight of the men, that they began to talk among themselves, discussing in half-clipped, boyish sentences what was going to happen to them; never expressing the deep fears that each held in his heart, but yet sharing a common unease.

'Are we going to Ur?'

'They beat slaves.'

'You did not hear what I heard.'

'What?'

'About cliffs.'

'What of them?'

'When they run short of food . . .'

'Us, do you mean?'

Then, after an interval of silent walking, watching an eagle swoop overhead: 'I wish I'd never come.'

'Too late now.'

Only Irad walked by himself, thinking of fishing with a spear, and did not join in. 'I could catch fish as well as them,' he thought, swinging his arm through the air with a deadly stroke for his imaginary victim.

They had an easy journey that day, following the stream along the valley, and then up and over another shoulder. The grass was very pleasing to the eyes of Jemimah, who made passing snatches at it as she ambled along between Sam and Shaul. Shaul had taken to the little donkey, and walked beside her silently, sometimes picking a handful of grass and holding it out in front of her nose to keep her going. The hard living out of doors was beginning to do him good. The puffy bags under his eyes had disappeared. And he looked leaner and stronger, and moved with more spring in his step. But he still kept away from his father.

It was Enoch who first spotted the smoke from the coppersmiths' fires—a thin thread going straight up from the opposite cliff. It was the first sign of any settlement that they had seen since the beginning of their journey. And the boys were a little cheered by the sight. But it was getting late, too late to cross the valley before sunset. Enoch decided that they must make their camp a little way down the hill, and start off the next morning. The boys willingly helped Shamashazir gather wood, glad to be of use—all except Irad, who kept to his resolution and demanded to be taught how to fish.

'Hi,' said Sam, laughing. 'A lad like you could never keep still.'

'I'm not a lad like anyone,' Irad answered, scowling. 'Try me.'

'Come then, O master of hunting,' said Sam. 'But if you move an eyelid, or let your breath sound above the glide of a hawk, I'll throw you in the stream, for the fish to eat.'

'Of course,' said Irad, in a determined and masterful manner that made Sam feel dubious. But the boy kept his word, held his spear as Sam told him, followed his instructions meticulously, and brought his first fish triumphantly back to the fire.

When they had eaten, the three shepherds and Shamashazir went to worship the Great Spirit. And the boys listened to the sound of their singing through the trees. And they wondered; for in the Village of Kenan, as in most other cities and villages in those days, the people made offerings and said prayers to their dingirs at sunset. If they did not do so, there would be no rain, and no corn to eat; or their enemies would set fire to their houses at night; or wild beasts would run off with their children; or some other terrible calamity would happen. For life was hard and dangerous. They sat round the fire expectantly, waiting for the Ishak to begin their prayers for them.

But the Ishak did nothing. He neither moved from his position nor spoke. The seven more nervous cousins began to cast anxious glances at one another, thinking of the wild mountains and the dark night before them.

Then, suddenly, the Ishak turned his head and looked at them in the gathering dusk. He must have read their thoughts; for he said:

'We are a people without a god. We have deserted the dingir of our fathers, and no other god will have us.'

The seven boys swallowed uneasily, dismay clutching at their hearts; for they knew that this was the most terrible thing that could happen to a man.

Then one boy summoned up enough courage to say what they were all thinking: 'Take us back to our village, O father of our people. We want to go back.'

'These mountains are evil,' said another.

'Slaves are beaten.'

'We were cowards to run away.'

'We are ashamed.'

'The mountain dingirs are more terrible than the Corn Dingir.'

'We have heard them moving in the night.'

'We've seen them. We know.'

They all began to urge the Ishak to take them back—all except Irad, of course, who was feeling wonderfully content after his successful fishing and his huge meal, and was afraid of no mountain dingirs.

But Zepho clung tightly to his father's arm. The Ishak could feel him trembling. And Shaul came out of the bushes and watched his father's face.

'What do you say, my son. Do we go or stay?'

For answer, Shaul gently stroked Jemimah's ear. 'I'm going to be a slave in Ur,' he said.

'I shall stay with my sons,' said the Ishak. 'But you eight sons of my cousins are free to go as you came.'

Shaul glanced at his father, his habitual look of suspicion relaxed. Then he sat down in the circle among the others, and began to dig into the moss with a twig.

The seven looked at Irad hopelessly. They had had enough of wandering on their own, without food or fire; and they might never find their way back to Kenan at all. They gave up the idea and decided to stay, feeling themselves greater cowards and more shameful than ever.

That evening, all the stories told round the fire seemed flat and uninteresting. There were no adventures so exciting that they could make the boys forget the terrors of living without a god. Shaul was rubbing away at a reed with a blunt flint, absorbed in his thoughts. The boys fidgeted. No one seemed to be listening, until Irad broke the spell by suddenly asking Shaul why he hadn't run away before. 'I'd have run away before they got me and shut me up in that hut,' he said.

'I tried to,' Shaul gulped, looking round startled, as if he felt invisible eyes watching him.

'Did they catch you then?'

Shaul did not answer.

'They wouldn't have caught me,' Irad muttered to himself.

'You'd have had to live alone in the mountains if we hadn't come with you,' said one of the cousins.

'I wouldn't care. I'd have been better off without you. Didn't any of them run away without being caught?' he asked the Ishak.

The Ishak nodded.

'How did they do it? Tell us!' the other boys urged, scenting the only kind of story that could interest them that night.

But the Ishak shook his head. 'There is nothing to tell. Now and again a boy has disappeared, and his footsteps have been found leading to the mountains. But the mountain dingirs are no friends of the Corn Dingir. They defend all those who run away from the village. It is not safe to go searching for them.'

'We know,' said Sam. 'We know the way the mountain dingirs have with strangers; we know, O Jemimah, beloved of my eyes.'

Jemimah gently woffled the back of his neck with her nose as if she knew what he meant.

Shaul laughed. 'Did *you* help the others to escape?' he asked Sam.

Sam looked wise. Among the tribes, if your enemy thought you had magical powers, it was foolish to undeceive him.

But the Ishak Moab stared straight at Sam. 'The last boy to run away successfully was the brother of my father. Unless you are the son of a very old man, your father was not born at that time.'

Sam's dark skin turned darker. He was ten years younger than the Ishak.

'Then it was the dingirs,' said Shaul. 'What did they do?'

'When my uncle ran away, they rolled great boulders down on the warriors who went seeking him.'

'And did he come back when he was grown up, and become Ishak?' asked Zepho.

'He never came back. Only once some footsteps were found in the vineyards. They had a crooked toe. I saw them myself when I was a boy. And my grandmother, who was an old woman, swore that they were her son's. But many men have crooked toes. And a boy's foot alters.'

'I bet it was his!' said Irad.

The next morning, when they climbed the slope again, to take a bearing by the sun of the direction they must go, they were disappointed to see no sign of any smoke from the copper-smiths' fires. The trees stretched away to rocky cliff at the bottom of the valley. And only a solitary eagle broke the silent emptiness of the forest.

'They've gone!' said Shamashazir.

But Sam did not think so; copper-smiths never moved about. If they were smelting copper, they burnt charcoal, and blew up their fires red hot. 'And red-hot fires give off no smoke.'

'There is truth in that,' said Shamashazir, thinking of the copper-smiths in Ur.

Enoch took the direction by the shadow of the trees; and they set off downhill through the forest, Zepho with his father, Shaul with Jemimah and Sam, and the other boys trailing behind. Before the bottom of the valley, they came across the first signs that men were living near. The undergrowth had been cleared of fallen trees and branches. The bilberries had been picked, and some of the bushes were broken and trodden flat. Farther down, towards the stream, whitened bones lay in the grass, and well-trodden paths led up to it and ran along its banks. But they saw no human being about; and it was curiously silent. 'They can't be at work,' said Sam. 'In a valley like this, you could hear the chink of metal ten arrow-shots away.'

They followed the path that led downstream; and came to a flat, well-worn rock, above a deep, clear pool. Enoch picked a fine long black hair off a fern, and said he thought the women must use the pool for getting water and for washing in. Just above the pool were stepping-stones that had been put in place by human hands, and were worn bare of moss by constant use. Sam was right. This was not a passing tribe, but a permanent home for a people who lived in caves.

From the pool a well-worn path zigzagged up the cliff. They stood at the bottom looking up at it. 'The caves'll be up there,' said Sam. 'Give them a hail, O Enoch son of Enoch.'

Enoch put his hand to his mouth and gave the yodelling mountain cry that meant 'Friend'.

But there was no answer.

'Queer,' said Eb.

'These people are a small tribe,' said Enoch thoughtfully. 'They have no sheep. The men could be out hunting. And the women would be afraid.'

'If there are only women, can't we take Zepho? Then they will know we come in peace,' said Shamashazir.

Enoch agreed, and telling Sam to stay there with the boys, he led the way across the stepping-stones and up the path, with Zepho following close behind.

Tall trees grew up the cliff; and the path wandered in and out, choosing the easiest way. Here and there steps had been cut, which delighted the little boy. He wanted to stop and run up and down them.

Half-way up, the trees stopped, and the path came out on to a platform of rock, that overhung a steep drop down to the stream below. Bare white bones were scattered about, and fine grey ashes from long burnt-out fires grimed into the cracks and blew in little eddies over the surface, giving the whole place a grey and sordid appearance. At the farther end were the charred remains of a more recent fire, in front of the small entrance to a cave. 'People were here a few moments ago,' said Enoch. 'They must be hiding in the cave.' Then he raised his voice and cried: 'Hail, O Copper-smiths of the Mountains! We come in peace to buy and sell.'

But there was no answer.

'Tell them we have corn,' suggested Shamashazir.

'If I shout "corn" in the manner of a shepherd,' said Enoch, 'they'll think it's some treacherous trick. Shepherds never have corn to sell. You call—the traders' call of Ur!'

So Shamashazir cried out: 'Corn for your copper and cloth for your wool,' as he had heard Serag cry when the caravan passed by a village. They listened for an answer. They thought they heard a faint murmur coming from inside the cave.

Meanwhile, Zepho, standing and waiting in silence behind Enoch and Shamashazir, began to look round for something more interesting to do. His mind went back to the fascinating steps cut in the rock. Unnoticed, he tiptoed past his father. A little lower down, a path branched off from the main path and ran along the side of the cliff. He made for it, with quick, pattering footsteps.

'Zepho!' his father shouted. 'Zepho!' And the name echoed round the hills.

There was a sudden buzz of voices from inside the cave, a shuffling of goatskin against stone, and an old man came creeping out. His face was deeply furrowed and grey with dirt; his beard, which should have been white, was long and grey and ragged; his hands trembled; but his eyes were bright and restless. 'Who called?' he said.

'I, Enoch son of Enoch, come in peace. I bring corn, to trade with the copper-smiths for a copper pot.'

'We are no copper-smiths,' said the old man haughtily.

Behind him, men were pushing out of the cave—two evil-looking, scowling men, carrying large boulders, followed by several young lads armed with spears and arrows; and a wild woman, shouting: 'Since when have shepherds taken to selling corn?'

Shamashazir began to explain; but the old man interrupted him. 'You are not a shepherd,' he said, fixing Shamashazir with piercing eyes.

'I come from Ur. My name is Shamashazir son of Teresh. I...'
Again the old man interrupted him, pointing at the Ishak Moab. 'And he? Does he also come from Ur?'

Every man turned to look at the Ishak.

'I come from the Land of Milk and Honey,' he said with a voice of shame.

The old man narrowed his eyes slightly and let them wander to Zepho. 'I have heard of it,' he muttered; and was silent, looking at Zepho. The little boy became aware of his intent gaze, and overcome with shyness, went and stood close beside his father.

Meanwhile, a few dirty, naked children, becoming bold, began to look cautiously out of the mouth of the cave. The woman shooed them in again, and then began to question Shamashazir about the corn.

Enoch called down to Sam to bring it up.

But the moment the woman's back was turned, out came the children's heads again, like young fox-cubs savouring the air. And then, as no one took any more notice of them, they stood up and boldly ventured forth—thin, dirty, shock-headed, with lean bellies, and ribs that could be counted. They were followed by three or four very shy young women, dressed in goatskins fastened together by strands of human hair. They were so shy they could hardly bear to be looked at by the strangers; and hid behind the backs of the young men, huddling together and bashfully giggling, until the older woman told them to blow on the fire. Then they all knelt round the pile of dead ashes, and began to blow with their mouths, until glowing embers appeared among the grey. One of the young men fetched an armful of small sticks and dried ferns out of the cave; and the fire was soon sparkling and crackling again.

The old man welcomed the strangers as his guests, inviting them to sit down on the ledge of hard rock and wait for food. But all the time he was speaking, his eyes were following the movements of Zepho, who had joined the girls and was watching the rekindling of the fire.

Sam brought the corn up. And behind him came Shaul—nearly as excited to walk up the strange mossy steps as Zepho had been. At the top he looked at the dirty children; and they looked at him, measuring each other with their eyes like strange dogs meeting.

Sam set the basket in front of the old man, who slowly stretched out a trembling hand and dug his fingers into the grain. An expression of ecstasy came into his eyes, and his worn old face lit up in a sorrowful smile. Lovingly he gathered up a handful, letting it trickle through his fingers.

The Ishak Moab watched him curiously. 'This man,' he thought, 'was once used to eating corn; but for many years he has never seen it. He greets it as a father would his long-lost son.'

The young women, having made the fire burn brightly, came crowding round the basket, curious to see this new thing that so excited their grandfather. Overcoming their shyness, they watched him with silent fascination, until Shamashazir broke the spell by saying that if one of them would bring him an earthenware crock he would fill it for them; and they could bargain about the price. They began to laugh at the word 'crock'. They had never heard it before.

'It means "pitcher",' said Shamashazir. But that was funnier still.

'What do you keep your nuts and berries in?' Eb asked. 'And what do you fetch your water in?'

The girls fetched an empty goatskin tied at the legs by some creeping plant.

'Have you no baskets?' Shamashazir asked. But 'basket' was another word that made them laugh. It seemed as if one rough copper pot was all they possessed. They brought it out and showed it proudly to Shamashazir, who put several handfuls of corn into it and set it down near the heat of the fire, where he could stir it with a stick. They watched him with awe as if he were preparing some great magic, until one girl, bolder than the others, asked if she could try what it felt like.

Shamashazir gave her the stick, and she put her hand bravely towards the copper pot, and then stopped and fell suddenly backwards in a fit of giggles, overcome by the awful excitement.

When a goat was roasted, and the corn was parched, and the children had brought in handfuls of berries, they all sat down—

crowded together round the fire as best they could in the small space the ledge offered. One of the villainous-looking men cut up the goat with his hunting-knife, while the older woman handed it round, carefully dividing it up into small bits, and seeing that everyone had a fair share. For the young men and the children were always hungry and ready to fight over their food. They ate like wolves and finished at an astonishing speed. Only the girls, watching the strangers and trying to copy them, ate more daintily. And the young men laughed at them and teased them.

The moment they had finished eating, the mountain people began timidly to ask the strangers for stories, and their eyes shone with excited expectancy. 'Tell us about the great world on the other side of the mountains,' they cried.

Shamashazir was asked to begin. And he told them the story of Noah and the Flood. And the people of the mountains listened, leaning forward with wide-eyed astonishment.

'What a great tale,' cried some of the young men. 'All that water! But who is this Great Spirit—this Lord of all the Earth—who drowns the whole world when He is angry? Tell him to keep out of this valley; for we live on a mountain.' And they laughed.

But the old man said, 'Hush,' to them. 'I heard such tales as these when I was young. There is no happiness when the dingirs curse.' He began to rock his body to and fro, moaning.

'Why does he do that?' asked Zepho, alarmed. The moaning reminded him of Shaul waiting for his death. 'Is the Corn Dingir coming?'

The old man looked at Zepho and became still.

Then Eb told the story of a great battle that the tribe of Enoch had had with another tribe. And the men clenched their hands and beat their chests in excitement.

But all the while he was speaking, the old man was watching Zepho. When the excitement had quietened down, he turned to the Ishak Moab, and said: 'You have not spoken, O stranger from the Land of Milk and Honey.'

But the Ishak answered that he was only a slave. He could not speak before his host. Hadn't the old man a story to tell?

'My story,' said the old man, 'is a story of great wrong.'

'No, it isn't,' cried one of the grand-daughters. 'They are both good stories.'

The old man shook his head and was silent for some time, while they all sat round him expectantly. Then he looked up again, and his eyes were drawn as if by a magnet to Zepho.

Zepho grinned. 'I can tell a story—the biggest and best story in the world.'

'Ah,' said the old man slowly. 'Let us hear the story of the Little One with a Face of Magic.'

Zepho settled himself down with crossed legs, holding on to his feet and rocking his body to and fro. 'My story,' he began proudly, 'is about Shamashazir of Ur, and Enoch son of Enoch. Once upon a time there was a boy called Zepho and his father was the Ishak. And he had a brother called Shaul. And they gave him wine, and tied him up in a hut like all the others.'

'Ah,' said the old man, nodding excitedly. 'That was the custom among the corn people!'

Zepho looked at him disapprovingly for interrupting, and went on: 'And Shamashazir came. And he had a donkey. And Zepho liked donkeys. And Shamashazir said that the plough in Ur had copper tips and wheels, and it made the corn grow better than the Dingir.'

It was a truly childish story, the way Zepho told it. But the old man was listening to it with rapt attention. His hands were trembling and his lips were quivering; and he leaned forward eagerly as if he were afraid of missing a single word.

Zepho went on until he came to the part about the Frog Spring. Then, suddenly, the old man seemed to choke. The wild woman elder jumped up and ran to him, patting him on his back; but he waved her away. 'It is nothing,' he said. 'Let the child go on with his story about the Frog Spring. Tell me, child, where was this Frog Spring? Was it near the village or was it near the mountains?'

'It was near the mountains,' said Zepho. 'One side of it was vineyard; and the other side was rough grass where you can't go because of the mountain dingirs.'

'And the path. Was there no path after the Frog Spring?'

'No, the path stopped. And it was all hard lumps made by the oxen's feet when they went to drink.'

'And the boy Shaul,' the old man whispered. 'What became of him?'

'He is over there,' said Zepho, pointing to his brother.

The old man turned and gazed at Shaul; and saw and understood the look in his eyes. 'You are also a man without a god and without a tribe,' he said.

But Shaul did not answer.

'We have our own tribe,' one of the wild men growled. 'And what does a man want with a god?'

'Be quiet, you,' the woman snapped. 'Let the strangers tell their stories. Day after day, year after year, I have listened to the same story. And now these men come with tales of wonder from the wide world; and you start wagging your tongues again. Be quiet, I say, and let the strangers talk.'

'All right, all right,' the man answered. 'We said nothing. We're not stopping them. It's you with your cackle who broke into the young cub's silly tale.'

The woman clenched her fists. 'You . . .' she began. But the old man told them all to hold their peace; for he had a story to tell that they had never heard before. There was immediate quiet. And the old man began: 'My story is the story of Irad son of Zepho.' At the words 'Irad son of Zepho' the fingers of the Ishak Moab, which were clasped round his knee, suddenly tightened, so that the knuckles showed white.

'This Irad lived in a village far, far away, where corn grew in the fields, and grapes in the vineyards; and every man built himself a separate hut for his family. And they had bread to eat, and apples, and figs, and olives. Have you tasted bread, my brother?' he suddenly asked Zepho. Zepho said eagerly that he had; *and* he'd eaten apples and figs and olives.

The old man sighed, and then went on:

'Now Zepho, the father of Irad, was Ishak of that village, and the Ishak had many duties. He led his people to battle; and he saw to it that the fields were ploughed, and the corn seed sown when the moon was full. He saw to it that songs of praise were sung to the Corn Dingir, and that gifts were made . . . .'

The old man paused. 'But at the time of the sowing,' he went on, 'it was the custom for the Ishak to give to the Corn Dingir his dearest possession.' He stopped and began rocking his body to and fro again.

'I know what it was,' said Zepho anxiously. 'It was his son.'

'Aah!' the mountain people gasped.

'The Corn Dingir made the corn grow high and thick and green. If the Ishak did not give his son, the corn grew thin and poor, and the people starved.' Suddenly the old man's voice changed from the voice of a story-teller to that of a man pleading for mercy. 'I had many brothers older than I, so my childhood was happy. I played with my three younger brothers among the olive-trees; and we caught frogs in the well.' The old man paused again, sorrowfully thinking. Then he continued with his story:

'When I was fourteen I knew that my own days were numbered. At the next sowing of the corn my hour would come. I watched them bringing in the harvest. Then they took the ploughs down to the fields. And every day more furrows were made—more soil was turned over, and less and less stubble was left between me and my death. I could bear waiting no longer. When the stubble was no more than a wide strip, I told my brother Nik that I planned to run away. He looked at me sorrowfully and his face went pale. "You must come with me," said I. "We must steal some food and hide it in a crock down by the Well of the Frogs. You must hide it, because already they are watching me." He agreed. And we stole the food, and he took it down to the Well of the Frogs. We had planned to go that night; but as the day drew on, storm-clouds gathered over the mountains, and lightning flashed. My brother, who was a timid boy, was afraid. "It is the mountain dingirs," he said. And he tried to persuade me to give up my flight. But I wouldn't. When the darkness came down, I left him—and started out alone.

'But outside the village gate, a feeling of shame came over me, that I should leave my younger brother to take my place. And I turned round and went back. Another idea had come into my head. By the side of my father's hut stood a bundle of fishing-spears. I picked out the sharpest and stoutest, then went over to the fire and pulled out a lighted brand; for I thought that if I killed my father, a new Ishak would be chosen and all my brothers would be safe. I had heard that a man could be killed by driving a fishing-spear into his eye. I took the lighted torch in one hand and the fishing-spear in the other; and I went into my father's hut, my heart beating and my head swimming with the wickedness of the thing I was to do; but I was desperate. And when a man is desperate his thoughts are violent and evil. Inside the hut I held up the lighted torch and looked at my father sleeping peacefully. And the horror of the thing I planned came over me. I stood, helplessly looking down at his sleeping face, thinking, "It is my brother's life, or it is yours, my father," and trying to nerve myself up to the deed. Then suddenly his eyes opened—and he lay looking up at me calmly and fearlessly. I dropped the torch and fled. At the Well of Frogs I found my hidden stores in the crock, bread and cheese and dried raisins. It was the last bread I was ever to eat.'

The old man paused again and then went on, mumbling to himself: 'For years I wandered in the mountains, feeding on berries and rabbits that I learned to catch. Then I grew more daring, and stole lambs from the shepherds; and ventured into the fields at night, for corn on the ear, or grapes from the vines. But I never spoke a word to man, woman, or child.'

'Ooh,' said Shaul suddenly. When he had thought of running away he had dreaded the loneliness of the mountains more than anything else.

'But one day,' the old man went on, 'I met my Ruth. She had strayed away from a shepherd tribe, picking berries. And I carried her off and lived with her in a cave. She was the mother of my daughter here and my sons. But she died.'

The old man was quiet for some time, thinking of his dead wife. 'But,' he added, 'her death does not lie so heavy on my heart as the deaths of my three brothers.'

There was silence for some moments after the old man stopped talking.

Then Zepho whispered: 'He has a crooked toe.'

And the Ishak Moab stretched out his hand to the old man, and said, 'O Irad, brother of my father!'

When the excitement of meeting their new-found relatives had died down, Old Irad said, 'I saw the boy Zepho had the face of my brother. But I could not believe that Moab had ever lived to grow up, and to have a son of his own!'

'I can explain that,' said the Ishak. 'After you ran away, your next brother was sacrificed, but before the year was out and it was Moab my father's turn, the Ishak Zepho was killed in battle. A new Ishak was chosen. So Moab your brother grew up in peace. I am his son. My name is Moab also.'

Old Irad sat very still and thoughtful. And when the woman elder began asking questions as to why the Ishak was travelling with Enoch and Shamashazir, he seemed to be so wrapped up in his thoughts that he took no notice of what was going on round him, until the eight cousins were called up from where they had been feeding with Sam at the bottom of the cliff. The Ishak explained exactly how every one of the eight was related—who was his father and his grandfather and his mother and his grandmother. It took a long time. And the old man stared intently at each face, trying to see some resemblance to faces he had once known.

After that the gathering gradually broke up. The two villainous-looking brothers retired to a warm corner to sleep; two of the young men, who were much more friendly than their elders, took Eb hunting with them; while Shamashazir, used to feasting and merrymaking in Ur, enjoying himself by talking about the wonders of that city to a circle of young girls who had quite forgotten their shyness.

The woman elder was talking to the Ishak. She wanted him to stop with them and make his home in the mountains. 'Father will die soon,' she said. 'He is already feeble. And my two brothers care for nothing but their bellies. Stay with us. We are the people of your father's blood. Stay with us, and teach these young ones some law and the customs that my mother used to talk of. You have been an Ishak. You must know things that a woman like me, born in the mountains, has never heard of. It's not right for an Ishak to be a slave among a strange people.'

But the Ishak Moab, who was used to the comfort of a hut and a village with a wall round it, and corn to eat, and women to grind it for him, looked at the bare, cold walls of the cave and the wild mountains, and decided that slave or no slave, he preferred the comforts of the City of Ur. He shook his head. And his hand went again to the little leather pouch, tied to a string round his neck and hidden beneath his clothes.

While these conversations were going on, Enoch, who missed his long days alone with the sleep, had climbed the cliff upwards from the mouth of the cave. He was looking for peace and quiet away from all this chatter of a reunited family. But one of the young girls with the extraordinary name of Prickle, with her friend Ruth, followed him up. Enoch had no difficulty in eluding Shamashazir's stalking. But these two were brought up in the mountains. They were his equal in silent movement, and every bit his match. He could not shake them off. In the end he had to give in and let them talk—or rather, let Prickle talk. For Ruth was as soft and quiet as her name, and seldom said anything but 'Mm' or 'Yes'.

'Why do you go away from the others?' asked Prickle.

'I am not a corn grower. I am no relation to you. I come from the tribe of Enoch. My people are shepherds.'

'That's no reason why you should go away. I think it is because you like being followed.' Prickle fixed him with her large, innocent eyes.

Enoch jumped to his feet, furious, and then stood feeling rather stupid because Prickle was laughing at him.

'I like being alone,' he said.

'Why?'

He was not going to say why. He tried to look dignified, and said nothing.

'Our grandmother,' said Ruth, who was lying face downwards on the ground playing with the lichen in the rocks. 'Our grandmother came from a shepherd tribe. It was a great and powerful tribe and owned hundreds and hundreds and hundreds of sheep. It was called the tribe of Enoch.'

'Yes,' said Prickle, 'the tribe of Enoch, that's what it was called.'

'You are lying,' said Enoch, sitting down again on a rock. 'In my tribe girls who lie have their tongues burnt with a brand from the fire.'

'It wasn't a lie,' said Prickle. 'It was the truth.' And she looked at Enoch again with her large, clear eyes.

'It was a lie,' he said. 'You are a tribe without a god, so how can you know the difference between truth and lies?'

'We can,' said Prickle, but she hung down her head.

'What is a god?' Ruth asked curiously, speaking into the lichen. Enoch looked down on the back of her head scornfully. At first he wasn't going to answer.

'What is a god?' she repeated, as if she were asking, 'What is a basket?'

The desire to show off his superior knowledge overcame the boy: 'A god is the spirit which the tribe serves and which looks after it and guides it. Every tribe has a spirit like this. The tribe of Enoch serves the Lord of all the Earth,' he finished proudly.

'I've heard of Him,' said Ruth in her soft, dreamy voice. 'He is the one that looks after me.'

Enoch nearly choked with fury. But neither of these girls could see what there was to be angry about. Prickle looked at him astonished, wondering why his skin had suddenly darkened; and Ruth went on playing with the lichen as if nothing had happened.

'Go away!' said Enoch at last. 'Can't you see I want to be left alone?'

But the girls made no attempt to go. Prickle, hugging herself and smiling mischievously, sat down beside Ruth, who went on quietly with her little game of arranging the lichen into a pattern.

'Don't they teach you obedience in your tribe?' asked Enoch angrily.

'What is obedience?' asked Prickle, looking up at him round-eyed.

'Doing what your Ishak tells you.'

'Oh, what Grandfather tells us. Of course.'

'Well then. Go!'

'We don't obey boys. We order them about. Aunt orders my father about. She's older.'

'I'm not a boy!' said Enoch. 'When my father dies I shall be Ishak of the tribe of Enoch.'

Prickle stared at him in astonishment. '*That* great tribe,' she said. Then she tapped Ruth on the arm, and got up gingerly as if she had suddenly become afraid of Enoch. Ruth looked at her; and then got up herself, leaving her little pattern of lichen arranged on the ground. And the two walked nervously away, occasionally looking uneasily back at Enoch.

Now that they had gone Enoch felt rather sorry to lose their company. 'Strange,' he thought. 'They knew about the tribe of Enoch when it was great. They lied themselves; yet they believed me.' And then he began to wonder if they *had* lied. Perhaps after all their grandmother, who was called Ruth and came from a shepherd tribe, had really come from the tribe of Enoch. Enoch was surprised to find that the idea quite pleased him. He got up and went to the edge of the cliff, where he could look down on to the platform below, thinking that perhaps he might see them again. But neither of the young girls was there.

The woman elder was by the fire, parching corn in the copper pot, with Zepho beside her giving help and advice. Old Irad was rocking his body to and fro, mumbling and moaning, half to himself and half to the Ishak, who was sitting very thoughtfully beside him.

Enoch lay down. The midday sun and the meal of goat's flesh had made him drowsy, and the words of old Irad drifted up from below like a half-heard chant.

'What you have told me of my father Zepho's death weighs down my heart with a yet heavier burden of sin,' he was saying to the Ishak Moab. 'When I ran away all those years ago, I said, to comfort myself, that I was only robbing my brother Nik of one year of his life; for at the next time of sowing it would be his turn. All these long years I have lived in the mountains and thought these things to comfort myself. "One year of life," I have said; "no, less than one year. For the last months of the life of the Ishak's eldest son are worse than death." I know . . . I have lived through them. But now you come from the village of my father and tell me this thing that brings a greater curse upon my head—the curse of Cain himself. For by my cowardice I have taken a whole lifetime from my brother Nik. Nik the gentle, who put the food for me down by the Frog Spring, and should have lived to be Ishak of his people when my father died . . . And he was only twelve years old.'

He stopped, but the Ishak Moab did not speak. There was nothing he could say.

The old man went on: 'The curse of Cain is terrible to bear, and none can escape it. I am a man without a god and without a tribe. There is no more place for me among the living. There is no place for me among the dead.' The old man groaned in anguish. And the Ishak Moab, sitting beside him, heaved a deep sigh.

'When I die,' the old man went on, 'no man will greet me at the gates of death; and the Dingir of the Underworld will spit on me. My sin will be on the heads of my Ruth and all my children; and on the heads of my grandchildren for ever and ever, to live as outlaws and robbers, godless and tribeless; and to die in shame.' And the old man burst into heart-rending sobs; so that Zepho went pale and dropped some of the corn into the fire.

'Don't you mind him,' said the woman elder comfortingly.

But the Ishak Moab was thinking of his own sons who were dead because of the curse of Cain. And he wondered if they had made a new Ishak, and if they had sacrificed another boy. And all the time he was twisting the ring on his finger, the ring without which no Ishak could reign in Kenan. Without an Ishak all his tribe would be godless and cornless, and would die of famine and starvation. He bowed his head, and groaned, 'O Great Spirit, have mercy on my soul.'

Enoch lay on the rock high above them, young and strong, free and happy, trying to calculate how long it would take them to get to the Lake of the Kingfishers with their party of fifteen, and no corn and no cheese. He wished the old man would stop his moaning monologue. It made it difficult to think. His thoughts became cloudy. . . . What did he care for the sins of a heathen old man. . . . The Lake of the Kingfishers was a day's journey from the four eagles' cliff . . . and that was three days' journey from the spring of . . . what was the name of the spring . . . the spring of Cain. . . . And then it must have been that he fell asleep. For he was back in the Land of Milk and Honey, walking among the grape-vines and the olive-trees, and looking at the fields.

In one field there was a man ploughing. But how fast the oxen were pulling the plough. He floated over the ground to have a better look. The plough was running along quite smoothly, instead of lurching about as he had been used to seeing it. And it was running on two round discs. Enoch knew at once that these must be wheels. The harness of the oxen was different, too. It was joined together by rings of brass, and brass studs. And the tip of the plough was covered in a dull grey metal that he had never seen before. The man who was driving the plough did not look like a man of Kenan, but like his friend Shamashazir. 'Is this place the City of Ur?' Enoch asked the man, looking round for any signs of a great city like Jericho.

'This place is Canaan,' the man answered, pointing to a village of square stone houses with flat roofs, that stood on a little hillock near by.

Enoch went to look closer at it. It was very different from the Village of Kenan that he had known. A dusty road ran up to it, and passed in through an arched gateway. And people in brightly coloured robes with striped cloths over their heads were coming in and out. Enoch watched them, fascinated. He had never seen so many people since the time of the great battle against Jericho. There were women carrying pitchers of water on their heads; and men with donkeys, laden with all sorts of plants and things that Enoch had never seen. And then a body of men came by with short skirts that clashed and jangled as they marched. They carried great shields of shining metal on their arms, and heavy metal swords; and more shining metal on their heads that glittered in the sun. They were a terrifying sight. And the people in bright clothes moved off the road to let them pass. Enoch hid among the olive-trees.

When the noise of the armed men had died away, and the dust they made on the road had settled down, Enoch came out of his hiding-place and looked about. The road was empty, except for the vaguely familiar figures of two men, walking painfully along towards a well in the distance. Enoch found himself following them, wondering all the time where he had seen them before.

As they came near the well, he saw that there was a man sitting on a stone by its side. He sat curiously still, looking down the road towards the two who were coming, as if he were waiting for them. And the two vaguely familiar figures went on. And Enoch followed behind, slowly catching them up. As he went he began to see that the man by the well was no ordinary man. A quiet, still glory shone from Him—the glory of the Lord of all the Earth. Enoch was afraid to go any nearer. He stopped; but the two other men went on. They came to the end of the road. They came to the well. They knelt before the Lord of all the Earth, and He laid His hands on their heads, while Enoch watched.

Then he said, 'My children!'

That was all He said; and then He was gone.

But slowly the two figures stood upright and turned their faces towards Enoch. They were the faces of the old man and the Ishak Moab of Kenan.

When Enoch woke up he was trembling. A cloud had come over

the sun and the valley was very quiet. But the presence of the Great Spirit was in his heart and he felt very small and humble. For some time he sat with his hands over his eyes, until the voice of Shamashazir made him look up. Shamashazir had come right up to him without being heard. 'I had a dream,' said Enoch, his voice trembling.

Shamashazir, saying nothing, dropped down beside him. He had never seen his proud and daring friend in such distress. He sat and waited for him to speak, flicking bits of moss over the cliff, pretending to notice nothing unusual.

Then at last Enoch began, and with stumbling words told him his dream:

'It was a man with the Great Spirit shining through him. And he spoke with the voice of the Great Spirit. . . . "My children!" was what he said. He said it to the Ishak Moab and the old man.'

Shamashazir knew at once what the dream meant. He leapt excitedly to his feet. 'The Lord of all the Earth has lifted the curse,' he said.

'Yes,' said Enoch quietly. He felt humbled and ashamed before the glory that he had seen. He got up more slowly, and led the way down to the platform below; with Shamashazir walking behind him, trying to control his excitement at the thought of the joy of the two, when they heard the news.

The old man, tired out with his grieving, had fallen into a doze. The Ishak Moab still sat beside him.

The boys stood before them, not knowing how to begin.

'We have a message for you,' said Shamashazir. 'Enoch son of Enoch has a message for both of you.'

The Ishak saw their serious faces, and his anxious and guilty heart told him of calamity. 'It is the shortage of food,' he thought. 'There are too many mouths to feed; and they have decided to throw some of the boys over the cliff.' He leapt to his feet. 'Let it be me,' he said. 'I am ready.' If he gave his life for the boys he might find forgiveness at the gates of death.

'Have no fear, brother,' said Enoch.

'Brother!' Enoch the Proud had called him brother?

Shamashazir was speaking to the old man. 'Wake up,' he was saying. 'There is good news for you.'

'Good news?' The old man opened his eyes.

'There is good news,' repeated Shamashazir—'from the Lord of all the Earth.'

The surprise of Shamashazir's words made the Ishak Moab's knees tremble. He hardly heard what followed. 'Enoch son of Enoch has had a dream,' Shamashazir was saying. 'And in it the Lord of all the Earth sent a message to you, Moab of Kenan, and to the son of your brother.'

'To me?' said the old man, his voice trembling. 'The Lord of all the Earth? A message to me? Good news, did you say?' His eyes filled with tears. 'Your faces are shining. I cannot see.' He held up his arm as if to keep out a blinding light.

'The Lord of all the Earth has freed you from the curse of Cain,' said Enoch. And he knelt down and slowly and clearly began to tell the old man everything he had seen and heard in his dream.

Old Irad was very still, but when Enoch came to the words 'My children' he gave a sudden gasp and fell sideways. The Ishak caught him and laid him on the ground . . . motionless.

The woman elder, who had been sitting in the mouth of the cave, got up and came over to them.

'Your father is dead,' said the Ishak Moab.

Supper was a very quiet meal that night. The brothers had brought
back a sheep which they had stolen; and part of it they roasted and
gave to their guests. They heard the news of their father's death
indifferently. To them he meant one less mouth to feed, and nothing
else. But the younger men and girls felt a great change had come
over their lives. Their grandfather had kept the family together
with some sort of order. The two brothers, who would now be the
heads of the tribe, were wild and rough men, men without mercy of
kindness. The young girls turned their eyes longingly to Shamashazir and Enoch, and even to Eb. They were the kind of men whom
they could admire and look to for protection. They were all
thinking the same thing; but none dared speak. It was the woman
elder who first broke the silence:

'Is this forgiveness that I heard you talking about, for my father
only, or for the whole of the tribe?'

'A father stands for his family, and the Ishak for his tribe,' said
Enoch. 'The tribe was cursed for one man's deed.'

'But you aren't an Ishak any more. You are just our father,
Moab,' said Zepho.

The Ishak turned the golden ring on his finger, and said, 'I am
not an Ishak, and yet there is no other Ishak of Kenan while I.
wear this ring.' And he held out his hand for them all to see. It
was a beautiful ring and Shamashazir guessed that it had been made
in Ur.

'Then somebody ought to go back and tell them. And stop them
killing any more boys,' said Zepho.

The Ishak shook his head. 'They would never believe me, my
son.' And there was silence, until Shamashazir asked if he might
look at the ring more closely.

The Ishak took it off, and handed it to him over the head of
Zepho, who was sitting between them. It was made of gold set
with stones of lapis lazuli, and was very old. It lay in the palm of
Shamashazir's hand, while Zepho's chin came pushing over the
crook of his arm. Zepho's eyes suddenly shone with a secret
purpose. His hand shot out and seized the ring.

'Look out!' said Shamashazir.

But Zepho had put it on, and was waving his hand above his

head with the ring dangling round his first finger. 'I am the new Ishak of Kenan,' he shouted. 'Look. And when I'm grown up I'll go back to Kenan and find my mother. And I'll make them stop serving the Corn Dingir. And I'll tell them they have to serve the Great Spirit; and I'll fight them and tell them, until they do what I tell them.' He jumped to his feet, waving the ring, until his father gently pulled him down.

It seemed as if Zepho's high spirits had broken the spell of death. For the young girls all began to talk among themselves about Ur; and the woman elder turned to the Ishak Moab and began to plead with him again to stay in the mountains. 'Now that my father is dead, you can be our Ishak, and teach all these wild children how to live as my mother's people lived in the tribe of Enoch.'

Enoch heard what she said, and looked at her, surprised; and Prickle jumped to her feet, clapping her hands. 'There,' she shouted. 'You see, we weren't lying. Aunt has said so.'

Enoch was thoughtful for a moment while all the other girls, who had been listening to Shamashazir, began to shout that they wanted to go to Ur. Only Ruth sat silent, watching Enoch from under her soft lashes. Shamashazir, too, looked at his friend. He could guess what was passing in his mind. 'If you come to Ur,' he said to the girls, 'you'll miss your freedom. You will be slaves in some rich man's house. You won't be allowed out into the streets alone. You will have to sit on the roof-tops most of the day; and learn to spin and embroider, and how to buy food in the market, and how it should be cooked, and how to tell stories to children.'

'No,' said the woman elder. 'You wild things could never live a life like that.'

'*We* don't want to go to a city,' put in one of the young men. 'Why can't we join the tribe of Enoch? The shepherds live a good life in the mountains; and we are no longer outlaws.'

'Ah!' said Shamashazir. 'If you did that my father could send a thousand sheep to the tribe of Enoch.' He looked at Enoch. But Enoch looked at Ruth.

'Would you like to join my tribe?' he asked rather shyly.

She lowered her eyelashes and blushed. 'Yes,' she whispered.

'So would I,' said Prickle. And one by one, all the other girls agreed that it would be better than going to Ur.

But the woman elder shook her head. She knew her two wild brothers would never leave the mountains, nor subject themselves to the rule of the Ishak of Enoch. She would stay with them, and look after them when they were ill, and bind them up when they were wounded, and keep them from fighting each other to death when they felt quarrelsome.

'But,' said Enoch, 'these young men are not enough to look after a *thousand* extra sheep. They are not used to shepherds' work. Two hundred are as many as we can accept from your father, O Shamashazir of Ur.' He spoke solemnly as if he were already Ishak, and he bowed towards Shamashazir.

'Two hundred? Why, that is nothing,' said Shamashazir, disappointed. 'You can't make the tribe of Enoch great with only two hundred sheep.'

Suddenly, young Irad, who had wandered up the steps again to do a little eavesdropping, broke into the discussion. 'What about me?' he shouted, throwing out his chest and striding into the middle of the gathering. 'I could look after a hundred sheep.'

The girls laughed. 'We know how you corn people live! You've never seen a sheep except to eat it! And you can't hunt! And you're afraid of mountain dingirs and lions!'

Irad the brave looked rather abashed at this feminine scorn.

'I'm not afraid of mountain dingirs or of lions,' he said. 'And I can fish.'

'No,' put in Sam, coming to his rescue. 'He's no corn grower. He led them across the mountains on his own. He'll make a good shepherd.'

'And what about the others?' Shamashazir asked.

'I'll have them all if Father agrees,' said Enoch unexpectedly. 'I'll tell him my dream.'

Irad stood on the very edge of the cliff, and shouted down to the others below: 'Do you hear? We are all going to be shepherds. We're not going to Ur to be slaves. We are going to hunt, and to eat sheep. Hurrah!'

A cheer rose from the seven at the bottom of the cliff.

But when it had died down, Zepho said quietly, 'I am not going to be a shepherd. I'm going back to Ur with Shamashazir, to learn about ploughs with wheels and copper tips; and how to grow corn without the Corn Dingir; and how to be as wise as Shamashazir; and how to rule my people properly. And you are to come too, Father.'

The Ishak laughed happily—the first time for many years. 'And what will you do, my son Shaul?'

Shaul scratched his head, thinking for a moment.

'Are there donkeys in Ur?'

'Of course,' said Shamashazir.

'Then I'm coming with you, Father. I'll feed the donkeys.'

The Ishak's face was shining with happiness.

They *all* joined in the prayers that night and they *all* sang: *'Oh come let us sing unto the Lord and rejoice in the strength of our salvation.'*

And the next morning they set off on the last stage of their journey, leaving only the woman elder and the two surly brothers alone in the caves.

They had no belongings to take with them; so they spent no time in packing. They simply bathed in the pool at the bottom of the cliff for the last time, put the remains of the sheep that had been killed into goatskins, and the corn back into the donkey's baskets, picked up their babies; and they were ready.

Back in Ur, after the news had come from the mountains that Shamashazir was dead, and they had got over the first shock, the days passed monotonously for most of the family. Naychor was getting used to being treated as the eldest son. He had already taken his place beside his father at the feasts, which they still held when the caravans returned. But Haran and Dinah, listening through the cracks in the floor above the guest-chamber, thought they were never as merry as they used to be; and even the stories seemed to have lost their excitement. Teresh seemed an old man; and none of his guests ever knew what incident in their tales of adventures was going to remind him of his son that was lost. They talked with caution and restraint.

But to his family, Teresh was gentler, and spent much more time with the rest of his children—as if he were afraid to lose them too. Quite often he would take Naychor away from his school-work; and let him spend the day poking about in the warehouse; learning something of the men who would one day call him master. Naychor had his heart's desire—he was somebody important. Men treated him with respect and obeyed his orders. But curiously enough Naychor was no happier. There was something unreal about being the head of the family, and it made him feel uneasy; as if he were wearing his brother's shoes.

Haran was quiet too. He could not really be happy when his father was so sad. And he loved Shamashazir. He could not help feeling that it was partly his fault that Shamashazir had gone away and been killed. If only he had left that stupid Image alone. Oh, no. It was very wicked to call the Image stupid. The Teraphim would hear him and be very angry. 'Well, anyhow, I didn't mean it like that. And you've got a better Image now, so you ought to be pleased,' he said aloud, hoping that the Teraphim might be about, to hear him. He gently put back the fig that he was stealing from the larder, and went out into the marshes to look for frogs. Haran was getting good. He tried very hard not to cause any more trouble, but sometimes he found it very difficult. And he felt that he must burst out and do something really mad and mischievous as he used to. But the moment he started to make any plans, he remembered the horrible laughing croak of the raven when he broke the Image; as if that ill-omened bird were always sitting just over the top of the wall, watching for him to slip up.

Sarah was quieter too. She had cried for a whole day when she had heard Shamashazir was dead; and ever since, every night and every morning, she had brought a special bowl of her favourite food down to the Teraphim, and asked him to look after Shamashazir in the Underworld.

Dinah was the only one of them all who remained exactly the same. She could not believe in Shamashazir's death. She refused to treat Naychor as head of the family, and spoke Shamashazir's name with the other names of the living, when she repeated the prayers for guidance. Dinah was going her own way and thinking her own thoughts, living a secret life of her own. She was always persuading the cook (or one of the other servants who took her to the food markets with them), to go on just a little bit farther, to the house of Illi Silli.

'I can't understand why she does it,' said the cook. 'There's nothing there to please a girl's fancy. Nothing—except mud—mud on the walls—mud on the door. The servants of Illi Silli are no friends of water. They must fear to put their hands in it as a farmer fears floods. And then, when she gets there, there's nothing that pleases her. And she comes home as cross as the brother of my mother's aunt.'

But one day they met Mushinti in the narrow street outside her house. Dinah greeted her politely. Mushinti stopped, and looking at Dinah with her head tilted slightly on one side, and her eyes twinkling, said: 'I think I know you.'

Dinah bowed. 'I am Dinah, the daughter of Teresh the Stern.'

'Come into my house by *daylight*,' said Mushinti, laughing. 'There is a very good view from the roof.' Dinah blushed, but to Mushinti's astonishment, she said: 'Yes, m'm,' and followed her in. As they stopped to wash their feet in the hall, and as they crossed the central courtyard, Dinah seemed all the time trying to twist her neck round to peer into the rooms that they passed.

'Do you want to see the factory?' asked Mushinti.

'Please!' said Dinah. But in the factory she walked impatiently from room to room, not at all interested in the ovens or images —until they came to Uz, as usual covered with clay—then she stopped, and smiled.

Uz stood up. He was half a head taller, his skinny limbs were filling out and becoming smooth and strong. He smiled back at Dinah radiantly through the clay. And Dinah stood looking at him, saying nothing; and he stood looking at her, saying nothing, until Mushinti, laughing, left them alone together.

Then Uz took a very deep breath, as if he were making a great resolution, and said: 'Would you like to see my clay-and-wood-and-stone animals?'

Dinah gulped, then nodded, and whispered: 'Yes.'

But now Uz didn't have to go into a corner and take out a brick to show her his work. His animals were all in another room, arranged on a shelf. And Dinah held her breath when she saw them.

Uz asked her which she liked best. And when she had taken an interminably long time making up her mind, and at last chose a goat, he gave it to her to take home.

She found Mushinti talking to a man in the guest-chamber. 'Here is the daughter of Teresh,' she said, as Dinah came in. 'This man has come from beyond the river and he brings news for you.'

'News of Shamashazir?' said Dinah, holding her goat tightly in both hands, her eyes sparkling with eagerness.

'I have seen him at the Village of Changing Beasts, where he was waiting for his cousin Serag to come across the mountains.'

'Then he *is* alive! I said he was!'

'He was alive when I saw him.'

'And well,' Mushinti added; 'but he limps with one leg.'

'I must go and tell Father!'

But when she told Teresh, he could not believe her.

Half a moon later, a travel-stained man arrived at the door and wanted to see Teresh. He announced that the caravan was on its way, and that Shamashazir was with it. But Teresh said that he had a shifty eye, and that many messengers invented good news in order to earn money. He gave the messenger a meal and a cloak; and told him to keep out of his sight.

But after that, Haran and Sarah and Dinah kept a nightly watch for fires on the other side of the river. Seven days later, Naychor joined them. And then Teresh himself began to come every evening to watch the twilight turn into the darkness over the smooth water.

Then one day Naychor said that he saw a faint haze of smoke at sunset; and the whole household came up on to the roof-top to watch.

'O dear kind Teraphim! Sweep all the mist off the river so that we can see,' said Sarah.

Haran was almost beside himself with excitement, and could not stop talking.

And then came the fires—one by one they appeared—and among them Serag's signal fire, which told them it was his caravan.

'I shall burst!' shouted Haran.

'You will,' said Dinah. 'You had better look out.'

Teresh gently put his arms round his youngest son's shoulders. 'You'd better have a day off school tomorrow, or there will be trouble. I don't know if Shamashazir will be there; but you can all go down to meet the boat.' And then he added with almost a twinkle in his eye: 'If you want to.'

'Are *you* coming, Father?' Dinah asked.

'I don't know.'

'You must come.'

But Teresh turned away and went downstairs alone.

'He doesn't believe Shamashazir is really here,' said Dinah. 'But I know he is.'

The first thing in the morning there was more news of Shamashazir—from a fisherman, who had got it from his cousin, who lived on the other side of the Great River. And Teresh decided that he would go with them. All that morning they could none of them keep away from the roof-top. And the whole family stood waiting for the tiny ferry-boat to come into sight—and then for it to pass mid-stream, when they could go down to the quay.

'It's big enough now,' said Sarah.

'No, it isn't,' said Naychor. 'You can see it much better from up here.'

'It's much bigger!' said Dinah. 'Why, it will be here at any moment.'

But still Naychor said it was too small; and Teresh agreed with him; it was better to wait on the roof-top. They all stood silently watching the tiny sail.

'How quiet it is,' said Dinah, looking round to see why it was. 'Where's Haran?'

Where was Haran? He wasn't on the roof-top; and they agreed that none of them had seen him since breakfast. 'He's probably gone down to the quay already,' said Dinah. 'He's terribly impatient. He can't wait for anything. Can't we go and find him?'

Teresh agreed that they might as well. If they left Haran by himself on the quay there was no knowing what he would do in his present excitement.

But Haran wasn't on the quay. Nor had any of the porters that they asked seen him.

'It's his own fault if he misses Shamashazir's home-coming by doing something stupid,' said Naychor. But Teresh could not help feeling a little uneasy. The naughty Haran was very precious to him. He sent Naychor round the quay asking every boy he found hanging about if he had seen Haran anywhere. A good many of them did not know who Haran was. Only one ventured the remark that he thought he had seen such a boy down on the quay the first thing in the morning.

'But I would have guessed that,' said Naychor when he told his father. 'He came down here so early he got tired of waiting, and is somewhere mooning about the streets, forgetting the time.'

'He will come,' said Gimkarsida. 'When a caravan arrives, every boy in the city knows it; and all the streets are so full of chattering rumours that Haran will come down at the last minute.'

Dinah heaved a great sigh. 'I said he'd do something awful.' She missed sharing her excitement with Haran. She thought of how they had watched the boat getting smaller and smaller all those moons ago—taking Shamashazir away from them. Now it was getting larger and larger. They could actually see the dark figures of men on the deck and the man at the helm. She held her hands tight clenched with excitement, while Sarah danced about beside her.

'What if he isn't there after all?' said Naychor.

'I can see a boy—I can see two boys—and another. There're three boys,' shouted Sarah. 'And one of them's jumping about all over the place.'

'They are too small to be Shamashazir,' said Naychor in a superior voice.

'The biggest one's standing quite still. He's not too small.' And Sarah began to jump up and down, more than ever, with excitement.

'That's not Shamashazir,' said Naychor.

The ferry-boat turned and tacked. All the figures stood out clearly, and some of them began to wave. The jumping boy stopped jumping, and joined a man standing alone in the bows, both waving frantically. The family at the quayside waved back, but no one said a word. They were too excited. They all knew the *man* was Shamashazir, standing in the bows waving to them—and the boy beside him?

'It's Haran,' said Dinah as the boat drew in. 'He really has burst —this time.'

'How could he get *there*?' Sarah asked. 'Has the Teraphim carried him?'

Naychor had the answer ready: 'On a fishing-boat that went out early this morning.'

'What, one of those tiny little things in that great river! Why, Haran's never been in a fishing-boat before.'

In another moment the boat glided up to the quay. Ropes were thrown to the waiting longshoremen, and Shamashazir jumped on to the quay and was among them again. Shamashazir, the length of a thumb taller, with muscles that rippled under his skin, and the faint marks of scars on his arms and chest. He stood and looked at them; and they at him. He was Shamashazir, and yet he wasn't Shamashazir. He was different. There was a strangeness on him— a strangeness of the far mountains, the dusty roads, and the wild forests; and the strangest of adventures. The stern face of Teresh grew soft with joy at the sight of his son alive again, and tears welled up in his eyes.

But Dinah was the first to speak. 'I knew you weren't dead,' she said. 'I knew it all the time; but nobody believed me.'

'I believed you,' shouted Haran (who had come off the boat), waving his arms and jumping about.

'I told you, you would burst,' said Dinah.

Haran put his head to the ground and turned a somersault and two or three cartwheels, until he landed smack into the stomach of a rich merchant who had come to meet the caravan. Then he stood upright, and dodging the merchant, began to explain to his family that the two other boys they had seen on the boat were Shaul and Zepho, sons of the Ishak of a heathen tribe, that Shamashazir had rescued.

Shaul bowed to Dinah, and then began to look round at the seething crowd that had collected on the quay. Porters shouting, donkey boys cursing, travellers exchanging news, and boys putting up as much din as their lungs could manage. Shaul had eyes for only one thing; and that was the donkeys. He had never imagined so many in his life—and for him Ur at once became a heaven. 'I am going to be a donkey boy,' he said, breaking away from Haran and plunging into the turmoil.

But the sight of so much noise and so many people was too terrifying to the brave and resourceful Enoch. 'It is like a great flock of noisy sheep without a shepherd,' he said. And he went and stood on the very edge of the quay, until Shamashazir took him by the arm, and began to tell his father how Enoch had found him and saved his life. Enoch looked at Teresh, and decided that he liked him. He was proud like himself; and when Teresh took him by the shoulders and kissed him on both cheeks, he made no objection.

Zepho, too, did not like the noise and the crowd. He stood beside the Ishak, closely clutching his father's hand. He held on tightly to it, all through the jostling of the narrow streets, and through the darkness of the Eastern Gate. But the bridge over the canal he liked. And when they got to the house of Teresh and he found that it overlooked the marshes on one side; and that he could see field of barley growing when he stood on the roof-top, he felt much happier, thinking of plough with wheels and copper tips.

All the family were allowed to sit up for the feast of welcome that night—even Sarah and Haran. And Shamashazir found himself in the place of the story-teller, with all faces turned expectantly towards him. Night after night he had told stories over the camp fires, gradually learning the art, so that he had become more skilful than his cousin Serag; yet now that he was faced with his own family he suddenly felt shy and afraid to begin. The familiar rows of little waving lamp flames along the walls of the guest-chamber, the familiar noises and smells of feast day from the kitchen, the whole rich stench of Ur, which drifted as far as the marshes even to the edge of the new city ... all these things made him feel like the young Shamashazir who had sat at the feast for the first time, and listened with awe to his cousin Serag. And the whole of his long journey seemed like a dream. But at the far end of the table was the pale face of the Ishak of Kenan and close beside him, his new friend Enoch, sitting there quietly watching the strange men in this strange new world.

Shamashazir straightened up, and began to speak of his visit to Kenan to buy corn, and of all that followed. But he left out all mention of the Lord of all the Earth.

Sarah listened with tears running down her cheeks; and even Haran was still. Until Shamashazir reached the part about Jemimah, you could have heard a gold pin drop on a rush mat. Then Haran burst into a loud guffaw, Dinah began to giggle, and Gimil Mama's fat belly shook like a jelly.

But Shamashazir said nothing of Enoch's dream or of the old man's death; until the children had been sent to bed, the guests had gone, and he was alone with his father.

The two sat in silence for a little time in the soft light of the many lamps, each feeling the change that had taken place in the other, and in himself. Teresh looked older. A sadness had crept into his fierce eyes; the sadness of a trusting animal that has been beaten. And Shamashazir saw his father no longer as a law, and an authority to be obeyed, but as a man who had had his own battles to fight and his own decisions to make. He felt guilty now, not for disobeying the law, but for causing his father so much sorrow.

Teresh, looking at his son, saw sympathy in his eyes—the sympathy of a man and a stranger; and the words that he had meant to speak died on his lips. Instead he said, in a rather puzzled voice, 'My son, you have defied the Teraphim and the laws of all dingirs; and yet you have returned safely from your journey.'

Then Shamashazir began to tell his father how, and why, he had decided the way the caravan should take, and all that had followed this decision.

When he had finished the whole story, right down to the death of the old man, Teresh said in a trembling voice:

'The God of our fathers has sought you out among men. He will bless you and make a great nation of you.'

Shamashazir gulped. He was young. The immensity of his father's seriousness took him aback. Suddenly he felt the responsibility heavy on his shoulders. A great nation! A city as big as Ur, and he the king? He wanted to be a shepherd on the hills. He drooped slightly and was silent, trying to catch again the feeling of the last happy days of his journey with his friend Enoch. But he couldn't. With a burst of resentment towards his father, he said, 'If the Lord of all the Earth was the God of our fathers, and you knew it, why didn't you tell me?'

'Our forefathers were simple shepherds, unaware of the greatness of the earth and its nations. When I saw the thousand times ten thousand people that lived in Ur and Erech and all the cities of the Land Between the Two Rivers, like the sand upon the sea shore, I saw that one god could never listen to the prayers of so many voices. It seemed to me that my father had great wisdom when he put a Teraphim upon the altar and worshipped it.' Then he lowered his voice. 'But the Lord has chosen you out,' he said. 'He will grant your requests, my son.'

'But, Father, all this time I have been learning to have no requests but only to obey. It is true that one God cannot hear the voices of so many people. Yet His voice comes to the whole earth like the light of the sun by day and the stars by night. And only the clouds of men's sin come between them and the voice of the Great Spirit. How shall I, with my requests, tell the Lord of all the Earth what to do?' Then he remembered Enoch's dream and the message that had come from the Lord of all the Earth to two miserable and despairing people. Truly the ways of the Great Spirit were unfathomable.

Teresh had no answer. He had grown a little afraid of his son. He looked at the floor and realized that he could hardly make out the pattern of the bricks. 'The lights are dwindling,' he said. 'We had better go to bed before the oil in the lamps runs out.'

And so, the next day, the Teraphim was removed from the altar, and the Lord of all the Earth was worshipped in one Chapel of the City of Ur. But Naychor took care of the Image that Uz had made, partly because he liked good craftsmanship, but mostly because he remembered how the Teraphim had cleared him of suspicion when he was unjustly accused. . . .

EPILOGUE

All this happened nearly four thousand years ago. It is a story that had to be strung together from clues buried deep in the earth, from legends and customs handed down from father to son, and from a few words written in a very old book. Some of it is true; but not all of it. For many of the clues and signs left by Shamashazir and his three brothers are lost, and in four thousand years legends alter. So I have had to make my imagination fill the gaps.

If you looked at the same clues and signs as I have, you would write a different story, and you might give Shamashazir a different name. You might call him Abram or Abraham, his father Terah, and his brother Nahor. But whatever you wrote about them, some of it would be true and some false; and so I prefer to call them Shamashazir, Teresh, and Naychor.

Haran, of course, will always be Haran.

TITLES IN THIS SERIES

THE ARMOURER'S HOUSE *Rosemary Sutcliff*
AYO GURKHA! *J. M. Marks*
THE BEETHOVEN MEDAL *K. M. Peyton*
BOWMAN OF CRÉCY *Ronald Welch*
CASTORS AWAY! *Hester Burton*
COLONEL SHEPERTON'S CLOCK *Philip Turner*
THE COSSACKS *B. Bartos-Höppner*
DEVIL'S HILL *Nan Chauncy*
DOWN THE LONG STAIRS *Winifred Cawley*
DROUGHT *Andrew Salkey*
THE EAGLE OF THE NINTH *Rosemary Sutcliff*
EARTHQUAKE *Andrew Salkey*
THE EDGE OF THE CLOUD *K. M. Peyton*
ELLEN *E. M. Almedingen*
FLAMBARDS *K. M. Peyton*
FLAMBARDS IN SUMMER *K. M. Peyton*
FLY-BY-NIGHT *K. M. Peyton*
GOOD-NIGHT, PROF, LOVE *John Rowe Townsend*
A GRASS ROPE *William Mayne*
AN HOUR IN THE MORNING *Gordon Cooper*
HURRICANE *Andrew Salkey*
I MARCHED WITH HANNIBAL *Hans Baumann*
IN SPITE OF ALL TERROR *Hester Burton*
THE INTRUDER *John Rowe Townsend*
THE JOURNEY OF THE ELDEST SON *J. G. Fyson*
JUMPER *Nicholas Kalashnikoff*
KNIGHT CRUSADER *Ronald Welch*
KNIGHT'S FEE *Rosemary Sutcliff*
THE LANTERN BEARERS *Rosemary Sutcliff*
THE LARK IN THE MORN *Elfrida Vipont*
THE LARK ON THE WING *Elfrida Vipont*
THE LATCHKEY CHILDREN *Eric Allen*
LILLIPILLY HILL *Eleanor Spence*
THE LITTLE BOOKROOM *Eleanor Farjeon*
LITTLE KATIA *E. M. Almedingen*
THE MEMBER FOR THE MARSH *William Mayne*
MINNOW ON THE SAY *A. Philippa Pearce*
NORDY BANK *Sheena Porter*
ONE IS ONE *Barbara Leonie Picard*
PARCEL FOR HENRY *Paul Ries Collin*
PASTURES OF THE BLUE CRANE *H. F. Brinsmead*
PENNINGTON'S SEVENTEENTH SUMMER *K. M. Peyton*
PIPPI GOES ABOARD *Astrid Lindgren*
PIPPI IN THE SOUTH SEAS *Astrid Lindgren*
PIPPI LONGSTOCKING *Astrid Lindgren*
PIRATE'S ISLAND *John Rowe Townsend*
RANSOM FOR A KNIGHT *Barbara Leonie Picard*
RIDE A NORTHBOUND HORSE *Richard Wormser*
RIFLES FOR WATIE *Harold Keith*
RIOT *Andrew Salkey*
A SAPPHIRE FOR SEPTEMBER *H. F. Brinsmead*
A SEVERNSIDE STORY *Frederick Grice*
SIRGA *René Guillot*
SONS OF THE STEPPE *Hans Baumann*
TANGARA *Nan Chauncy*
THE THREE BROTHERS OF UR *J. G. Fyson*
TIGER IN THE BUSH *Nan Chauncy*
A TIME IN A CITY *Gordon Cooper*
TIME OF TRIAL *Hester Burton*
TOM'S MIDNIGHT GARDEN *A. Philippa Pearce*
WARRIOR SCARLET *Rosemary Sutcliff*
WHEN JAYS FLY TO BÁRBMO *Margaret Balderson*